Juno's Peacock

by

Heather Robinson

By the same author:

Wall of Stone – historical fiction set in Roman Britain
mybook.to/WallofStone

Celebrating Wiltshire – a mini guide book to the beautiful county of Wiltshire, disguised as a quiz.
mybook.to/CelebratingWiltshire

Stour Valley Way in Pictures – potted histories and photographs of the Long Distance Footpath which starts in Wiltshire and finishes in Dorset.
mybook.to/StourValleyWay

Historic place names and their modern equivalent used within this story:

Pompeii	-	Pompeii, Italy
Misenum	-	Miseno, Italy
Puteoli	-	Pozzuoli, Italy
Sinessa	-	Mondragone, Italy
Brundisium	-	Brindisi, Italy
Roma	-	Rome, Italy
Isola Tiberina	-	Tiber Island, Rome, Italy
Britannia	-	Britain
Isca Augusta	-	Caerleon, Britain
Glevum	-	Gloucester, Britain

Chapter One

She walked the streets not knowing where to go or what to do. Decima could feel the heat bouncing back at her from the stone walls as she checked the urge to run along the paved Via del Vesuvio, noticing but not registering the burning at the peak of the mountain ahead. Her mind was full of the cruel words her mistress, Rufina had ravaged at her, and her cheek was showing the red welt of the brutal slap. She was exposed...oh, the hurt of the truth constricted her breathing.

Decima had always thought her mother was a slave-girl who died during childbirth, but today's angry words from her mistress had told how she, Lady Rufina, had found her twelve seasons ago, tied by strips of leather to a cypress tree on the remote slopes of the mountain. Tied so she couldn't wander off, even though she was barely beyond the age of crawling at that time. Abandoned, unwanted, exposed by her father, thus legally dead and available to be taken as a slave.

"I spared you from death and this is how you repay me!" Rufina had raged, striking the girl with the back of her hand, the ruby set ring on her middle finger adding painful venom to the blow. Rufina had glared with bitter malevolence, her nostrils flaring with emotion as her voice dropped to a controlled snarl. "You were nameless when I found you. I designated you Decima, my tenth lost soul saved. You are my property and now, with this breath, I cast you aside and declare you nameless again." Decima retreated under the intense hatred, shaking and breathing in shallow gasps. Rufina snapped her fingers towards the head slave who folded out from the shadows, indicating he detain the girl who was trapped in the courtyard, her mistress standing between her and the only exit. "Imprison her with shackles in the threshing room. Choose her death for me, crucifixion or the arena, it matters not."

Decima was too stunned to struggle and the head slave led her quietly out of the cool courtyard with its lush green foliage glistening with water droplets from the finely spraying fountain, leading her in silence down the vine covered portico to the kitchens. The kitchen servants averted their eyes as the two passed by, their superstitions greater than their curiosity. All had heard the curse from their mistress and to look into the eyes of a condemned soul was to invite the wrath of Jupiter, king of gods, sky god, god of rain who uses the thunderbolt as his weapon.

The head slave, still with a firm grip on Decima's thin upper arm, furtively picked up a small knife as the pair swept alongside the benches and a bolt of fear shot heat through Decima's chest at the realisation of what he would do. He was meaning to give her a quick cut-throat death. Favourable indeed to the slow death of crucifixion where the crows peck at your eyes before you are dead. Favourable also to being fed to the wild animals in the arena for the pleasure of the mob. Favourable, yes, but also imminent and the urge to live was rising in protest.

"I did not steal from Lady Rufina," she gasped, struggling for the first time. "The topaz choker was a gift to me." The strength of the head slave easily overcoming her efforts to disrupt their journey, Decima had no choice but to stumble along beside him as they descended the steep flight of steps to the lower levels of the villa that contained the threshing room, stores and stables. "Master Philo gave the choker to me." The head slave stopped abruptly and with a shaft of pain searing his expression, locked his gaze with Decima's.

"Philo is her Greek lover! You must have known. Everyone knows, though the mistress pretends to be discrete. He gave the same choker to Lady Rufina. You chose badly in giving the Greek his pleasure." There was resentment in his voice and he pulled her roughly onwards. As they entered the threshing room, there was a loud rumble from the bowels of the villa and a violent shaking threw them both sideways against the wall, knocking the knife from the head slave's hand, but his grip did not loosen on his charge.

"His pleasure was my duty not my desire," she said plainly with wisdom borne of innocent truth. The head slave reached to retrieve the knife and the ground shook again, thwarting the attempt. He looked at Decima with awe.

"The gods shake the ground as they speak to defend you," he whispered, releasing his grip on Decima's arm and moving a step away. "Exposed, yet you are twice saved child. The gods must have a purpose for you." Cogency came to his voice. "Leave quickly by the grain shaft. You are small enough to pass through, but do not run on the streets or you will draw attention to yourself. Go!" Decima did not hesitate for life could swing on a door hinge and her life-blood was potent.

The grain shaft was narrow, but she wriggled her way upwards, focusing on the growing circle of light as she made her way closer to the street above. If she'd had an ounce more fat covering her hips, she would not have made it. Emerging onto the street with relief, she scrabbled free from the villa which had so nearly become her prison. Fighting the impulse to run, heeding the head slave's warning, Decima walked towards the forum, trying to organise her thoughts. Where should she go? What should she do? The heat in Pompeii was rising with the sun and the shadows were shrinking. Soon the flagstones would blister her bare feet, so she turned away from the forum with its open areas, in favour of a narrower side street where shade from the tabernae walls still lingered. Feeling wholly alone with just the echoing words of her mistress for company, Decima walked along the city streets using the raised flat-topped crossing-boulders to avoid the stinking mule dung and dog excrement that buzzed with flies. For more than a sundial segment she meandered with no resulting plan other than she must leave Pompeii.

The city was sounding different. It seemed to Decima that every dog in the vicinity was barking or whining, and there was no birdsong, she realised. Reaching a crossroad and seeing a large dog snarling aggressively, straining to be free of it's leash, in the narrow street opposite, she turned left into the wider Via del Vesuvio to avoid the animal. The leather restraints on the dog reminding her of the hurtful truth spoken by her mistress. Exposed...tied...abandoned to die, and now cast aside by the mistress too. She must leave the city, but how?

A cry went up behind her, breaking into Decima's thoughts. A muleteer was trying to control his beast which was stamping shod hooves and nervously flicking its head causing the beads edging the cloth placed above its eyes to deter insects, to bounce and dance fiercely. Decima recognised the muleteer from receiving deliveries at the villa. The mule was usually such a docile creature, perhaps the dog has upset it she thought. The animal kicked out several times, up-ending its baskets of luxury goods, its master cursing the air blue. Decima collected the strewn items and guarded the baskets, waiting for the muleteer to calm his beast. Regaining the rein and wiping rivulets of sweat from his neck, the muleteer thanked her.

"The peak burns and the mule goes mad," he said, nodding towards the mountain and pressing a gemstone to her palm in gratitude. "I see your day has been no better than mine," he was referring to the obvious welt on her cheek. Decima looked down in shame, immediately raising her hand to hide the wound.

"It is nothing," she muttered, wincing in disparity to the comment as her hand touched the lesion. The mule began stamping again, distracting the muleteer who decided to turn about and head back to the forum. Decima continued towards the mountain, heading for the gate in the city walls at the top of Via del Vesuvio, for she now had a plan. The gemstone was her ticket. From the Via del Vesuvio city gate she could take the track down to the port and catch a boat across the bay. Looking up at the peak, it did have a rim of orange as if it were aflame. How strange this day was.

Once free of the city walls, Decima gave in to the urge to run. The sparkling stars of the blue sea in sight, alluring, teasing and calling her to hurry. A new life was waiting across the water. Praying to Jupiter that a berth be available and ready, her rangy legs throwing up puffs of dirt as she sprinted down the dusty track to the port. Praying also that the gemstone would be value enough to buy a passage and vowing to fulfil whatever purpose the gods wanted of her in return.

Her escape from Pompeii came to fruition upon a fishing boat that was rowed from the harbour just as the gods roared in bitter argument, spewing their fury in a fearsome, billowing, black stream of ill-temper that exploded from the mountain. Day was turned to the darkest night of death as Decima's boat left the harbour, the oarsmen increasing their strokes as they watched in awe, with ash and pumice beginning to coat the water around them. Exposed...cast aside...condemned, yet she was thrice saved for a purpose the gods were yet to reveal.

Chapter Two

The captain of the fishing boat intoned a rhythm for his crew to follow as they rowed across the bay. His voice was a resonant and steady chant of normality amidst madness, congruent with the prevailing terror. With every oar-stroke the fishermen were distancing the boat from Pompeii. Saving her from the exploding mountain but taking her away from all she had known. She was no longer Decima, slave girl to Mistress Rufina. She had no home, no family and no name. She tasted the bile of despair, yet its bitterness was sweetened by the richest honey of freedom. *The gods shake the ground as they speak to defend you. Why? What did they want of her? Was she now their messenger?*

Her new name came unbidden from this thought. She recalled Philo's teachings of the Greek goddess Maia, as the mother of Hermes the Messenger god. A beautiful nymph and a shy goddess. She had liked the idea of a goddess being shy. From now, she would use this nomen, Maia.

A loud cracking noise rent the air. The captain ducked away from the black sky, as if by dipping lower he could dodge the sound. With fear freckling his expression, he ceased his intonation and the oarsmen faltered. A series of larger waves caused the vessel to rise and fall dramatically, but the boat stayed afloat. An eerie calmness followed. Then came a cloudburst of molten rock. The ocean that had given the captain his livelihood, was hissing spit at him, seething the hatred of a scorned woman and the mountain continued to disgorge its fiery guts behind them. The captain's fear was brandished as rage and he shouted at his men.

"Row you curs! Pull as if the whorehouse is unfettered tonight." The captain leant on the rudder steering them in the direction of Misenum across the bay where the naval war fleet was berthed. The water became safer as they left the explosion behind, the rowing hard work against the wind, but no-one complained as it was blowing the death-cloud away from them.

*

Two triremes were pulling out of the port of Misenum as the fishing boat arrived. The waters had become clearer and safer as they'd progressed across the bay and were twinkling their familiar pastel beauty of marine blues and greens in the sunlight. The black cloud was visible over Pompeii and the eruption looked like the tallest pine tree as its menace branched out above the peak, but Misenum was unaffected.

Maia had never seen a war galley at close quarters before and the three tiers of oars reaching out along the length of the trireme's slender hull were an impressive sight. The order to 'lift oars' could be heard and the galley came to glide alongside the fishing boat.

"What are the conditions in the bay?" shouted Gaius Plinius Secundas, the naval commander.

"There is death at Pompeii," replied the captain. "The mountain rains fire rocks into the sea and the noise is like that of four storms. The waters grow dark and dangerous as you near." There was little time for more shouted conversation as the trireme slinked by. The commander saluted his thanks and the oars were dipped into the sea once more. It didn't take long for the warship to clear the harbour with its huge engine of man-power.

Another trireme was leaving its dock. The small fishing boat crept gingerly along, seeming inadequate as a seagoing vessel in the company of the sleek war fleet. The captain steered a route to keep clear of the bigger vessels, hugging the honey-coloured sandstone rocks of the western side of the harbour. The port was full of noise and activity as more of the naval fleet, the largest in the Known World, was preparing to sail.

"That's Plinius's villa on the cape," the captain said to his crew, turning his head and nodding at the bluff they had passed. "On the end there. Lives with his sister and her boy scribing his notes. Spends more time at his villa than out on the seas," he grunted. "No wonder the pirates enjoy so much plunder. Yet he is not short of courage to be sailing towards Pompeii this day." The captain had been shaken by the ferocity of the eruption. "There is death at Pompeii," he said again.

Maia had been listening and stood up as they neared the wharf, the tension showing in her fierce grip on the side rail. She would run as soon as she was off the boat. The captain's words had given her a plan.

The fishing boat jolted as the crew moored. Maia waited as a rope was thrown round a wooden post on the quayside and deftly knotted by one of the oarsmen. To her dismay, she realised it would be impossible to disembark anywhere other than via the landing ramp. That meant passing the captain and she had hoped to avoid further contact with the crew. She sent a swift prayer to Feronia, then scolded herself. Decima would have prayed to Feronia, the goddess who grants freedom to slaves, but Maia does not!

With a drumming pulse, Maia moved towards the landing ramp and with no choice, took the offered hand of the captain to disembark. The hoof of a fawn in the paw of a bear. She met his stare. Did he know her secret? The captain's appraisal dropped to her bare feet as she jumped to the ground. She felt his grip tighten and shame coloured her face. For a moment she thought he would trap her, but the burly seaman released his grip. Maia ran. Her bare feet, dirty and toughened, kicking up dust with each stride and shouting 'slave' as loudly as any orator at the forum.

She would need shoes.

She ran towards the Cape, taking the left fork where the path split. There was no paving away from the wharf and the ground sloped steadily upwards, the dirt path becoming less obvious as it merged with the low growing scrub turned brown by the summer's heat. Maia stopped running as she crested the bluff, welcoming the cooling breeze against her back. It was more noticeable atop the headland than at the wharf. The top of the villa that belonged to the naval commander could be seen ahead. Beyond that was the growing plume rising from the peak. What of her friends at Lady Rufina's villa? She chewed at the inside of her top lip, a habit that displayed her anxiety. A movement in the scrub brought her attention back to her own predicament. A snake slinked away and Maia's heart rebounded at the sight of it. She hurried on.

Her plan was to find the service door to the villa. She had given seed-bread to those in need who pleaded at the door in Pompeii. If Fortuna was showing her good face the staff may sneak her into the villa for a night. She had seen it happen at Lady Rufina's. Something to eat and a safe place to sleep were her priorities. Then she must find shoes. She must dress like a free-born citizen. And her hair, she must braid her hair as she had braided that of her former mistress.

"What you do is who you become," she whispered, trying to recall the beginning of the saying but it wouldn't come to the fore. Philo the Greek, proud of his heritage, liked to quote the philosophers. She'd not understood many of his quotes, but this line had stuck in her mind. *What you do is who you become.*

Chapter Three

The villa was surrounded by a stone wall taller than Maia by a forearm length, crenellated and punctuated with deep niches. Each niche was filled with a different statue: deities, sea creatures and forest animals. The stone had been lime-washed giving it a mottled, chalky texture. Red roof tiles topped the villa itself, which rose as a cube behind the wall. Only the top was visible. Maia guessed the main entrance was to the left in the direction of the dusty trail which linked the cape to the town and port, so she followed a path to the right in search of the service entrance.

She found the gate shaded by a pair of Aleppo pine trees which marked the start of a neatly hoed olive grove that glided to the headland edge. The olive fruits were recently harvested. A bronze polyphallic figure of Mercury was fixed beside the gate. An assemblage of bells hanging from its oversized erections, two of which extended from the messenger god's ears. She rang the bells without hesitation.

The service gate was made from solid oak, an arched design fitting snugly in to the stone curtain wall, so Maia could not see if anyone was answering. A goldfinch caught her eye as it landed atop the wall to her right. She watched the little bird with its blood-red face and yellow-flashed wings fly over to the olive grove, then back again to the wall. Seven times it came and went. Her confidence was beginning to waver with the wait, but she had no other plan and with hunger pressing, she gave the bells another strong rattle, overplaying the chimes.

"Patience if you will," a man's voice called out in irritation from behind the gate. "I am coming." Maia chewed at her top lip. The peep-hole in the gate was opened, the small rectangular piece of wood scraping aside. Two eyes stared out at Maia, beautiful in rich brown but unnerving in their scowl. Maia did not have to act to look a pitiful sight.

"I am hungry," she said. The man's scowl seemed fixed as he assessed her. Maia was regretting coming to the service door. What was she thinking? Decima was the slave girl; Maia was not. She must be bolder if she was to be convincing. "Forgive me, hunger has stolen my manners. This day has been exhausting. You cannot know the fear." Truth before the lies. "I am Maia Secunda, second daughter to a wealthy moneylender...and the gods have saved me from the exploding mountain." The tremble in her voice was real as the enormity of the day overwhelmed her. "I am hungry," she repeated swallowing a sob.

"Where are you from?" he asked.

"Pompeii...I have come from Pompeii."

"Why have you come to the master's villa and not taken refuge in the town?"

Maia had not expected such reluctance to open the door.

"I saw the naval commander as we entered the harbour. Such a brave man to be heading to the peak that spews the anger of Vulcan. A saviour. He shouted to me from his ship that food and shelter would be available here." Each lie that followed to prop up the first became easier to utter. "I would not be turned away he said."

The door was opened to her.

The man whose eyes had scowled through the peep-hole was older than his voice betrayed. Maia was surprised as it was uncommon for a slave to still be employed at such an age. An African, from the land of lions, he introduced himself as Uday. His receding crown shining and smooth above a circle of closely cropped white hair. Maia followed his limping frame along the corridor in silence, heartened by the drifting smell of cooking but unable to calm her dancing nerves. He led her to the kitchens.

"Sit!" he ordered indicating the bench at the table in the centre of the room. Maia willingly did as instructed, eyeing the plate of stuffed dates with envy. It was not the food of the poor and she felt the eyes of the two other kitchen staff upon her; both girls similar in age to her and with the same dark skin as Uday. "Master Gaius will want to speak to you for his uncle has set sail for Pompeii and the Mistress is a-bothered by it. Bring a bowl of the porridge, Ebele," he said, pointing to a pot put to the side of the range. The taller of the two girls did his bidding and brought a full bowl to the table. "Eat!" he directed Maia. "It may not be overly warm but hunger will add spice to any meal."

Maia accepted it gratefully. Her nerves beginning to settle as she ate, only to have them stab with a sharp intensity when Uday said quietly, "a hungry daughter of an equestrian would have eaten from the plate of stuffed dates without hesitation." Maia reddened but remained silent. "Master Gaius is not a fool. Your feet..." he flattened his lips to a hard line and gently shaking his head looked down at her dirty feet, leathery around the heels despite her young age.

Maia remained resolutely silent, averting her gaze from his as if by not looking she could ignore the truth of his words. *The gods have a purpose for me. They will guide me.*

The doorbell clattered a new arrival to the service door.

"Perhaps this is the delivery of the honey we have been waiting for. I do hope it is this time! We should never have let stocks get so low. The Mistress will be cross without it to sweeten her wine," he worried. "Find the girl an oatcake to eat." Uday limped away.

As soon as he had left the kitchen, the two girls hurried across to sit at the bench with Maia, eager to learn her story.

"Have you escaped your master?" asked Ebele directly. "This is my sister, Hadassah. Uday is our father. We were born in this house but Father was born a free man. He used to tell us stories of his life in Africa and talk of escaping, but no longer. The heart has gone from him since Mother died of a fever last year."

"You will be whipped if you are returned and branded a runaway," said Hadassah, absently touching her forehead where the letter F for *fugitivus* would be burnt on the flesh, a mixture of fear, excitement and incredulity bending her voice from its normal timbre.

"Pompeii is lost," replied Maia. "The mountain is exploding. I do not think there will be anything left to return to." Maia began to tremble with the enormity of it all. "My life there is buried," she said in a whisper, as much to herself as to Ebele and Hadassah. Could it truly be so? "I will make a new one." Maia lifted her chin a little as she spoke, determination growing as her thoughts were shared as words.

"You must find your way to Roma," said Ebele, her eyes alive with her dead mother's dreams. "We are told there are enough patrons there to fund every opportunity. You must seek out a patron to support you."

"If it is as you say and Pompeii is lost, you can do that as a free citizen, as the daughter of an equestrian as you said. There will be no-one to deny your words," added Hadassah, making the possibility seem easy.

Chewing at her top lip, Maia looked from one girl to the other, her breathing ragged as it matched her dancing pulse. She reached a hand up to the ugly welt on her cheek. The pain from touching it sliding to her heart as an ache of the cruel reminder of her exposure. She would tell no soul of that. Her heart was filling with hope, her mind filling as quickly with problems. "You were not deceived by my story. You saw the slave I am, so how will I convince those in Roma?"

*

Uday returned to the kitchen looking relieved and carrying the honey.

"I see you have finished your meal," he said to Maia. "You must wash whilst I inform Master Gaius you are here. It would do well for you to look clean before the Master. If you are lucky he may write a letter of leniency to avoid a flogging. It cannot be promised. Hadassah, you are similar in size to Maia, swap her tunic for a clean one of your own." Maia started to repeat that Pompeii was lost but Ebele spoke over her so that Uday did not hear either girl. "There is too much talk," he complained and turning his back on them, gave his attention to unpacking the delivery.

Ebele led the way in silence along two corridors turning left then right before entering a room filled with neatly folded linen and clothing, and a waist-high wooden pedal stool which had a large decorated bowl and matching pitcher on top of it. There was one high window, its shutters open to the early evening breeze which ushered in the scent of the jasmine flowering nearby.

"I have something that will help you build a new life," said Ebele, bold and direct as the situation demanded for there was little time to assess or do anything other than act on a whim.

Maia washed her face and hands quickly in the bowl of water, the coolness of it was refreshing. Hadassah helped her change to a clean tunic, the freshly laundered linen feeling good against her skin. Ebele then surprised Maia by producing a highly decorated ebony box which she placed on the nearby bench.

"Come and sit here," she said to Maia, patting the bench beside the box. Hadassah gasped when she realised what her sister was going to do, for she knew what was inside the box.

"Yes...yes," she breathed. "Oh, Ebele, it is the right thing to do. Oh, Maia...there is hope."

Ebele opened the box. It was Maia's turn to gasp.

"They are beautiful," she said, looking upon a pair of sand-yellow leather shoes, with closed toes, an exquisite cut-out pattern along the sides and long laces to tie.

"Mother made them," explained Hadassah. "They were her treasure."

"Her 'freedom shoes'," added Ebele. "That's what she called them. She would put them on when Father told us his stories of Africa." Ebele knelt in front of Maia who realised what she intended. Her pulse quickened. She should refuse the shoes. The words to do so formed in her head but two more smothered them. *Freedom shoes.* Maia was mute.

"We must be quick," urged Hadassah. "Father will be here soon to take you to Master Gaius. You will look so fine!"

It took Ebele and Hadassah little time to comb and plait Maia's hair, the braids just long enough to loop and pin above her ears in the popular fashion. Uday limped through the door as Ebele was fastening the shoe laces. He stopped abruptly when he saw the soft leather shoes on Maia's feet. All three girls froze as the room filled with the loudest hush. Each holding their breath not knowing how Uday would react. He stood still, a flicker in his left cheek muscle below his eye showing his tension, his wide nostrils flaring with emotion.

"Take them off," he said curtly as he moved across to the shelving.

"But Mother would want..." began Ebele.

"Take them off," interrupted Uday.

"But Father..."

"Take them off. The shoes are too big! We need some rag. Here, rip this." He handed a muslin cloth to Hadassah. "That's it, pad out the toe of each shoe. Hurry now." Maia put the shoes back on. "Better," he said with a satisfied snort. Ebele jumped up and hugged her father before looping a woollen cord of the same sand-yellow colour round Maia's thin waist, bunching the tunic into shape. Maia was so slight it wrapped around twice with still enough length to add an attractive knot.

"We must go, for Master Gaius is waiting and eager to return to his studies. His time is precious. Mistress Marcella will receive you too." Uday limped to the doorway and Maia followed, her back a little straighter, her walk a little slower, her deportment more confident than when she had arrived. *What you do is who you become. Could it be this easy?* Uday held the door open for her to pass and she saw a glisten to his eyes as he looked towards his daughters. "I will tell you of the lion that roamed our village in Africa," he said to them. "It is a story your mother would have me tell despite it's gruesome content. It is time we looked forward by remembering the past." So he retold how a boy from his village had killed the beast of the jungle, but not before the lion had torn his father to shreds. It was a tale to warn of the strength of a lion and how it must be respected.

"The gods brought me to you," said Maia with thanks. "I will fulfil the purpose they have for me and return to repay your kindness. Truly. I swear it!" said the liar.

Chapter Four

A little before dawn, Misenum was subjected to a violent earth tremor. Maia, Uday and the two girls were all woken abruptly by the crescendo of noise and the shaking of their cots and a pitcher smashing on the floor as a pedal stool was up-ended. The window shutters banged as the building shook. The quake stopped before they had time to gather their wits. One shutter continued to rattle.

"Is everyone safe?" asked Uday urgently as he climbed from his cot as the gods quieted their baying.

"I think so," replied Ebele, her voice quavering with fear. In contrast to the tremor, the hush of the early morning seemed to deepen beyond the normal pre-dawn stillness. She reached a hand out to hold her sister's arm for comfort.

"Our cot has shifted," said Hadassah, "and why is the shutter still banging?" The two girls were both kneeling in their shared cot, cowering from the ceiling afraid it may fall on them. Maia had been sleeping on a thick blanket on the floor and was closest to the fallen pedal stool.

"That was a stronger quake than usual," said Uday. "Girl...are you all right?" Her name had slipped his memory.

"Yes...yes, thank you. Deci..." Maia just stopped short of giving her old name. A bolt of fear at her carelessness reddened her face and she was glad of the darkness to hide it. Unwelcome memories had been triggered by the violent tremor and she recalled her flight from Pompeii in flash-shot detail. "The gods shook

Pompeii like that before the mountain exploded. I am Maia," she added.

"Sit with my daughters in their cot," said Uday. He was not as calm as his voice portrayed.

"Is the villa safe, Father?" asked Ebele. "The shutter still rattles. Should we go to the courtyard?"

"It has come unhinged by the shaking is all and the wind has turned to blow across the bay, thus it continues to rattle." A bell tinkled before Uday could say more. Hadassah let out a small cry at the sound of it, for their nerves were taut and the noise was startling in the post-tremor calm..

"Should we go to the courtyard repeated Ebele?"

Uday was undecided for a moment. The bell rang again. "No, wait here. I will come straight back as soon as I have attended Mistress Marcella. Stay together." He limped his way quickly towards the main reception room but found both the Mistress and Master Gaius before he reached it sitting together in the open forecourt looking out to the sea. A growling rumble started up again and seemed to roll rapidly towards them gaining in anger and noise. The grounds heaved once more causing Uday to stumble upon the mosaic floor as if aboard a listing ship. He kept from crying out but Marcella did not. The violent shaking came again. Two pure-white marble statues toppled over, the arm of Venus breaking on impact. Uday stayed on all-fours looking up at the surrounding courtyard walls in fear and wishing he'd not told the girls to stay in their cots.

"Gaius, we will surely be buried alive under our very own pillars. Look how they totter." Marcella had to shout to be heard above the rumbling earth. "It is as if all the legions have gathered to stamp their hobnails upon our terrace." Within minutes, the quake was over but their fear was not. "We must leave the villa. I am afraid in this confined space."

"You are right, Mother. Uday, rouse the household and bring the carriage to the front gate as quickly as you can. We will be safer away from all buildings. Mother, wait here whilst I find your stola. We will make our way to the front gate together." The silence following the tremor was eerie and Gaius, glancing at the clepsydra in the bedroom, noted the marks on the water-bowl were giving a time reading of six o'clock. Yet the dawn light was dim.

*

Uday was full of concern for his daughters and cursed his dragging leg as he broke into a loping run as best he could, banging on doors as he passed along the corridor.

"Rouse yourselves! To the front gate. The villa is toppling!" Bursting through the doorway to the kitchen, he was greeted with cries of alarm and a loud clatter as the damaged shutter gave up its tenuous hold to fall to the floor. All three girls were huddling together.

"Dress quickly! We are leaving," said Uday without preamble. "I must prepare the carriage. As soon as you are ready, go to the front gate. Wait away from the walls for I fear the gods have not finished arguing." With that said, he was gone.

In the darkness of the room, Maia saw an opportunity. It only took a moment for her to tuck the pouch containing the yellow leather shoes under the belt of her short tunic which she'd been sleeping in, before quickly putting on her longer tunic. She didn't belt this one, instead leaving it loose to hide the package.

"Follow us," said Hadassah and gave her other hand to Ebele who led them all down a corridor, across the courtyard gardens, through a reception room and out to the front gate. More of the household joined them. Maia avoided looking at any of them, trying her best to be invisible. There was trepidation amongst the group. Were they right to be leaving the villa? Where should they go to be safe? This was working to Maia's advantage as they cared little in wondering who she was in the unnerving circumstances. Maia chewed on her upper lip and keeping her head angled down, looked at the growing throng by peering furtively beneath her brows from behind the two sister-slaves. A ruby brooch was dropped to the ground unnoticed by all except Maia.

Uday arrived with the carriage. The mare pulling it was unusually skittish and Uday was struggling to keep her under control. She was stamping her hooves and bucking her head, ears pricked and eyes full of terror. *The horse runs mad like the mule on Pompeii,* thought Maia, her eyebrows matting with a frown. *Did the animals listen to the gods more closely than people?*

"Where is the daylight this morning?" Ebele asked in a hushed voice, directing her question at no-one in particular and looking around as if she might find an answer in the sky somewhere. "It's as if the sea fog descends and yet there is none. The air is dry."

Marcella and Gaius appeared at the gate and boarded the carriage. Marcella's ample frame taking up more than her share of the seating. They started moving with a lurch causing a cry of surprise from Marcella, followed by a cross retort.

"Get that animal under control!"

"My apologies Mistress," replied Uday in a tight voice.

"I will be spilled to the floor if this continues!"

"Stay calm, Mother," said Gaius, at the same time as the mare stamped a sideways shuffle before rearing up in a skip causing the carriage to weave, stop, then lurch forward again. Gaius jumped out to help Uday and between them they succeeded in managing the beast so the carriage made progress more smoothly down the hill from the Cape towards the town. Maia, Ebele, Hadassah and the rest of the household slaves were hurrying behind in the strange half-light, the brooch digging in to Maia's palm. She was now a thief as well as a liar.

*

As they neared the theatre and public baths in the town centre, the road became busier with folk milling around, unsure if they should stay or go. Some recognised the carriage of Plinius and chose to follow the family's judgement to flee.

Not long after passing the town boundary stone, where the buildings gave way to open land, with the road continuing a route betwixt beach and grasslands, Uday halted the carriage. Gaius helped his mother alight.

"We will wait here," Gaius said in an authoritative voice to his household slaves. We are safer here without walls around us. We'll sit a while." He pointed at Ebele and Hadassah. "Bring the cushions from the carriage for your mistress to sit on." His gaze flicked past Maia who was standing nearby, then came quickly back, drawn by a suspicion he couldn't fathom. Maia averted her eyes. Gaius frowned but had no chance to contemplate his suspicion. brought away from his thoughts by his mother's worried voice.

"I do hope the villa doesn't collapse further," fretted Marcella. "Your uncle will be devastated to lose his statues in the courtyard."

"Statues can be replaced; people cannot. I can hear Uncle using those very words. He would have told us to leave had he been there." His absence was a void, both of them wondering how he was faring, both unspeaking of that question for fear of malediction. The ground rumbled and shook again but not with its previous intensity.

"That gentle shake from the gods we are used to," continued Marcella. "Perhaps their spite is lessening. We may have over-reacted in fleeing the Cape."

"Well, whether it was right to leave or not, it seems we've started a withdrawal. There is quite a crowd leaving Misenum now." Gaius nodded towards the families filling the road. "They follow like ants." He shook his head, a little irked that the lower class were seemingly unable to think for themselves. The noise of an earth tremor began again.

"Look out!" shouted Uday in warning. "The carriage is rolling Master, look out!"

Yet the ground is flat thought Gaius in puzzlement. "Fetch rocks to wedge the wheels," he ordered jumping up to lean his weight against the carriage to still it. The ground was strangely undulating and he felt an unbalance as he moved and collided with the carriage front a little harder than intended. With the help of his household slaves, they steadied the coach and the earth became flat and solid and quiet once more.

"The sea is disappearing," cried Hadassah, pointing to the beach, quite forgetting to correctly address her mistress who she was supporting. Her misdemeanour was overlooked such was the sight before them.

"What is happening, Gaius? I have never experienced the like of this." Marcella was ashen.

"Extraordinary," muttered Gaius as he watched the sea being sucked away leaving fish stranded on dry sand as the ocean retreated. There was no time to study it further as a second warning cry went up, this time from the crowd behind them. The cry was full of terror. *A death cloud, a death cloud is come, look!* They all turned to see a dreadful black cloud coming across the land towards them. Complete in its funereal, inky gloom it was swallowing both land and sky looming large with a portentous omnipresence. They watched as it sank down over the bay, first hiding the island of Capri from sight and then the Cape. Pewter-coloured powdery ash started falling lightly upon them, soft and silent like big, dusty snowflakes. Cries came from the crowd.

We are cursed!

The Cape is gone!

Run for your lives!

The world is ending!

Death is come!

The cloud was suddenly torn by a tongue of magnified lightning followed by a rent of spurting flames.

The god Vulcan means to destroy us!

Run! Run!

Gaius saw a new danger.

"Mother, let us leave the road whilst we are able to," he said urgently, aware of his mother's lack of mobility. "The crowd has turned into an hysterical mob. We will be knocked down and trampled if we stay here."

"Leave me, Gaius! Save yourself. I am too old and plump to run. I will hold you back. Please..." She beseeched him to go but he did not, instead taking a hold of her by the elbow and leading her firmly to the grassland verge where he sat her down. His heart was thumping, his mind reeling from all that was happening, but outwardly he stayed calm. He would not show fear before his mother.

The cloud engulfed them, eerie and dark. Gaius heard Uday calling for his daughters. Some people were praying aloud, others were wailing that the gods had abandoned them all. Women were shrieking, children crying. Men too were wailing. Gaius fought down his own panic at the sudden sightlessness. The light of the world had been snuffed out. He still had hold of his mother's arm but the cloud was such a dense black that even being so close he couldn't see her. No silhouette, no vision. This was surely the last night of humankind. He resolved to keep his dread in check as was befitting of his rank in society. He would be worthy of his uncle's respect in death.

*

Maia ran. She saw the wild, frightened mob coming with the cloud of a thousand storms behind. She heard their shrieks and tasted their fear and she ran. Keeping to the dusty path she once more felt her life-blood rise in the urgency to live. With each stride she could feel the freedom shoes bumping against her ribs serving as a reminder of what she could be. She was quick and stayed ahead of the crowd but even the swiftest warship could not have outrun the death cloud that advanced like a huge, surging wave. Maia dropped to her knees covering her head with her arms as the darkness washed over her like a flood.

She had never felt more alone.

Something brushed her nape, ever so lightly like a breath of a kiss. Fear shafted her chest as images of a forked tongue of the most deadly snake appeared in her mind unbidden and irrational. She felt its touch again on her forearm. Fear prompted Maia to move. *This is not my time to perish, not like this.* Crawling, she felt her way using the grass-ridged edge of the track as a guide. The ground beneath her felt powdery to touch and as her sight adjusted to the darkness, she could see a sheen of light grey covering the ground. Another breath brushed her eyelashes, then her nose. To look up was a mistake and she spluttered as the falling ash quickly smothered her face. The smell was of burning, the taste on her lips acrid, but the image of a snake slithering at her heels disappeared with this new sensation. A fresh thought took hold. *There must be an edge to this darkness, it blows on the wind.*

Maia kept crawling, the stolen brooch still tightly wrapped in her small hand.

Chapter Five

In the great port of Puteoli, so named because of the permanent stench of sulphur that arose from its mineral springs, the sky was clear and blue. Dominico had been in his warehouse, which adjoined his home, since daybreak, hardly aware of the world beyond those walls. A merchant's son and a merchant himself. His paternal grandfather had raised the family's status to the equestrian class by selling the family land on Sicily.

In his thirtieth year he was happy with the success of his business of exporting delicately decorated blown glassware. Puteoli glass was finding a name for itself amidst the mass of exported goods. The harbour was a great emporium for the Alexandrian grain ships that would arrive laden with grain destined to feed the masses in Roma, and leave full of exported goods: blown glass, mosaics, wrought iron and marble. He wanted the name of Dominico di Stefano Siciliano to be the most popular of the Puteoli glassware.

In an attempt to achieve this notoriety, and to numb the grief of losing his only child, a daughter, to a fever, Dom had worked long hours over the last two years seeing very little of his wife, indeed seeing little of anything other than his business. He'd spent long days deliberating over the design of a new-style perfume vial, sweating alongside the glass blowers in the furnace room as they perfected the new product; arguing intensely with the artist when he'd wanted something different to his vision.

Overseeing the production of the new-style perfume vials had consumed him. Alone in the warehouse now that his staff had gone home, the room still hot from the furnace which would burn continually, it was with a mixture of pride and wonder that he held a vial to the lamplight, turning it slowly to inspect its artwork. A delicately blown glass droplet that resembled a flat-bottomed tear drop shimmering with an exquisite picture of Venus, her flowing hair painted in shades of gold, her dress an alluring deep red. Dom was beguiled by its beauty. A perfect miniature of the most famous image of the Roman goddess of love.

"Justification," he muttered, nodding with satisfaction, thinking back to the disagreement he'd had with Claudia in choosing his artist. His wife had wanted him to employ her cousin's husband. He was a noted muralist but his work did not transfer to the miniature as well as that of Calix, the young Greek who'd responded to Dom's advert which he'd called out in the forum. It had been difficult choosing the inexperienced Greek over a family member, especially as he didn't much like Calix. He was headstrong and sly, an untrustworthy combination, but there was no disputing his artistic talent. This being his first commission, Dom had negotiated a far lower rate than Claudia's cousin's husband was asking.

He'll want an increase, thought Dom with a resigned shrug and small snort, still with a smile gently lifting his lips into a curve. *I'll commission a drawing of Aphrodite next, that should please His Greekness.*

With the daylight fully gone, he checked the furnace temperature was low before locking the warehouse and returning via a short connecting passageway to his home. He was eager to share his excitement of the new product with Claudia. She'd not been interested in the new venture in her grief. Or was it that he had locked her out in the need to deal with his own darkness? Dominico sighed. Either way, it was time to show her the fruits of his labour. A celebration was needed. And an heir. It was time to try again for a son.

He frowned at the thought. Their marriage had always been difficult in that area. Perfunctory rather than pleasurable and with little return. One child conceived, one child lost. It had been a marriage of convenience, a solid Roman combination with Claudia bringing her own family riches to the union. Closing his fist around the glass vial, he sent a prayer to Venus: *let our union be ardent, let it be fertile, let us produce a healthy son and let him live to survive me.*

Making his way quickly through the empty atrium, he crossed the courtyard taking the steps down to the sunken pool and up again the other side two at a time. The air felt fresh and he relished the coolness after the heat in the warehouse. He could smell thyme as he bruised the leaves of the plants as he trampled across them. Expecting Claudia to be eating in the triclinium at this hour, he was drawn up short to find their house-slave clearing the table, set for two people he noticed.

"Where is the Mistress?" he demanded, his anticipation turning to irritation.

"Mistress Claudia is attending a guest, Master. I have just taken a bathing ewer to the guest quarter." Dom's eyebrows raised in surprise.

"Who is the guest?"

"A young lady, Master Dominico. She is come from Pompeii where's there's been a terrible disaster." Dom's eyebrows met in a glower at this reply.

"What disaster? What has happened?"

"I'm none too sure, Master. The girl was hungry and dirty and spoke of a death cloud."

"A death cloud? Did she appear addled of mind?" Dom absently wiped a finger across a speck of dirt on the table and frowned again when it smudged a black ash mark along his hand.

"She'd been tearful, Master as I could see streaks of clean skin down her cheeks. Without that I would've thought she be wearing a mask of grey for the theatre. The Mistress thought to feed her, then bathe her." The house-slave stopped talking as he could see a glower threading through his master's eyes. Dom's excitement had withered with the absence of Claudia to greet him. The house-slave thought to change the subject. "Can I fetch you a meal, Master?"

The change of tack worked to arrest his lowering mood. "Yes..." he said hesitantly, then more decisively, "yes, it smells good. Please inform Mistress Claudia that I am eating and would like her to join me as soon as possible."

*

It was an hour before Claudia came to the triclinium. Dom had long since finished his meal, and was sitting in thought, his lips pursed and resting on steepled hands. Any residue of excitement about the perfume vials had gone, replaced with a festering resentment that was aimed at the guest who had occupied his wife when she should have been attending him.

Claudia glided across the triclinium, her chin tilted upwards to compensate for the forward lean in her walking posture when she was hurrying. It was a most peculiar gait, with a half-twist of her hips negating any rise and fall in her step.

"Oh, Dominico, there has been the worst disaster at Pompeii," Claudia said without greeting him as courtesy would demand. Dom's eyebrows raised in surprise before quickly sinking to a frown, irked by her lack of respect rather than the news. Claudia read his look. "Forgive me, I have not asked of your health or how your day has been." She dropped her gaze to the floor and Dom immediately regretted his response seeing all her animation disappear. An ebullience had been absent since Cornelia, their first-born, only born, child had died. A loose curl cascaded over Claudia's face, reminding him how unruly her hair was when it wasn't sculpted with pins to tame it.

"I have been waiting," he said brusquely. More brusquely than intended.

Then Claudia surprised him with an angry flare.

"That is too bad Dominico," she said. "I would not have kept you waiting without good reason and you know this. There has been a dreadful disaster at Pompeii. I don't have much detail to tell you, but it seems the peak exploded. Can you imagine such a thing? At

Pompeii of all places!" Claudia's anger began to settle as she related her story. "I'd been visiting with Liliana who was speaking of it. The news was so grave that I was eager to get home, so left before her son arrived."

"So news of this disaster is from Liliana ," interrupted Dom. Claudia ignored his barbed comment but flashed him another scowl before continuing.

" I know what you're implying yet I believe her. I don't know how she gets the news before most people but she does."

"She is a gossip, that is how. And her news is often exaggerated!"

"It looks as if it is true this time," replied Claudia conceding that point. "A poor waif was sitting beside the path. Oh Dom, she was just staring, unseeing. Nay...not unseeing for there was terror in her eyes, and trauma in her trembling. She was covered in ash and it took all my courage to approach her for I feared she was from the Underworld. I've not seen the like of it before. Oh, I prayed hard to Pluto as I brought her home with me Dom. I *had* to bring her home ." Claudia dropped to her knees in front of her seated husband, taking his hands in her own, imploring him to understand. "I had to. I saw Cornelia beside her."

A pain screwed into Dom's chest. Claudia saw it fill his eyes and she looked down rather than hold that gaze, but seeing it told her he understood.

"She has eaten, bathed and is resting in the guest quarter," continued Claudia quietly.

Dom frowned and pursed his lips pulling them to one side of his mouth creating a skewed expression. He was considering his choice of words before speaking this time.

"Who is our guest?" he asked.

"She hasn't spoken much," replied Claudia, rising to sit beside Dom. "Her name is Maia and she spoke of a death cloud. I didn't think it helpful to question her too much."

"And the paterfamilias, who is he?"

"She did not say. Maia is all she offered. I haven't pressed her

Dom, she is in trauma. By her clothes I would say she is the daughter of an equestrian. Unmarried, unless her stola was lost."

Dominico poured some wine from a ewer. "Shoes?"

"Yes, she was wearing shoes. And a pretty ruby gemstone brooch was in her hand. She was gripping it as if her life depended on it, poor mite. I cannot imagine the terror."

"Not a slave then."

"Definitely not a slave." Claudia's expression showing she disagreed with that idea.

"Well, she raises a lot of questions this Maia. We will learn more tomorrow," concluded Dom. "Tonight, we have something to celebrate." His happier demeanour was returning as he showed the perfume vial to Claudia. He felt a change in both of them this evening.

Chapter Six

Dominico rose early the next morning and walked briskly through the upper town of Puteoli, passing the rectangular courtyard of the food market. Tossing a coin to a beggar sitting against one of the surrounding porticos, he made his way down the uneven steps towards the lower town. The hues in the sky were vivid but fleeting in their appearance as the dawn light aged quickly. The air was fresh.

Most people were going about their daily business unaware of the disaster unfolding down the coast. This would not be the case by the end of the day if the news from Pompeii was true. Dom remained sceptical, but he couldn't afford to ignore the possibility. If it was true then Claudia had made a very astute business observation as they'd retired last night. Having gone to their sleeping quarters buoyant, his mood had turned to restless concern for his business by the early hours as her echoing words denied him sleep: *Pompeii is the pinnacle of luxury, the crest of pleasure, the apogee of enjoyment. If the gods have turned against it then the investment from the rich that props up trade in Puteoli will be hit.*

Dom wanted to negotiate a new shipping consignment for his glassware before the news broke. Whether it was true or not, rumour alone could damage trade. And if Liliana was talking of it, the voices in the forum would soon be repeating it. A deal agreed this morning would be binding until the next quarter day and would give him breathing space should a downturn occur.

Turning the corner, he stopped momentarily to look across

the port. He could see the enormous travertine blocks, weighing six or seven tonnes each, that made up the extensive mole protecting the harbour. Four decades earlier, Emperor Caligula had erected a floating bridge from the stone mole across the bay, an incredible feat of engineering that some say only proved his madness was real. Nothing remained of the timbers of this great structure now but the tale of Caligula riding his horse across the bay was still spoken of.

Dom could see the berth he wanted to visit from his vantage point and set off down a second flight of steps mulling over his opening gambit. He was nervous, this was important and the shipping captain was a sharp negotiator.

*

"You will make your lip sore if you keep chewing at it," said Claudia gently. Maia stopped immediately, flicking her gaze downwards in a guilty way. "You have no need to be nervous of meeting my husband. He is a kind man."

But is he easily fooled? Maia's confidence was in crisis. She had been at her lowest ebb when Claudia had found her. Tired, hungry, bewildered and ready to give up this world of freedom for the safety of slavery where food, clothing and a home were provided. This was the whisper of Decima, the slave she had been.

"I have some clean clothes for you to wear," said Claudia, nodding to a house-slave who came forwards placing fresh linen of high quality on the bed beside Maia. "I will leave you with Gwendolyn, my personal maid. Gwen will help you dress and braid your hair in your chosen style. She is a very capable hairdresser. You may use my powders too...for your face." Claudia tapped her own cheek at the place of Maia's wound. They'd not spoken of how the gash had come about. Maia flushed with the memory of it and the shame that was Decima rushed forth shouting far louder than the earlier whispers. "Come to the courtyard when you are ready. Gwendolyn will show you the way."

*

The transformation in the young lady who came before

Claudia in the courtyard an hour later was colossal and Claudia took inspiration from it. She could see a new glow emanating from Maia and it folded joy into her own mood.

"Yesterday you looked a vulnerable child, today you are a confident young lady full of resilience. I take heart that I am doing right by you," beamed Claudia as she rose to take Maia's hands in greeting.

"You are most kind," replied Maia. "I do feel more like myself this morning." She smiled at the lie. *What you do is who you become.* Claudia smiled with her, unknowing of the deception.

"Come," said Claudia leading Maia gently by a hand to sit on the blue and white tiled seat beside the shallow pool. A small fountain was spraying fine droplets of water across the pool wrinkling the glassy surface, almost tinkling in sound. "The sun is warming at this hour. We will chat whilst we wait for Dominico to return. He has gone to the port on urgent business. I am hopeful he will have further news of Pompeii to give us. Bring us lemon-water to drink, Gwendolyn, and a small platter of dried fruit. Bread and olives too."

As a slave, Maia had acquired a talent for listening and she found it a useful tool that morning, letting Claudia rattle along with conversation that held no substance. Maia added enough to the conversation to not appear ignorant, succeeding even in steering away from potentially difficult topics. A couple of hours passed easily, each relaxing in the other's company. Maybe it was being relaxed that tripped Maia, her guard having been lowered.

"Your hair is braided in such a distinctive style," said Claudia suddenly after a short lull in their conversation. "I have been trying to recall the name of the lady who it is styled on. There is a frieze dedicated to her near the upper town." Maia's blood ran cold. "She is famed for rescuing exposed infants from the Vesuvius peak. Oh, her name eludes me. It is frustrating! Nay, I cannot recall it." Claudia held her palms open and upwards shaking her head in defeat. "It will come to me later. Has this style become fashionable in Pompeii? Perhaps you know this lady?"

Maia couldn't speak. Her heart had tangled itself in her throat so suddenly, so violently, that air to her lungs was restricted. Was she to be undone by her choice of hairstyle? How foolish to have mimicked Lady Rufina's unusual method of braiding. She had not realised the extent of Lady Rufina's renown.

"I cannot..." gasped Maia, her face flushing crimson as the blood-chill reversed to a burn, the heat of it streaking down her neck. She jumped up, felt faint and sat back down heavily reaching an arm out in search of something to steady her. Claudia came to her side quickly, calling to Gwendolyn to bring fresh water.

"All will be well, hush," she soothed, gently patting the back of Maia's hand. "Breathe slowly. Here, sip a little more lemon-water."

Maia did as instructed, her mind reeling to think of a plausible explanation to her strange reaction. It was Claudia who supplied an answer.

"Forgive me Maia," she said earnestly. "I spoke without tact or thought, forgetting the trauma you have been through."

"I cannot speak of it," replied Maia, blurting out the words unsteadily, her eyes round and wide like a frightened doe.

"And I shall not make you. Come, let us go inside where it will be cooler. I thought Dominico would be home by now. We have been sitting in the high sun too long."

Chapter Seven

Dominico had refused Calix a pay increase for the third new moon running. Saturnalia had come and gone and although the daylight hours were lengthening, the cold with it was strengthening. Storms were expected to disrupt the grain ships for another month yet and he felt sure trade this coming summer season would remain constricted in the bay.

The impact of the disaster at Pompeii had affected people so acutely that the city had been left beneath the ashes. No attempt had been made to recover it. Pompeii had been a lavish playground for the rich and the shock of its sudden demise was devastating. Pompeiians had offended the gods. Vulcan had paid no heed to their wealth in his anger and the rich were currently fearful of enjoyment and the economy of the area was suffering, just as Claudia had predicted.

The effect of the tragedy was rippling on in Puteoli with many of the survivors having migrated there. A makeshift camp had arisen on The Circus, a much smaller version of the racing arena of Roma, and not really big enough for the number of refugees that squatted there. Mercifully it was not too far from the public baths but still the place was beginning to stink and as soon as the weather warmed, the stench and flies would become intolerable. Emperor Titus had promised to give generously from the treasury funds to ease the suffering of those affected by the eruption. Dominico hoped he meant what he said. Politicians were often unreliable with their promises, although his father, Vespasian had been solid in power.

Dom raised a swift prayer to Minerva that Titus would not undo that good and return Roma to the wasteful reign of Nero.

Some of the refugees, like Maia, had been taken in to homes by patrons. Some families had felt it their duty to help; others had hoped for a favourable connection; the opportunistic were looking to gain financially. Dom also knew of families who had shut their doors to the Pompeiians, too afraid to shelter those who must have upset the gods beyond repair. One thing united them all though: they had expected the placements to be short-term. Not one of the patrons had thought these people would never be returning to their homes and businesses on Pompeii. This had only become clear as the psychological damage to the inhabitants emerged. Maia was a classic example. Four months on and she still could not talk about her life there.

Or *would* not, mused Dom as he drummed his fingers on his desk, although he wasn't sure of his doubts. Maia was an enigma to him. Mysterious, beguiling and shy, although he'd seen flashes of a tough confidence beneath the shyness. He felt a nudge of distrust from her silence; pleasure at seeing the happiness her living with them gave to Claudia; confusion from something he couldn't define about her and an irritating lance of uncontrollable jealousy when she directed her ambrosial smile at Calix. Damn the girl for arousing him, or perhaps he should thank her. It had resurrected his marital lovemaking at least. Claudia was not to know his thoughts were not on her as they coupled, and an heir was needed.

He probably should thank Maia for the continuing services of Calix too. Dom was convinced the young Greek would have left his employment without the daily lure of seeing Maia at the workshops. The disputatious nature of Calix, and the fact that Dom inwardly agreed that the artist's work merited a higher rate of pay, had not made negotiations easy but Dom had remained resolute that a rise could not be given with trade as subdued as it was.

Dominico swept his hands up in exasperation through his black curls that piled high on his head accentuating his long face. The curls were glistening with oil. The months since the peak exploded had been a trying time in a hundred different ways and at the centre of most of those problems was Maia. Young, inexplicable, alluring, diffident, exasperating Maia. She was a mystery that wouldn't unravel. Claudia had all but adopted her as their daughter. A god-sent replacement for their own Cornelia. That didn't work for Dom. Claudia was convinced Maia was from a rich family. Dom was not so sure, but he'd kept his doubts quiet. The girl was breathing welcome life into them regardless of her past, yet her mystery troubled him a touch.

His thoughts were interrupted by Claudia sweeping into the room.

"What has happened?" he asked, sensing her worry.

"Liliana's head slave is here with grave news of her health. She has been sick with a fever for far too long. It is worrying. I wish to read the latest scrolls of De Materia Medica to see if there is any advice on what we can give with valerian. I'm told she has had a heavy dose of that already."

"What about crushed poppy seeds? " Dom reached the leather casket which contained the medical scroll down from the shelf and passed it to Claudia, who sorted through the scrolls until she found the one she was looking for. Undoing the red ribbon that secured it, she carefully unravelled the sheet of papyrus. It was beautifully scribed and illustrated and Dom was pleased he'd gone to the trouble of buying the fifth volume in the encyclopaedic set by Pedacius Dioscorides. It had been difficult to obtain and expensive because of that.

"Poppy is for aches. I'm looking for a herb to bring her temperature down. She feels hotter than a firestone I am told. I will visit her to check for myself later."

"Quarantine may be wiser," he cautioned, raising an eyebrow.

"Don't be ridiculous, I must help where I can. I know you don't think much of Liliana but her friendship is important to me. I will never forget her kindness when I was at my lowest ebb. I will visit the asclepion as well and pray before the statue for her restored good health."

Dom held both hands up in a gesture of placating defeat.

"Buy a new charm if it eases your mind but let the slaves do the nursing," he added, before kissing Claudia's forehead. "I hope the God Asclepius visits Liliana in her dreams with an answer to her sickness. I need to speak to Calix about our next glassware project. The boy has some interesting ideas that are worth considering. See if you can encourage Maia to go to the asclepion with you."

"You know she has a fear of public places," replied Claudia distractedly as she was concentrating on the medical scroll.

"It is time she overcomes those fears," Dom answered, his brow creasing into a frown as an unexplained sense niggled at him. "I have an idea that may help her with that." He got up to go. "It will help us too if she agrees to my request," he added as he left the room. Claudia looked up after him quizzically for a moment before shrugging away the mild confusion to concentrate fully on the De Materia Medica.

Chapter Eight

Maia was watching carefully as Calix added detail to the etching on the wax tablet. It was a new design for the glass perfume vials to add to the set which already included Venus and Aphrodite. Calix was adding a tiara of tiny flowers to the goddess's head. Maia watched in silence, not wanting to disturb his concentration nor break the intimacy of the atmosphere between them.

They were sitting at a bench in a corner of the back warehouse away from the furnace that was roaring with heat. Three glass-blowers, all sweating despite wearing loose tunics of thin cotton, were working their trade across the room from them. The furnace contained three chambers of progressively cooler temperatures that were required for the process. It was noisy and hot yet easy for Maia to ignore as she became absorbed in the aura that was Calix.

Today he smelled of spices. A rich aroma of musty cloves with subtleties of citrus sliding through. Last week his scent had been of lavender. Calix would visit the public baths every morning before coming to the workshop; a sweat in the hot room, a plunge in the cold pool, with a quick massage to complete the ritual where he would choose an 'oil of the week' as he put it. His hair was dark and wavy, parted off centre and chin-length so that it would cover his left cheek and eye, acting like a curtain when he was leaning over his artwork.

When the curtain was drawn, Maia had learnt to be silent.

Calix could be sharp-tongued if you broke his focus. Art was his passion, his craft, and he wanted to make it his livelihood as well. Aspirations of riches to raise him up in status drove him to work hard. To have talent and motivation was a sound foundation for success, yet his pugnacity would likely hold him back. A useful trait in a politician but not so helpful for a young artist who could not afford to annoy his employer. Dismissal was easy.

Calix sat upright and studied his work critically before nodding gently showing his satisfaction.

"I am happy with that," he said. "What do you think?" He passed the tablet over to Maia. "Hold it by the edges so you don't smudge the wax." Maia studied the tiny image and, after a moment of silence, turned her eyes upwards without moving her head as she felt the intensity of Calix's stare. A light flush came to her cheeks unbidden.

"What...?" she asked.

"Who is it a picture of?"

Maia felt the heat in her face burn stronger. "A goddess of course."

"But which goddess?" he asked impatiently. Maia did not know. As a slave she had not had any formal schooling and situations such as this would set her pulse racing as it pierced her armour so easily. If she had been the daughter of the equestrian as she claimed, people were right to assume she had attended ludus and could read and write. The tutors were usually Greek slaves and the illustrated scrolls of both Greek and Roman gods were widely distributed and a favourite in the schools. So far she had managed to dodge such situations.

Much of her time in Puteoli had been in the company of Claudia who asked nothing of Maia but gave her everything. Maia knew she was a substitute for the daughter who had died and although she didn't try to replace Cornelia, she thanked the gods for guiding her to Claudia at a time when they needed each other. A mother's protection was invaluable and Maia had used Claudia's without remorse. Questions from Dominico that may have proved awkward had been brushed aside or answered by Claudia. She really had been the shield of three legionaries. If Maia began chewing on her lip, Claudia would read the signal and step in to help.

Fear of being recognised by someone she had known in Pompeii had kept Maia away from the forum, indeed she shunned all public areas and Claudia had accepted this without challenge. Whenever Dominico had encouraged her to visit the baths, the shield of Claudia had been raised: *when she is ready Dom, we can bathe as we need to here.* Cloth for new clothes had been delivered to the house and tailored by a slave. Maia and Claudia found gentle joy in brushing and braiding each other's hair. It had become a daily pleasure where they experimented with different styles. Maia had never worn hers in the style of Lady Rufina since that first time and Claudia had mentioned it only once, letting the subject drop when she saw Maia's distress.

"It must be a terrible likeness if you can't recognise which goddess it is!" said Calix grabbing the tablet back, his disappointment exploding as anger. In a flash he smudged a thumbprint across the design obliterating his work. He looked crestfallen. Maia was horrified.

"What have you done?" she whispered, her chest tight with emotion. She was about to say how beautiful the image had been when Dominico entered the room.

"*Futuo!*" cursed Calix under his breath. He never enjoyed talking to Dominico and his sudden drop in mood was not a good platform for a discussion. "I should give up painting and become a snail farmer," he said sullenly but not loud enough for Dom to hear.

"It was my fault," blurted Maia boldly before Dominico had even said good morning.

"What was your fault?" asked Dom, sensing the strained atmosphere. Calix was looking down with his face hidden behind his hair, struggling to contain his emotions.

"I smudged the tablet by accident and ruined Calix's work." Dom looked pointedly at Maia, pursing his lips as he let his silence worm into her mind. Was she lying? She covered it well if she was.

He felt he'd walked in on something more than they were telling but couldn't decipher what. "I am sorry," she added in a very small voice. "The picture was beautiful."

"It was not good enough," sulked Calix. Dom raised both eyebrows at that admission as Calix was usually full of swagger where his artistry was concerned. The boy's mood was like a cape of irascible gloom.

Dom sniffed. "Re-do it and make it a priority. We need to get this new project moving." Dom was tapping a finger against the bench and speaking sternly, yet he was feeling smug. The situation had unexpectedly given him the upper hand in negotiating Calix's contract. That, and he found he was enjoying their obvious discord! "Maia, please accompany me to the atrium. We must let Calix work. He needs to prove his ambition does not outstrip his talent. Plus, I have something to discuss with you." He beckoned for her to follow him, turning back to Calix before leaving. "Which goddess was it?"

"The queen of gods, Juno."

"Hm..." Dom was pensive. "I suppose Juno sits well with the other two goddesses to complete the set, but it is an obvious choice. I was expecting something more from you, more flair in your selection. Still, if you get plenty of detail into your etching I will go with it. We are running a tight schedule with this project."

Maia gave Calix a puzzled glance. That had not been Juno on the wax tablet. Maia would have recognised the queen of gods. There had been a statue of Juno at Lady Rufina's villa. Why was Calix lying to Dom?

Chapter Nine

The night-time air was cool and Maia pulled the bed cover up to her chin, tucking one cold foot beneath the other in an attempt to warm it. Sleep felt a distant friend that evening with the events of the day rushing around in her mind. Sometimes clear, sometimes colliding but ceaseless and refusing to still.

Thinking of the statue of Juno at Lady Rufina's villa, she was surprised to find that her life in Pompeii seemed an age ago. It was but four Moons since she had fled Pompeii; four bleeds, she had marked them by placing a small pebble in the shallow dish that decorated the low bench in her room. Made of red-gloss pottery with carvings of different fish, it sat proudly at the centre and Maia would run her forefinger around its rim, relishing the silky feel of it.

She could recall the detail of the statue of Juno as if she had seen it that morning, and although she had not forgotten the life of a slave, such was the dramatic changes in her, coupled with the strangeness of time in all its distorting glory, *being* that slave-girl was remote.

What you do is who you become.

She seemed to be doing Maia well. Maia Secunda...a free-born citizen of Roma. Was that really who she had become? Claudia adored her and the feeling was mutual. And Dominico who she had not been sure of, clearly trusted her too, for today he had asked her if she was willing to assist in the business. An unprecedented move for their family, an admission of a slide in their financial affairs. The mere thought of it made her skin tingle: with pride, with horror, with fear.

Dom wanted her to sell the glassware products directly to customers from the front of the warehouse and to assist in the organising of a big promotional open day. What if someone from Pompeii, from her old life, came to the warehouse shop and recognised her? That was her fear. That was why she kept away from the town. Now Dom was planning to bring the town to her.

Yet the prospect of a wage, money of her own and a respected place in society was the better side of the coin. And something to do! How she would like to keep busy. It was what she was used to. As she lay there, her thoughts rushed along uncontrollably: she would be able to buy shoes and send them to Ebele and Hadassah. A pair of freedom shoes each when she had saved enough, assuming the two girls lived that was. Maia smothered that black thought as quickly as the death-cloud had smothered the Cape. She would buy them shoes. Oh...think bigger, her inner voice yelled without invitation: buy them their freedom! Maia's eyes widened at this sudden unbidden reflection. *Thrice saved for a purpose the gods were yet to reveal.* Was this why the gods had saved her? To buy these two girls out of slavery? Her heart was thumping wildly, the idea rooting as soon as it was planted. Once rooted, she knew it would grow, for if she returned to help Ebele and Hadassah, it would be a promise upheld, a layer of good to cover the guilty lies. Maia fell asleep with her destiny laid out to work as hard as she could in promoting and selling the Dominico di Stefano Siciliano Glassware despite her fears.

*

"I have never been inside an asclepion," admitted Maia to Claudia as they were making their way along the cobbled street in the direction of the upper town. Maia was chewing at her lip. The wind was gusty and still held an unusual chill keeping most people indoors and allowing Maia to partially hide her face beneath a palla. A lock of Claudia's springy hair had escaped its pin and was at the mercy of the gusts. It was strange being out in public; both unnerving and thrilling. The salt of the ocean could be tasted upon the air, giving a sense of freedom that Maia had forgotten, yet she kept her eyes looking down whenever they passed a person, irrationally afraid of being recognised as Decima.

"It is nothing to fear," replied Claudia casting a glance at Maia to see how she was coping. "It is a place of calm, not like the bustle of the public baths. There may be a few sick people sleeping beneath the large statue of Asclepius in the main chamber, but we will make our way directly to the ante-chamber to buy a charm. It should not be busy."

"But don't we need to lay the charm upon the hand of the statue of Asclepius? I don't think the god will visit your friend in her dreams with a cure if we do not." Maia had learned this from the head slave at the villa in Pompeii.

"You are right, the charm must be touched to the statue of Asclepius but there is a second statue for such things sitting in the atrium between the two chambers. It means we do not have to disturb the sleeping sick." Claudia patted Maia's forearm. "It is good of you to accompany me. It is a comfort. It was a fever that took my precious Cornelia and I am concerned for Liliana. We will pray together at the shrine."

"Have we far to go?"

The cobbled street had turned into a dirt path that veered away from both the upper town and the steps down to the port. The wind was throwing dust around in a swirling dance across the open tract of scrub.

"Do you see the big tree behind the pines?" Claudia pointed towards the woodland two hundred paces ahead that was swallowing their path. "The big downy oak tree stands at the start of a bridge that takes us to the entrance of the asclepion, so you can see we are nearly there. There is no river to cross, the bridge is symbolic, built in imitation of the Temple of Asclepius in Roma which is located on the Isola Tiberina. Talking of Roma, I must write to my sister to thank her for taking the milk and wine to the eternal home of our parents. It is much easier for her to visit the tomb along the Appian Way than I, yet I feel guilty for not attending the ceremony of Parentalia with her. I shudder at the thought of the dead feeling hungry and returning to haunt the living. Next year I will go with her."

Claudia continued to chatter as they walked, telling Maia how well her sister had married and how her social connections kept her busy entertaining the rich in Roma. "Her villa is well sited for it sits beside the River Tiber and is close to the Circus Maximus. I was once introduced to a member of the Imperial Palace at a dinner my sister was hosting. An uncle of a cousin of a cousin to Emperor Vespasian, or something like that. There was a time when Dominico and I thought of moving to the city to promote ourselves in the same circles, but then...well...I lost the heart for it when our daughter died and Dom has the business to run now, but a visit is overdue and I should enjoy showing you the wonderful buildings of our capital city. It is full of vitality and I marvel at how many people it homes. The forum alone is a spectacle to behold."

They reached the pine woods and entering into the darker light stilled Claudia's tongue and the pair made their way across the small plantation in silence. Beyond the pines was the big downy oak that Claudia had pointed out earlier, its branches bare from the winter months but with the potential of fresh spring life curling within its limbs. The colonnaded entrance of the asclepion welcomed them as they crossed the wood-slatted bridge that arched over dry ground.

Identical stone carvings of Asclepius were decorating the walls either side of the entrance. The curly-haired and curly-bearded god was draped in cloth that covered all but his right arm and muscular torso. He was holding a staff in his left hand with a serpent entwined around it. The beauty and solidness of the marble columns standing to attention along the building giving a wonderful sense of robustness, as if the edifice itself was protecting you.

Maia was in awe of the place; the building, the setting, the atmosphere. Inside was no different. They waited for their eyes to adjust to the torch lit interior. Flickering flames were adding soft, moving shadows which blunted the sharp corners of the atrium. To the right was the shrine and statue of Asclepius, the god's strong hand splayed palm upwards to receive any charms. Cushioned kneeling pads were scattered before the shrine for people to use when they prayed.

"Come," whispered Claudia leading Maia along a path of inlaid marble across the flagstones. The marble, its polished granite flecks shimmering, took them towards two archways. "The first archway goes through to the chamber we want, the second leads into the main chamber." she explained. Let's just peek into the main chamber so you can see what it's like.

A statue of the god, three times the size of a grown man, was dominating the centre of the room. Surrounding it were rows of pallets, twenty in total and all looking small beneath the giant stone figure. Just two of the pallets were occupied, with both the sleeping patients covered by animal skins as was customary. Claudia had been right when she said it was a place of calm. Maia could feel the tranquility, the peacefulness transferring to her own heart.

"Let us buy a charm," suggested Claudia.

Chapter Ten

Over dinner that evening, Dom and Claudia discussed the promotional open day for the business, throwing around suggestions, painting a mental picture of what they hoped to achieve. Maia listened. The list of jobs seemed endless: carpenters and decorators would need appointing to alter the front of the warehouse; invitations written and delivered; food and drink ordered; products labelled for display.

"We will need to order more crates, some smaller ones I think, and extra wool and sawdust for packaging," said Dom. "And we must make arrangements to shout about the open day in the forum."

"Yes, we need to shout as many times as we can. It is the best way to advertise. We need to set a date Dom. When are you thinking?"

"Soon, "he said eagerly, adding earnestly, "the business needs the boost or we may flounder."

Maia was still listening, her emotions a cauldron of excitement, concern, nervousness but overall of apprehensive anticipation, as if she was approaching a cross of roads full of mysteries that would test her. Claudia noticed her chewing at her lip and drew her into the conversation as a distraction to settle her growing anxiety.

"There is much to be done in a short period, Maia. Once the talking is over tonight, we will be full of action. There will not be time to think," she laughed encouragingly. "Thinking inwardly too much can be harmful."

Dom was momentarily shocked to realise that Maia was still in the room but took up his wife's cue.

"You have the knack of a slave at melding invisible," he laughed, not realising how near to the truth he was. Maia's heart lurched with his comment, her cheeks blushing. A slave would be expected to look down. Maia nearly did, she wanted to, yet forced herself to hold Dominico's gaze. To her surprise, it was he who quickly looked away, raking his hand through his hair. She had aroused him. Composing himself with a small cough to clear his throat, he returned his concentration to the discussion with Claudia. With Maia controlling his loins, his jealousy brought Calix to mind.

"Calix will need time to produce enough vials with the new design," he began. "We had a setback with that but the problem is not insurmountable if the boy works hard." Maia noticed his frown but succeeded in hiding her own distress at the reminder of how she had upset Calix. She longed to put their friendship right.

"Can he be ready in six weeks?" asked Claudia. Dom indicated by a wave of splayed fingers that it would be touch and go. "A few weeks more then. How about coinciding the opening with Ludi Florales, will that work?"

"That's it!" Dom stood up in a moment of euphoria. His mind was racing, all thoughts of Maia, Calix and his own ardour expelled in an instance. "Calix must draw the goddess Flora with all her beautiful flowers. Flora will compliment Venus and Aphrodite much better than Juno. How did the boy not think of it? Claudia, you are a genius! We can pile the benches in the warehouse with flowers too. Add 'order flowers' to the list. Buy the most colourful, best scented blooms you can source. We will make this a public holiday celebration to remember." Leaning across the bench he planted a kiss full on Claudia's lips taking her by surprise. He usually kissed her forehead. "Yes!" he said wearing a satisfied grin and he left the triclinium consumed with ideas and excitement.

"Well...he is pleased," giggled Claudia, patting the couch

indicating Maia should sit beside her, both of them feeling as if a whirlwind had just whipped through the room.

*

It was late afternoon on the next day before Maia was able to see Calix alone. Everyone had been busy setting in motion the preparations for the open day. Maia had spent the day in the tranquility of the courtyard garden where the fountain was tinkling an accompaniment to the birdsong, making invitations by cutting papyrus sheets and decorating the top corners with bows of gold braid. A big pile was stacked in a reed basket and weighted down with a polished stone to stop them from springing up and scattering in the breeze which fluttered rather than gusted today. The air was warmer too.

Dominico and Claudia must be inviting the whole of Roma, she had thought, by the number in the pile. A smaller basket was filled with lengths of red ribbon she had cut to tie each papyrus invitation once the hired scribe had finished his work. Claudia was buying extra ink ready for his arrival tomorrow. Maia had painstakingly separated the ends of each piece of ribbon and curled the frays using a wooden spatula. It had been fiddly work but the end result was worth it.

She had looked into the warehouse a couple of times throughout the day, but Calix had not been alone on either occasion. With her tasks completed, she tried again and caught him just as he was leaving to go home.

"Was it Flora you had etched before?" she asked without preamble, the question having been bubbling on her lips all day.

"It was not," stated Calix in a flat voice, his manner making it obvious he didn't wish to engage in a long conversation.

"The goddess was wearing a garland of flowers, so I..."

"It was not Flora," he interrupted, his voice a tone more angry than flat.

"It wasn't Juno either. Why did you lie to Dominico?"

"Not your business," he snapped with an even icier edge.

"Do not be cross with me, Calix. I prefer it when you are trying to make me laugh."

"For that I have to be happy." A sneer crept into his expression, a blend of morosity and offence. He saw guilt flicker through Maia's frown. It was the response he was hoping for. Staring at her now, he waited for her reply but she remained stubbornly silent beneath his penetrating gaze. He gambled by pushing past her to go. He was through the corridor, out the door and more paces down the street than he wanted to be before he heard her running to catch him up.

"Calix, please...the fault lies with me, not your talent." He gambled again by ignoring her. "I did not have the schooling you think I had in Pompeii." There...it was said. Maia was shaking with emotion. It was a big admission that she should not have made. The slippery slope to the truth. Calix stopped, turned and stared at her with a warm intensity that scrambled her emotions further. So it was possible to unravel her mystery, he thought. He had her first secret and knew there must be more, for this admission raised its own questions. Why had she not been schooled? Why was she trying to hide this? Her intrigue was enticing and his anger had dissolved. Moving closer, he placed a forefinger under her chin tilting her head upwards so she met his gaze.

"So my etching was good, Maia Secunda" he said gently. Maia could only nod, captivated by the intensity of the moment, breathing in his scent of spices, her pulse was racing. The intimacy was beyond anything she had experienced coupling with Philo the Greek. She thought Calix would kiss her but disappointingly he didn't, pulling away instead. He said nothing more, just smiled a crooked, boyish grin full of charm at her, his hair cascading forwards. I have your first secret, he thought, feeling his loins stir with the power of the words: a secret he could use against her.

Chapter Eleven

The next week was a happy one in the Dominico di Stefano Siciliano Glassware business. It was productive too. Calix had regained his concentration and was working long hours on the new design. The goddess Flora was looking like his best work to date. It would definitely be colourful with the mass of tumbling flowers in her hair, and the same matching flowers on her stola. Dom had spotted Calix and Maia smiling in close conversation on a couple of occasions, their differences clearly resolved. Dom had been too busy to give leave to any jealousy though, his mind consumed with all manner of preparations and his body exhausted by the end of every day so that sleep came easily.

Claudia was flourishing under the hectic workload, industrious in arrangements and full of ideas he would not have thought of, efficient in the detail. Dom speculated on how accomplished his wife would be in the social circles of Roma, concluding she was a natural like her sister. It must run in the family, he thought.

A visit from Liliana's house-slave added to the buoyancy in the town house, bringing the welcome news that Liliana was much recovered from her illness. Claudia had given the slave an invitation to the Glassware Open Day for Liliana, along with a message to say she would visit in a week or two, by when she should be on top of the arrangements.

That did not happen.

The arrangements taking on a different, much busier, turn on receipt of a letter from Claudia's sister in Roma.

*

"Is Maia not accompanying us for dinner tonight?" asked Dom as he joined Claudia by the sunken pool in the courtyard. They had decided to eat outside, making the most of the lack of flies in the early evening springtime air. Claudia kept a palla around her shoulders, but it was warm enough to enjoy a meal beneath the stars.

"She has plans to eat with Calix at the Castello," replied Claudia. Dom gave a grunt of disapproval. "It gives me great pleasure to see her confidence shining," she reasoned in reply. "Calix is good for her and the Castello has several food outlets for them to choose from." Dom had a different opinion but chose to hold his tongue, unsure if his thoughts were clouded by a foolhardy envy or not. The evening was too pleasant to spoil and, despite his disapproval at Maia's absence, he soon cheered to the idea of a chance to talk to Claudia alone. They'd not had the opportunity for a good, frank political discussion recently. His wife usually surprising him with her knowledge and insights when they did.

"It looks as if our fears that Emperor Titus was to be a bad ruler like Nero are not coming true, despite his dalliances with the Jewish Queen," he began.

"Far from it. He seems to be continuing with the policies of his father and my sister writes that he is enjoying excellent relations with the Senate."

"Well, his first act as Emperor was to order a halt to trials based on treason charges. That will have pleased the Senate. None have been tried and put to death since his succession!"

Claudia laughed at that. "That is true. He is planning two weeks of games to celebrate the opening of the Flavian Amphitheatre too apparently. He is playing his tali pieces well."

"It is a shame Emperor Vespasian didn't live to see his commission completed. I have heard it is quite a structure. It's made of stone, how about that. Roma's first permanent amphitheatre, and not before time, especially as we have lost the old one in Pompeii. Roma's amphitheatre stands alone I believe, on the site of Nero's Golden Palace. I should like to see it, and the games, but the timing with the business is not good."

"There will never be a right time to take a break from Dominico di Stefano Siciliano Glassware," admonished his wife. "We should go for the opening games. It would be desirable to visit my sister and introduce Maia to Roma."

"Is Maia ready for Roma; is Roma ready for Maia?"

"She is coping well with the bustle of the Puteoli forum now. And eating out at the Castello. I think she is ready. Whether Roma is ready for Maia, I cannot answer," she laughed again. "Regardless, it would be suicidal to refuse the Emperor's invitation."

Claudia's last words didn't register with Dom immediately as he continued to talk about Maia. He stopped mid-sentence. "What did you say? An invitation from Emperor Titus?"

Claudia was smiling coyly. "Well, not quite yet, but I am hopeful he will extend you an invitation when he visits." She was waving her sister's letter at him.

"You are teasing me with riddles, Wife. Let me see that letter from Laurentia." Claudia watched with growing excitement as Dom took in the broken wax seal. "This has come via the Cursus Publicus," he said in astonishment, looking at Claudia for an explanation. "How has your sister managed to get use of the Emperor's postal service? The penalty for misuse is death!"

Claudia was still smiling. "Laurentia has been entertaining in high company and it seems our story of taking in a refugee from Pompeii and our struggling business because of the eruption has reached the ears of Emperor Titus who gave her permission to use the Cursus as time is pressing with arrangements. An Imperial tour of the area is planned and we are to receive the Emperor. He wants to meet Maia! I know it is headlines for the forums to shout: 'Emperor meets survivor of Pompeii'. Politics, good relations, oh I know all that Dom, but what a boost it will be for us! He has promised money to those hit by the disaster caused by the eruption, money from his own treasure chests as well as from the estates of those who died. My sister says Emperor Titus is personally overseeing the relief effort."

"This is incredible news." Dom continued to read the letter, pointing at a lower paragraph. "It says we are not to shout the news at the forum?" his voice raising in a question.

"For security reasons," explained Claudia. "We are to keep his visit to our warehouse a secret. The tour to Puteoli is being announced but not the imperial route. As Laurentia explains, it's a relief effort not a triumphal military parade. And although it will be used to promote the good of the Emperor, he does not wish to be seen as glorying in the disaster. You dance a fine line in politics. He plans to visit our warehouse in secret the evening before he tours Puteoli. An informal affair..ha...as if such a thing is possible with the Emperor. We are being so highly honoured that my heart flutters with the thought of it all."

"It is incredible news," Dom repeated, gently shaking his head in disbelief, but with a smile teasing at his lips. "It will be the making of us."

"Fortuna can be fickle Dominico. Never forget that she has two faces. She may show you favour as the cock crows, but bury you by dusk. We must not lack virtue, nor be idle."

"There is no chance of being idle. Our workload has just increased tenfold with the extra preparations. You must not mention the visit to Maia."

"Oh, you think I shouldn't, why?"

"She will tell Calix, who in turn will tell another and so the news will spread."

"You don't think we can take Maia in to our trust? Not even if we stress how important it is to keep the secret?"

"I fear the young Greek could charm a secret from Medusa without being turned to stone. We would be setting Maia an impossible task. It is kinder to keep it from her. And you are not to mention it to Liliana either or all of Puteoli will know before you have returned home!"

"Liliana probably knows already," replied Claudia wryly, conceding that her friend was a gossip. "I will not visit her until this is over Dom," she added sincerely. "I would not be able to conceal my excitement and Liliana is an expert at prising news from people. No, I cannot risk it...the Emperor...oh my goodness, the stakes are high!"

Chapter Twelve

It wasn't often that Maia allowed herself to think deeply about all that had happened since the gods had seen fit to save her from the exploding peak. Her friends from Pompeii had crossed her mind many times but she had deliberately turned her thoughts to other things rather than dwell on the past. When sleep was slow to come, she would resort to concentrating on rhymes she knew, pushing away other concerns by silently repeating the words in her head, over and over until sleep took charge. This tactic had served her well. The enormity of it all, the horrors of the events, the huge changes in her life, could have swamped her if she'd given them heed.

Yet today was different.

Gwendolyn had been unusually quiet whilst braiding and pinning Maia's hair, only muttering an apology for a sneeze whilst draping a palla around Maia's tunic and lacing the yellow 'freedom' shoes, still with the toes stuffed with padding to fit. It wasn't like her to be so taciturn. Maia put it down to the extra stress of the looming warehouse open day which was just two days away. Two days! Tensions were high in the whole household and Maia was pleased to be running an errand to the macellum to escape the heightened levels of anxiety for a while.

Gwendolyn's silence allowed Maia's mind to wander. She had first visited the macellum with Calix when they'd gone to the Castello to eat. The market hall had eighteen columns made of marble and grey granite. They had touched each one, smooth, cool and solid, together as Calix counted them. She'd had such fun. There was talk of plans to build a bigger hall with twice as many colonnades. Maia was resolved to learn to count before the new macellum was built.

With a lightness in her heart, Maia allowed her mind to drift back to her life in Pompeii. Life as Decima the slave girl, and found that the darkness that usually crept in around the edges of such thoughts, the shadows on her soul that would begin to close in, weren't there this day.

She let the memories meander on for a while after Gwendolyn had left the room, remembering the muleteer who had given her the gem which paid for her boat ticket; the head-slave at Lady Rufina's villa who had encouraged her to escape along the narrow grain shaft; the estate slaves as well as those in the house. Did they still live?

"I will look for the shrine today," she said out loud to herself, stealing her nerve. Calix had told her a couple of weeks ago that a new shrine to Venus Pompeiana had appeared near the asclepion. The goddess was the patron deity of Pompeii and unique to its culture, so it seemed likely the shrine had been built by other refugees who had escaped the disaster. The fear that she would be recognised and her lie unveiled had kept her away, but Calix had told her, rather impatiently, that she must make peace with the goddess, not abandon her. He was right. Venus Pompeiana would find a way to reveal her past if she turned her back on the goddess. She must take an offering to the shrine. The spring sun was not yet too hot for her to look out of place with her palla brought up around her face and head. She would be careful and quick, and the task would be done.

With a sense of relief at arriving at a decision, one that she knew would please Calix, and that alone warmed her heart, she smiled at the shoes upon her feet. She had grown accustomed to the feel of them now and marvelled at how well she must look with her palla of matching golden cloth which shimmered in the sunlight with the red silk thread flecking through it and the stolen ruby brooch clasping it together.

What you do is who you become.

There was no shade of Decima, she *was* Maia. Her transformation from slave girl to free-born citizen with a position in commerce, was complete. No-one from Pompeii would recognise her; she barely recognised herself!

Seeing the amphora which now decorated the low bench alongside the shiny red pottery dish made her wonder how many coins would be needed to buy freedom for Ebele and Hadassah. She had dropped the first one in there yesterday. Perhaps Calix would know. It would be foolish to ask Claudia or Dom. She could easily imagine the questions of their cross-examination. Calix would be less inquisitive as to why she was asking such a strange question.

Thinking about Calix brought an extra shine to her mood. Like them all, he was working long hours preparing for the warehouse open day, even helping the glass-blowers, sweating alongside them from dawn to beyond dusk, producing sets of the exquisite tear-drop perfume vials that surpassed anything Maia had seen in the expensive shops of Pompeii for delicate beauty. Stunning miniatures of Venus, Aphrodite and Flora, detailed, colourful and sparkling. She was so proud of his work. After the opening day, Dom had promised them all time off for the remainder of Ludi Florales and Calix had promised to take her to watch the imperial parade in Puteoli. He knew of a good spot to watch it from near the asclepion. Just a glimpse of Emperor Titus would fill Maia with awe.

*

A small crowd was gathering around the fountain of Neptune at the forum, listening to the latest news being shouted from the plinth. Despite the earlier confidence Maia had felt at not being recognisable as her former self, she fussed with her palla to ensure it was covering as much of her face as possible without looking obvious she was hiding, before mingling at the back of the growing throng. She wouldn't linger, but the clerk was sure to be shouting about the imperial visit and she may glean more information on the expected route, thus gain a better idea of the best viewing spots. It was so exciting, although hecklers in the crowd showed that not everyone thought the same way.

A voice close by called out an objection, ignored by the clerk who continued delivering his announcements unperturbed, but Maia gave the man a sideways glance, studying him surreptitiously. He had an ugly demeanour and a nose that had clearly been broken and not reset as the ridge of it had an unnatural kink.

The ugly man called out again and those near him started to mutter with one man taking a particular dislike to his belligerent attitude. There was a jostling that rippled out to Maia as people moved away from the two men anticipating the start of an argument. Fights in the forum were commonplace and it was not unusual for the security guards, privately hired militia comprising mainly of discharged legionaries who were not content to farm the plot of land given to them by the state on retirement, preferring instead to continue in a more familiar line of work, to arrest as many innocent bystanders as guilty parties when a fray broke out. Maia decided to leave immediately, frustrated at not hearing the news that may help with a better view of Emperor Titus, but not wanting to risk being caught in a problem that wasn't her own. Besides, there was much still to be done and the tide waits for none.

Hurrying up to the first of the eighteen colonnades of the macellum, Maia didn't hear the boots of the running security guards as she was immersed in mentally repeating the instructions from Claudia of the flowers she was to order; didn't see them either because of the huge pillar. A burly man in a leather breastplate was all she registered before being knocked over, landing with a thump in a sitting position. Shock was the worst of her injuries. Upright and walking one second, unexpectedly sitting on the paving the next.

The security guard was down on all fours several yards on, the collision having unbalanced him, his momentum keeping him stumbling on a few paces before downing on to a knee. They looked at each other. Maia, seeing the question in his expression, nodded quickly that she was all right, waving for him to catch up with his two colleagues who were shouting at the crowd to let them through. He hesitated a moment, still looking at her, then got up and ran towards the melee, deciding that was where he would be of most use.

There had been something comforting about the look from the security guard: a gristled kindness, a deftness of decision. Eyes that said they'd seen much worse, knowledgeable and caring but with an edge of hardness, but above all, honesty. If he had assessed her to be okay, then she must be. That is what his look and resulting decision said, and it cut through her shock settling her well.

She got up, brushing down her tunic and palla with her hands and readjusting the shawl around her face as before. Glancing back, she could see the guards were now in control of the forum fracas. "Thank Jove," she breathed and hurried on to the flower stall.

*

The sun was high in the sky and the shadows were short when Maia made her way from the town to reach the path that led to the asclepion. Even from that distance she could see the leaves on the downy oak had unfurled showing their fresh, young green shade displaying the promised life that had been hinted at when she came before with Claudia.

If she had understood Calix's directions correctly, instead of crossing the dry bridge to enter the asclepion, she needed to take the track to the left to find the shrine of Venus Pompeiana. It is easy to find, he had told her and she had laughed at that. People were prone to saying that when they knew where something was. It was never so easy when you were blindly following instructions. She would find it though, the gods would guide her, just as they had guided her along the road to Puteoli in the blackness of the death-cloud. She involuntarily touched the ruby brooch she had stolen that day which was pinning her palla together.

"Oh!" she gasped out loud when she realised what she was doing. *It is a sign. I must give the brooch as an offering to the goddess.* It was like sunlight spreading into the darkest cave when the notion came to her and her footfall across to the woods were the lightest they had ever been.

When she reached the bridge by the oak, the sight was arresting. The giant marble columns were sparkling, the sunlight picking out the minerals in the stone, quartz and pyrite, colours of rose, purple, silver, gold, all shimmering and twinkling like a night sky of coloured stars in daytime. It took her breath away and drew her across the bridge away from her intended destination. She had time for a quick look inside the beautiful asclepion.

As before, the reverence of the building both inspired and calmed her. She walked through the atrium noticing that most of the kneeling cushions were in use this time, a shadow of a frown slipping across her face. Nearing the archways that led to the two chambers, noises of the sick could be heard; sneezes, moans, coughs, the restlessness too much for just a few sleepers. With her curiosity and unease growing, Maia went under the second archway and was horrified to see there was barely a pallet left free in the main chamber.

"Upon my life," she breathed, raising her hand to her mouth in shock. "It is a plague!"

Retracing her steps to the atrium, she was met with another shock. Liliana was waiting for her.

"I saw you come in," she said by way of a greeting, lacking her usual manners. "Is there sickness in your house too? Is that why Claudia has not been to visit?"

The directness of the unexpected questions caught Maia by surprise.

"No, no, we are all well," she placated, concerned by the hysteria she detected in Liliana. "The preparations for the warehouse open day has taken our time."

"It will have to be cancelled. You must inform Claudia. Too many are sick. My entire household is succumbing to this fever, including my beloved son. It is beyond belief. All I can do is pray. I feel so hopeless." Then, with a fierceness to her tone as if she were addressing a slave, she instructed Maia to go home at once. "You should not linger where the sickness is! Go!"

Maia was shaken by the ferocity of Liliana's warning and, touching the ruby brooch again, decided she must go directly to tell Dom and Claudia what she had learned. An offering to the shrine would have to wait.

Chapter Thirteen

Claudia was pacing the triclinium, wringing her hands and impatient for Maia to return with Dominico. She'd sent her to fetch him from the warehouse as soon as Maia had told her what she had seen at the asclepion. It was a bad business: a plague outbreak! She slapped her thigh in frustration. Preparations for receiving Emperor Titus had been going so well and now this dreadful news. Had she visited Liliana as often as usual, she would have heard this news much earlier and they could have halted proceedings before they had invested so much.

The door flew open and Claudia turned to see Dom stride into the room, raking fingers through his black curls, looking every bit as perturbed by the news as his wife. Maia came stumbling in behind him.

"This is a disaster, we must get word to your sister immediately to cancel the Emperor's visit," said Dom. Leaning both hands on the bench, legs astride, he continued without waiting for any comment from his wife. "Call for Gwendolyn. We'll have to hire the quickest rider and even if they leave within the hour, I'm not sure if they'll reach Roma in time, but we must make every effort. Or should we attempt to intercept the imperial entourage? Would that make more sense?" Dom's thoughts were darting like minnows, visible by his rapid eye movements, darting but unseeing such was his inward focus. "Futuo!" he cursed, smashing a fist down on to the bench making both Maia and Claudia flinch. "You were right about Fortuna being fickle!" He was not a man to show rage often and

Maia slinked backwards trying to meld into the wall, just as she used to as a slave when the mistress was cross.

Claudia reacted differently, coming forwards, completely unafraid of his outburst. Confidence shines under such circumstances.

"Dom, I do not think we should cancel the Emperor's visit," she said firmly. He looked at her strangely, his eyebrows flicking up in surprise before knitting into an expression of incredulity at such a suggestion.

"What? We must. We cannot have it on our conscience not to warn him of a plague outbreak here."

"Let us be rational. Maia, I am not doubting what you say or saw," Claudia held up her hand towards Maia in a placating gesture as she was speaking. Maia was more than happy to obey the hidden request for silence given by the raised hand. "But Dom, you have never given heed to Liliana before. Have you not always said she is prone to exaggeration?"

"It is true the woman is a gossip and prone to making more of a situation than necessary, but it is madness to ignore the number of sick in the Chamber of Asclepius. That cannot be denied."

"How often do any of us visit the asclepion, Dom? Rarely!"

"Your point being...?"

"This could be more normal than we realise."

"Perhaps in the depths of winter, but at this time of year?" Despite his negative words, Claudia could sense Dom's attitude softening so pressed on with her argument.

"We haven't heard of any deaths being reported from this sickness, and Liliana recovered fully. I admit I was worried, but she did recover. Besides, no-one here is infected so it would be difficult for blame to be laid at our threshold. We should receive him, Dominico," she urged. "It will be the making of us!"

Maia was astonished at what she was hearing. Surely Emperor Titus wasn't coming to the warehouse, was he?

Dom put his hand on his hips and looked to the ceiling, puffing air through his lips. Claudia rang the bell a second time to summon Gwendolyn who had not yet arrived.

"No need," said Dom, indicating the bell with a wave of his hand. "We have come this far and you argue a case well, Claudia. Are you *sure* we should go through with our plans?" He looked earnestly at Claudia whose gaze did not waver.

"It will be the making of Dominico di Stefano Siciliano Glassware," she replied steadily.

"You have amazing strength, my wife." He kissed her tenderly and the intimate exchange touched Maia's heart. "We are gambling with the highest stakes, pray to all the gods that we win." Gwendolyn arrived, breaking the intimacy. "There is much to be done," remarked Dom, checking his stride and grunting as he noticed Maia. "You are indeed possessed with the stealth of a slave, Child. I forgot you were in the room. Well...it is not how we intended to give you the news, but now you know, I will leave Claudia to fill in the details," he said, winking at Claudia as he left.

*

Gwendolyn sneezed...twice. Claudia shot her a horrified look.

"Excuse me, Lady Claudia, I am not feeling my best today."

"I am sorry to hear it," replied Claudia with feeling. "When did this begin?"

"Two days ago, it started with a soreness in my throat and now I cannot stop sneezing."

"You may be relieved of your duties for the remainder of the day to rest but keep to your sleeping quarters, said Claudia decisively, trying to keep her tone level and only just succeeding. "I will check on you later."

"Thank you Lady Claudia, thank you."

"Dom is not to hear of this, Maia" instructed Claudia fiercely once her maid was out of earshot. "We will say Gwendolyn is running an errand for me if he asks. Is that clear?" Maia nodded, unaccustomed to such a sharp tone from Claudia. A jagged flint amidst soft chalk. Claudia noticed her chewing on her lip, something she'd not seen her do in a while and she made an effort to soften her voice, although inside she wanted to scream. "I cannot stress to you how important this open day is to the business, to us. I hardly dare to believe what is due to happen. My sister has given us the most incredible opportunity and I will not allow it to be scuppered at this late hour. We have come too far, invested too much, and without the Emperor's visit we are lost." Try as she might, Claudia could not keep her tone light. The tone of steel was back in her voice and joined by a glint in her eyes as sharp as any sword edge.

The atmosphere in the room was borne of the River Styx itself, with undercurrents to trap you in a swirling blackness. Desperation. Maia understood desperation, and with that understanding came a quiet confidence. Claudia, unknowingly, could not have a better collaborator by her side.

"We were going to tell you of the Emperor's visit over our meal tonight," said Claudia. "It has been so difficult for me not to confide in you. I wanted to share the burden," she explained with a short snort of a laugh, continuing in a bid to justify her decision. "But it being a burden is the very reason we kept it from you. The very reason why I have not visited Liliana too. She would have prised the news from me easily. In turn, that is the reason we did not hear of the growing number of sick in the town. If we had, we could have halted events before borrowing the money to pay for the extra arrangements to receive Emperor Titus. The reception has to be right. We have gambled the premises, our home, our livelihood, on making this a success. We must go ahead with the plans or we will having nothing. The Emperor is coming here tomorrow evening before he tours Puteoli town the day after. We are to keep his visit here a secret until the imperial tour is over. As a survivor of Pompeii, he particularly wishes to meet you, Maia. How do you feel about that?"

It was a question that had been bothering Claudia, one which she had chosen not to discuss with Dominico, knowing his response would be unwaveringly harsh in not giving any slack to Maia for her traumatic past. Claudia did not want Maia to fail with the eyes of

Roma upon her.

Maia's nostrils flared with emotion and she put her hand to her nose, pinching the end and resting the fist of her hand against her mouth, not knowing whether to laugh or cry. It was the highest opportunity to promote the business, and the rarest of opportunities for a rise in personal status, but there would be questions from the Emperor. Was she brazen enough to lie to a man who sat so close to the gods? The answer was simple...she must...for she was thrice saved so she may buy freedom for Ebele and Hadassah! It was her purpose. Her means to add coins to the amphora would disappear if Dom and Claudia lost the business. Condemned...saved...free to live. And live she would!

Claudia was not expecting to see the smile which slowly revealed itself as it grew wider than Maia's fist. Throwing open both hands and raising up her arms, Maia leapt to embrace Claudia and the pair laughed and danced with the joy of shared excitement.

"I have nothing to hide," laughed Maia. The biggest lie spoken so far.

Chapter Fourteen

The warm, evening sun was casting long shadows as Dominico and Claudia were waiting nervously in the atrium to receive the imperial visitors. Dust particles were dancing in the shaft of sunlight that was leaking through the window, the wooden shutters were open and the thin animal skin had been removed to allow maximum light into the room. The weather could not have been more favourable, producing a day bursting with freshness.

It was Claudia's idea to greet the Emperor alone and introduce him to their household as they toured the warehouse, giving demonstrations of the different skills and areas of the business as they moved round. The final day of preparing had been hectic and long, but nothing was longer than those last few minutes as they waited for their head-slave to lead the group through the door. The minutes seemed to string out like a spider's silk arcing on the breeze and they knew the visit would be contrastingly short, security dictating nothing lengthy.

"We rise or plummet, this is it," breathed Dom squeezing Claudia's hand as their head-slave opened the door and quietly and quickly ushered in Emperor Titus and four bodyguards.

"Ave, Imperator," they said together, both dipping forward into a curtsy-bow. The sweet trill of a songbird split the air giving its own greeting.

"It is good of you to come, Imperator," said Dominico.

"I am sorry for the troubles that have befallen you. The loss of Pompeii is immeasurable. I pledge to support those who have been affected by this disaster." Emperor Titus turned his attention to Claudia. "Your sister, Laurentia Corti has spoken of your plight and told me about the young refugee, Maia Secunda you have given a home to. She escaped the explosion of the peak on a rowing boat, I understand. I would like to hear her account of the event. Such an explosion is unfathomable to me. The peak has lost much of its height I am told."

"My sister has informed you well, Imperator. Maia is waiting for you in the warehouse. We thought it would be interesting for you to see the workshop in action."

"We appreciate your time is limited here, Imperator," added Dom, holding out an arm to indicate the direction of the connecting passageway to the warehouse.

The sweet scent of lavender drifted through the passageway as they trampled the dried seeds that had been liberally strewn across the floor.

"We have everything ready for the open day tomorrow," said Dom, opening the door to the warehouse, the furnace heat smothering them as the group entered. Blooms of spring flowers stood in tall vases all around the room. They would be replaced with fresh bunches tomorrow. The noise of the furnace disguised the unusual hush that descended on the room as Maia, Calix, the glass-blowers and household staff, with the exception of Gwendolyn who Claudia was appalled to find with a fever, all dipped forward in a curtsy-bow, each looking to the floor in respect to the Emperor. Dominico had not been told of the maid's fever.

Dom led the Emperor round the warehouse showing him the furnace and explaining the processes involved with the glass-blowing business. Titus gave time to talk to each staff member, taking interest in their answers. Maia was standing near Calix, the last two in line to greet Emperor Titus.

Nerves were dancing like gnats above a pond in Maia's stomach as she waited her turn. *Answer his questions with passion and, above all, with honesty*...Dom had lectured when he'd gathered his staff together earlier in the day. Maia could have laughed out loud. Her whole life was a lie. An accomplished thief with a tongue as deceitful as that of Mendacius, apprentice to the craftiest of all the immortals. That was what she had become.

Calix broke her introspection as he moved a hand to tuck his unruly fringe behind his ear, sharing a look with her that was full of excited anticipation. She could see he was bursting with the opportunity to garner the highest recognition for his work.

There was no more time to think as Dom presented her to Emperor Titus. With a nervous flush in her cheeks, she looked boldly at Titus feeling exposed as the fraud she was beneath his direct gaze. Yet it was the Emperor who seemed to lose his composure, looking strangely at Maia for a moment before stumbling over his opening words to her.

"I under-understand you...er...escaped the exploding peak that...er...has buried Pompeii."

"I did, Imperator," said Maia in a small voice, her slight frame looking fragile against his opulent physique. "It is difficult to speak of it," she added, adopting her usual strategy hoping it would work as well as it did with Claudia. There was a long pause as Titus looked around the warehouse, shaking his head, lost in his own imagination of the unfathomable disaster. Maia could barely breathe so tight was her chest with anxiety. How she wished she had given the ruby brooch in offering to Venus Pompeiana when she had been near the shrine. Was that only one sunrise ago? Time appeared to be warping, bowing like a cut sapling under stress. She sent a swift, silent prayer to Jupiter, asking the king of gods to mute the deity of Pompeii. *Please keep my secret for I have begun amassing coin to free Ebele and Hadassah.*

Everyone in the room was looking at the exchange between Titus and Maia. The Emperor looked at Maia again, another flicker of astonishment lacing his expression.

"I had questions for you when I heard your story, Maia Secunda, but now that I am here, I find I do not want to ask them. Your ordeal, the deaths, the loss..." he tailed off shaking his head again, his full lips pressed flat, sincerity in his words. Raising his voice he addressed the room, "I pledge my personal financial support to this business, Dominico di Stefano Siciliano Glassware." The room filled with cheers and clapping and Maia dipped into another curtsy-bow on legs weak with relief, not because of the promised money, but because she had escaped lying directly to the Emperor. The gods must favour her still.

Dominico moved in to present Calix to Titus. The Emperor took great interest in the young artist's etchings, admiring his work and giving heed to how he adapted a drawing into miniature for the glass perfume vials. Titus did his best to focus entirely on Calix's explanations, but he couldn't keep his gaze from flicking across to Maia.

Dominico ended the warehouse tour with a short speech thanking Emperor Titus for his pledged support, rousing his staff to another series of salutations as Claudia led the party back through the passageway.

*

"Did that really happen?" said Calix to Maia when the echo of their cheers faded. "Did I really speak to the Emperor? I thought I would swallow my tongue and be mute!" Calix impulsively grabbed Maia's hand, raising it high and twirling her beneath it, then using his other hand to cup her waist and pull her to him. She didn't resist, inhaling his happiness as well as his oils that were smelling of cinnamon today. "We have been noticed, my shy goddess," he whispered before kissing her fully on the lips. Maia came away from the embrace a little breathless. "The etching I smudged out was your namesake," he said, looking at her with an intensity that created a surge of melt water in her chest. "Beguiling, shy and beautiful."

"So why did you lie to Dom about that?"

Calix answered her question with one of his own. "So why did Emperor Titus give you such a startled look?"

"He did seem disquieted for a moment," replied Maia frowning.

"I should say, you disarmed him. Beguiling, shy and beautiful," he repeated, placing his finger to tilt her chin up as he'd done before. The melt water rushed in Maia again, her heart seeming to float without an anchor, adrift and helpless under his intimate gaze. It was the control Calix wanted. With their breath mingling, he was her world for that moment. A droplet of powerful, untroubled isolation. Their kiss was tender.

The noises of the warehouse filtered back in as they withdrew from the embrace, the droplet bursting, leaving Maia with a happy but self-conscious glow; the glow encompassing Calix and eclipsing all wrong, including the unexplained lie which seemed suddenly unimportant. Looking sheepishly at the other warehouse staff, she saw that they were going about their own business and not staring at her as she felt they would be. Maia was feeling wonderful.

"I must go to Claudia," she said, remembering the instructions she'd been given earlier. "Will you be here early tomorrow? There will be much to do."

"Before the sparrows fart," he said with a wink. "Sleep will not come after the great news we have had today." Calix smiled. "We met the Emperor!" he shouted, raising his arms in a crucifix and throwing his head backwards in the glory of joy. Maia bathed in his happiness.

The good news of the day didn't cease there either, for Claudia greeted her with the happy report that Gwendolyn was without a fever, sitting up in her cot and feeling much better.

"I am sorry she missed meeting the Emperor, but my relief that she is without the plague is immeasurable," said Claudia. "I have other news too: I am with child."

How wonderful this day was.

Until, that was, they received the dreadful news later that Roma was burning and Vulcan's wrath did not stop there as the god of fire saw fit to mimic his display of power simultaneously at the Dominico di Stefano Siciliano Glassware warehouse. It was sickening.

Chapter Fifteen

In all the excitement following the visit from Emperor Titus, the furnace was not dampened properly. The warehouse was burning fiercely before the alarm was raised by a late-night passer-by, the fire spreading with ease along the wooden tinders to the attached house. Dom, Claudia and Maia, their sleeping quarters being furthest from the fire, escaped to the street, but the household slaves did not. Dominico re-entered the burning building in the hope of saving them. He perished inside.

With the house and business in cinders, Claudia and Maia went to stay with Liliana. Within days, Claudia was burning with a fever as hot as the furnace that had ended her husband's life. Liliana had her driven in a carriage to the asclepion and here she, and the cherished child she carried in her womb, succumbed to the pestilence despite the furs covering her and Maia's constant vigil of prayer to Asclepius.

Calix found Maia sitting beside the big downy oak outside the asclepion, its massive boughs spreading shade across the dry bridge and darkening the entrance now that it was in full leaf. She was hugging her knees to her chest, staring at her shoes. The pink hues of dawn were slipping quickly to the light blue of early morning, the scornful cries of gulls splitting the air, the sound sliding on the breeze.

"Claudia has died," she whispered, not looking up. "The gods have taken her to Dominico."

"Her spirit will be judged with favour when she crosses the Styx," replied Calix sitting down beside Maia. "She will rise to Elysium."

"Without doubt. She was so kind, so very kind." They sat in sadness for a while, together but alone, each lost in their own thoughts. Maia was the first to speak: "I cannot stay with Liliana. Her generosity of heart does not match that of Claudia. She will make a slave of me." No sooner spoken was regret; *slave*. The word seeming to rumble in the air, increasing in volume like an approaching earthquake. It was a strange comment to make and produced a frowning, sideways glance from Calix. A blush rose in Maia's cheeks. *He has me undone.*

She fiddled with her shoes as a distraction, drawing Calix's attention to them. He'd not noticed the padding at the toes before. Poorly fitting shoes, no formal schooling, and a peculiar reaction to her own words, a confession almost...the layers were slowly peeling back and he saw an opportunity to dig beneath them and use it for his own benefit.

"It seems we both have predicaments without the backing of Dominico and Claudia," he said unexpectedly. "No work, no money, no homes."

"You have a home, surely you have a home?" replied Maia with a worried gasp. She had been about to ask if she could stay there.

"Only for a few more days. I will be evicted if I do not pay my rent by quarter end. I have debts...gambling debts...as well as rent owing. I've not been open with you." He gave a resigned shrug. "I thought my problems were solved when Emperor Titus pledged funds to the glassware business, especially with his interest in my commissions. I was riding high with the gods that day, but the glory was short-lived. Vulcan showed his strength with the warehouse fire to remind me of my mortality. I feel responsible for inciting the wrath of the great god of fire, yet it is Dominico who is dead and I am alive. For what reason? I am without work, the same as you. Without money, the same as you. And soon to be without a home like you. We are in strife together. Perhaps we should both present ourselves to Liliana as replacements for her household staff who have died of the pestilence."

"No...!"

Calix had been expecting a protest but was surprised by Maia's vehemence.

"It is surely preferable to being hungry and sleeping on the streets?" he probed. Maia dropped her head on to her arms that were folded across her knees to hide the hot tears that were threatening to spill. "I owe you an explanation as to why I lied to Dominico about the etching," Calix said softly, deliberately changing his tack. Maia didn't look up, so Calix tenderly hooked a lock of falling hair behind her ear before continuing. "I was confident the miniature was a good likeness of the goddess whose name you share. I chose her for you, to impress you, to win your favour, but my gesture was wasted and...well...then Dom interrupted us and I didn't want him to see my choice because he would have worked out how I felt about you before you did. That is not how I wanted it to be."

Maia lifted her head and, resting her chin on her hands, stared upwards catching sight of a bird flitting in to the high branches of the downy oak.

"It is irrelevant now. They are gone, did I tell you Claudia was with child?" Not waiting for an answer, she added, "and we are destitute."

"Maybe not," said Calix, throwing his last tali pieces. Pieces that he'd been waiting for the right time to pitch since a chance meeting in a tavern a week ago. "There are treasures beneath the ash on Pompeii. I met a man who thinks it is possible to dig through the deposits that spewed from the peak. Your family must have had riches. We could reclaim what is rightfully yours."

"Rightfully mine," repeated Maia with a curious snort, a vision of the choker that had led to her being cast aside and condemned by Lady Rufina jumping to mind. It was a pivotal moment as she looked at Calix directly, the truth twitching the corners of her mouth.

"Why spoil a good story with the truth?" smiled Calix deviously, pressing a finger to still her lips. I need your knowledge of Pompeii, you need my silence, we both need those treasures." Pulling a small knife from inside his tunic, he slowly and deliberately cut the pad of his thumb to draw oozing blood. Maia did not resist as he did the same to her and, intimately, they pressed thumbs together to share a blood oath. *Let the past remain buried, we dig only for our future.*

"I could never return to Pompeii," said Maia.

"You wouldn't need to, I would go if you could draw me a map of the streets and one of the villa rooms. Most have a similar layout."

"There is death in Pompeii."

"There is freedom for us in its treasures. I can think of no other solution." Calix stood up, stretching his arm out to Maia. "Come, we have said all we need to. Let us start our new life-journey. We can crawl back from this together." Maia accepted his hand and they made their way towards the town making plans with a small amount of hope.

"I will be meeting with the tunneller in two days and will need the street plans and outline map of the villa to show him. I have a wax tablet and stylus at home. I'll fetch it and I'll sketch it under your direction. We just need the main streets from the port and one of the villa layout where you lived. And we could mark where the richest villas are too."

"There were lots of those."

"To my ears, that is sweeter music than the fiddling of Nero! Let us hope." They parted at the next crossroads, arranging to meet at the forum when the sun was casting the shortest shadows. Maia was keen to collect her meagre belongings and escape Liliana's probing questions as soon as possible.

Chapter Sixteen

Looking at the ruby brooch, Maia once again gave a prayer of thanks to several gods, including the deity of Pompeii for not revealing, or at least smudging, her past despite her lack of an offering. Venus Pompeiana must have taken the circumstances of the plague and Emperor Titus's visit into consideration, she mused. It was humbling to still be in favour.

Apart from the brooch, Maia had little of value. The fire had claimed the amphora containing the few coins she had put inside to fulfil her mission to buy freedom for Ebele and Hadassah. There had only been time to grab the freedom shoes. Thinking of the girls gave credence to Calix's proposed idea of stealing from the villa's of Pompeii. For theft is what it was when you sliced away his soothing talk. It was troubling her now that he wasn't there to spin his magical words. *What you do is who you become.* Slave-girl, liar, thief, free citizen, noticed by the Emperor, now back to thief. Had her life peaked with Dom and Claudia? Was she rolling unchecked back down to her origins?

"What choice do you have?" she muttered to herself, feeling the small cut on her thumb. A blood oath is binding...*yet there is always a choice if you look hard enough,* screamed her conscience and amidst her scrambling thoughts came the idea of going to Roma to seek out Claudia's sister, the closest she had to family. Did Laurentia still live, she wondered. If not, she could seek patronage from Emperor Titus. He knew of her plight and would surely help...and so the seed expanded in seconds, flushed with initial growth until she scoffed it aside as nonsense. How would she get to Roma?

Her thoughts took another turn, the frieze dedicated to Lady Rufina jumping to the fore so strongly that Maia felt the breath of Juno on her nape. Was there a clue to her true family on the frieze? Why she should think of this now, she couldn't say. Claudia had only mentioned it that one time, the day she'd foolishly styled her own hair on Lady Rufina's, but Juno's breath was still upon her. She must find the frieze.

A bell tinkled, Liliana was summoning her like a slave. It was enough to light the embers of resolve in her, so tucking the ruby brooch into the hidden pocket she'd stitched in her tunic, she went to the triclinium.

"We need eggs," said Liliana forcefully. No mention of Claudia's passing, no tears, no wailing. Was the woman heartless?

"I will fetch some," lied Maia, grateful for an excuse to leave the villa. Liliana's attitude was making it easier to run away without giving thanks. With nothing to lose, she asked,"do you know of a frieze about a lady from Pompeii, it's somewhere in the upper town, who is famed for rescuing exposed infants from the Vesuvius peak?" Despite an attempt at keeping her voice level, it still pitched a little higher than normal. Preparing to turn aside the inevitable tirade of questions that was Liliana's style, she was surprised by a straight answer. Perhaps Liliana was not herself with the news of Claudia's death after all.

"The basilica at the forum is decorated with friezes carved into the stone of the walls inside. I recall seeing one depicting the peak of Vesuvius when my son summoned a suspect to court for a trial against our property. It was a difficult time, another difficult time." Liliana sunk into her thoughts, grief and memories taking her to a trance-like state, so Maia took her opportunity and simply left. She would not be enslaved by Liliana.

Walking away from the villa was a relief, although it did her no good to think further than a few hours ahead. At least she was walking the streets of Puteoli with a plan, unlike the day she escaped Pompeii and the exploding peak. There was plenty of time before meeting Calix to search out the frieze.

*

It was cool inside the basilica and surprisingly light. Maia had envisaged it being dark inside like a temple, but the high ceiling was ventilated with large open arches on each of the four walls, twelve arches in total, allowing sunlight to soak the dark corners. An orator was officiating a court hearing at the far end of the building where a cluster of people were gathered, his authoritative voice rising above the murmurs, otherwise there was just a smattering of people sitting on the benches that ran along one side, as well as a clerk and a scribe working at a desk piled with sheets of papyrus and parchments. Neither man looked up as Maia approached so she crept by, giving a sideways glance at the papyrus sheets as she passed, in awe of the neatness of the script, hearing the scratching of the reed brush as the scribe made his marks. Writing was an intrigue to her, she had mastered some of the letters but not all.

Making her way across to the benches, she could see a frieze running the length of the wall and curiosity mixed with a nervous excitement was putting her stomach in a flutter. As she approached it became clear that it wasn't one continuous frieze but a series of blocks, each separated by a colourful mosaic. The first block showed a carving of a fishing boat with a list of words which Maia couldn't read. The second stone carving was of a bridge which looked like that at the entrance to the asclepion. Again, with a list of words beside it.

Maia moved along the wall looking at each block, wondering about the stories behind the pictures, pondering if they related to Lady Rufina in any way. Then she saw the carving of Vesuvius, it's distinctive shape unmistakable. It had been a silent, looming presence over Pompeii every day in her life until the day the gods had argued so violently and allowed her to escape. Her pulse quickened on seeing it, a reaction to the trauma of the event plus anticipation that this could hold a clue to her family.

Tracing her finger along the relief, following the outline of the peak, she looked closely at the detail which showed a child tied to a cypress tree, then a close up of bound hands, followed by a third carving of the same tiny hands cut free with the leather bindings dropping away. This must be the frieze of Lady Rufina's rescues.

"That's a very poignant picture. The peak has changed shape since it exploded," said a man's voice, startling Maia from her scrutiny as she brought her hand to her mouth to suppress a yelp of surprise. The forum security guard who had knocked into her the day before the Emperor's visit was standing behind her. "I never forget a face," he added, "being observant is part of our training. I'm glad to see you are fully recovered from our collision. Didn't see you behind the pillar and I can see why now; you're stick thin. Took me by surprise at the time."

"It was a shock to be up-ended so suddenly but I landed with a bounce...sort of."

The guard grunted at that, thinking she was too bony to bounce. He was broad-shouldered and muscular from a life of hefting sword and shield, white scars on his forearms telling tales of old skirmishes, grey peppering his hair, and deep creases in his leathery skin, indicating he'd finished his military years.

"The Frieze of Rufina," he said nodding at the wall, his sentence ending with another characteristic grunt. Maia's heart skipped a beat. "Tells of a woman who saved exposed children from death, I believe. I'm not entirely sure of the story. Her father commissioned the frieze." Maia could hardly breathe, the shame of being exposed drenching her again. "Anyway, I am here on business so I'd better get to it. My name is Cletus Tettidius Castus.

"Maia Secunda. Is this a list of the children that were saved?" she asked, finding her nerve and pointing at the writing next to the drawing of Mount Vesuvius on the frieze.

Cletus looked closely. "I would think so. The clerk over there will be able to tell you for certain." Cocking his head to one side with a quizzical expression, he added, "you can find me here most days should you need to. Just ask for Clete." Intuition was the only reason he could provide for adding this comment before grunting an awkward smile that looked more like a grimace and tapping his finger to his forehead by way of saying goodbye.

Gathering her courage, Maia approached the clerk and this simple move was to start another dramatic change of course in her life.

"I must ring the noon bell to end the court session," said the clerk when she asked for his help.

"Oh, is it that late already? Please...it will only take a moment, the list of names is short and I have an appointment elsewhere at noon." Maia thought the clerk was going to refuse but something in her plea persuaded him to hurry to the frieze, looking agitatedly at the shrinking shadow through the window arches. A mark on the wall indicating when the sun was at its highest point.

"Let us be quick," he puffed. "This list?" he asked, pointing at the names beside the picture of Vesuvius. Maia nodded. "Is it the names of the children who were exposed on the peak?" Her eyes were wide with hope at what she might find out.

"Yes, it is."

"Does it give their nomen or mention their paterfamilia?" She almost swallowed the last word as her nerves tightened her throat. The clerk checked the shadow-marker again, which was all but met.

"Just praenomens." She chewed at her lip, the given name of an individual would not help. "Except for the name at the bottom, which has..." the clerk leaned in closer before standing straight again, and with a surprised raise of his eyebrows squinted more closely once more. Maia held her breath. "Yes..." he confirmed to himself, "it has 'Flavian' scribed beside it. "Decima – Flavian. I've not noticed that before. The bell, I must go," he flustered. Maia stood dumb, following the clerk with her eyes as he rushed away to fulfil his deed.

She stood there bewildered, her mind racing through unfathomable options. She had once thought her mother a slave-girl and was now thinking her birth line was Imperial. Ridiculous! The ringing bell cut through her racing thoughts. Calix! He would be waiting.

The forum was busier than when she'd arrived and shielding her eyes from the sunlight with her hand, she stood in the basilica doorway searching for Calix. She couldn't see him so made her way towards the fountain for a drink of water to slake her thirst. A juggler tracked alongside her tossing his wooden clubs, hoping for a coin and Maia had to check her stride as a tumbler flipped across in front of her. She ignored them both and the entertainers soon turned their attention to impressing others at the forum with their skills.

After drinking from the pump, Maia went to look for Calix in the covered walkway which had mature vines growing across the tiled roof and trailing down to the ground on both sides like finely woven curtains. It was dark and cool and before Maia's eyes had adjusted to the dim light, she was grabbed from behind and felt cold steel at her throat.

It was terrifying to think that her life could be taken so easily in a public area busy with people, but she couldn't cry out for help with the knife against her skin. Her captor was calm and discrete. *We probably look as if we are lovers embracing in the dark shade.* A strange reflection considering the threat, until she caught up with her subconscious thoughts and recognised the familiar spicy scent of Calix. Her emotions exploded in confusion.

"What did you tell the guard?" he hissed in her ear. "I saw you talking to him in the basilica. I can't trust you," he spat in a venom-soaked voice. "Not even after a blood oath."

Before she could answer, the knife was pulled away from her throat by a third person who was tackling Calix from the side and shoving her so roughly that she stumbled out in to the open of the forum and sprawled to the dusty ground, scuffing her knees as she landed.

Hearing a growl of pain from the tussle inside the walkway, she turned to see Calix emerge and take flight into the crowded, sunlit forum. Once again her gaze was met by a questioning assessment of her predicament by Cletus. For the second time, she nodded quickly that she was all right, taking comfort again that it must be so, as the veteran soldier's assessment agreed as he left her to chase after Calix, blood dripping from a gash in his arm.

Chapter Seventeen

Having lost sight of the chase, Maia was anxiously scanning the crowd for Calix and Clete. Why had Calix taken a blade to her throat? Where had Cletus sprung from? She'd not seen him as she crossed from the fountain to the walkway, yet only moments had passed before he'd rescued her. This day was not going to plan. What should she do? *You can find me here most days.* Clete's words were jumping around her mind. Perhaps she should return to the basilica and wait. Yes, that seemed the best thing to do. Walking quickly, she retraced her steps.

As with the forum, the basilica was busier than in the morning with a queue to see the clerk, so Maia tucked herself against the wall to wait and watch. She felt safer with the solid stone wall at her back. She could hear the orator calling names to start another court session at the far end of the building, his voice rising above the general hum again.

The queue to speak to the clerk slowly reduced and Maia chose to join it when just one person was ahead of her. Feeling vulnerable without the wall at her back, she was jumping at shadows and had still not seen anything of Calix or Cletus. Unfortunately, the query from the person in front of her was not straightforward and by the time Maia got to speak to the clerk her stomach felt it was crawling with worms.

"I must speak with Clete," she said breathlessly. The clerk, recognising her from earlier, scowled and gave a disdainful sniff.

"It's important I speak with him," she repeated.

It's important I ring the noon bell on time," was the petulant reply. "You made me late and now I have extra work as a punishment." Maia could feel her composure disappearing and with all her frustrations from the day gathering, she rushed at the clerk, taking both him and herself by surprise. Beating at his chest with her fists, screaming a wild attack, ferocious only in its turbulent hysteria rather than its strength, for she was too slight to do any physical harm, she released her frustrations on the clerk.

Within a moment, strong arms were pulling her away.

"You're keeping me busy," said Clete, adding his distinctive grunt, which quieted Maia as she recognised it, stripping her frenzied energy down to ragged gasps and trembles as the adrenalin worked out.

"The girl is demented, lock her up!" demanded the clerk. A chorus of mumbled agreement coming from the gathering circle of onlookers.

"I'll get things sorted," growled Cletus. "You have some explaining to do," he said to Maia marching her through the inquisitive crowd, a passage rippling open and closing behind them like barley being parted by an animal. He took her to an empty anteroom.

"Did you catch him?" asked Maia.

"Yes, he is in the cells."

"Is it you Calix owes money to?"

"So you know of that then?"

"He told me of his debts. Is it you?"

"No, but I was appointed to apprehend him by that person. He is in a group of low-lifes who are planning to tunnel into Pompeii to rob the villas. We've been watching them for some time but this little Greek weasel has given me the slip more than once. We almost caught him that day when you and I collided." Maia scowled, realising that Calix had been planning to rob the villas at Pompeii before the glass warehouse burned and not because of it as he had implied. "Apprehended an ugly bastard with a twisted nose but not the artist who I have since discovered worked with you?" Clete raised an eyebrow in question which Maia ignored as she was recalling how the ugly man's nose was so unnaturally kinked. She'd not been aware that Calix had been in the forum that day. "Are you part of the tunnelling party?" Clete asked directly, adding his customary grunt.

"No, I...no," Maia found she was uncomfortable lying to Clete. It was a disarming feeling for the accomplished liar she had become.

"Why were you interested in the Frieze of Rufina?" Maia was chewing at her lip, mute with fear of revealing too much of her past. Cletus, thinking she was just being stubborn, threw his arms up above his shoulders in exasperation, then banged them down on to the bench in anger. "Give us a day and that slimy Greek will talk, so tell me now if you're caught up in this thing. Damn it, Maia, if you share your friend's crime, you make it your own and I can't help you!"

"Why would you help me?"

"Damned if I know why!" Clete noticed Maia absently rubbing at the cut in her thumb. "You picked a bad egg to make a blood oath with," he said, having seen the same cut on Calix and making the correct deduction. "What did he promise you? A future? He cannot give you that. He is the lowest, the humiliores, and will be imprisoned by the judge. The gods will choose his fate: crucifixion if he's lucky, although my bet is he will be saved for the wild animals at the public games when the big amphitheatre opens in Roma. They are going to need quite a few condemned souls for that."

Maia caught a sob as Clete's tirade struck home, reminding her that this fate had been an option for her not long ago. She recognised the truth in his description of Calix's character but did not want to accept it. "Would he really have slit my throat?"

"Yes! Desperation makes a man unstable. Seeing you talking to me panicked him. Blood oath or not, he trusted you as much as an earthworm trusts a thrush." He could see his words had cut deep and he was sorry for it despite the truth in them. "I knew he was in the shadows of the walkway, I was watching him and waiting for my colleague to arrive so we could arrest him, but by the gods I didn't expect you to turn up there. I couldn't wait and my move had to be decisive with his blade at your throat. He was using you for information wasn't he? That makes sense," he said, nodding as the pieces fitted together. "So what do you know that he wants?" Cletus was leaning with his hands on the bench, his face close to Maia's, their eyes on the same level.

Maia liked those eyes; honest, caring, demanding. She did not want to lie before that stare.

But lie she did.

"I was to give him my ruby brooch in exchange for board with him."

Cletus narrowed his eyes as he weighed up her reply, letting the silence drag out, knowing from experience that many lies are undone by it, but Maia did not swerve.

"Do you still have this brooch?"

"Yes, it is my only treasure."

"Then why give it to the weasel?"

"My home was lost to a fire."

"And your family?"

"Gone...all of them." Maia's eyes brimmed with tears which spilled down her cheeks when she blinked, but she kept her hands from wiping them and no more came as she checked her emotions.

"Are you a refugee from Pompeii?" Clete noted the brief flare of her nostrils and knew it to be true even though Maia did not admit it. He couldn't fathom why. Pursing his lips, he withdrew from his intimidating position, cupping his cockled chin on interlocking hands which were steepled on resting elbows. Evaluating the girl before him, he was unable to marry what he saw with what he felt.

"I was foolish to believe in Calix," whispered Maia. It was a difficult admission to make and she looked away, the pain of the disclosure and the realisation of her ill-judgement, swamping all other sensitivities. "What you do is who you become...and I am wretched."

Clete gave a dispassionate grunt as he got up and turned away from Maia, tired of the discussion.

"I have one truth from you at least before I leave for Roma!" Maia looked up sharply as if a lifeline was being thrown to her. Was it possible she could get to Roma and find Claudia's sister after all? "All reservists are being recalled to help with the double disaster relief," continued Clete. "I leave at first light tomorrow. The death figures from the pestilence don't make happy reading. I'll be up to my knees burying bodies and you think you're wretched. What?" he asked when he saw her looking at him with an expression of hope.

"The gods have crossed our paths. Can I travel to Roma with you? I have family on the banks of the Tiber not far from the Circus Maximus." A partial truth; she would seek out Laurentia. Clete scratched the back of his neck with fingernails encrusted with his own dried blood from the slash on his arm, giving his guttural grunt. "I can cook and know a little of herbal medicine. I will dress your wound," Maia added with determination strengthening her voice.

"Roma is in a mess what with the fire and the plague."

"I have survived both, I am not afraid of either."

"You'll slow me down."

"I will not."

"I'll not be able to mind you once we're there. I have orders."

"I don't need minding. I will find Laurentia, she will not turn me away."

"No tears, I don't cope well with girl's bawling."

"No tears."

And so it was that Maia travelled to Roma with Cletus.

Chapter Eighteen

The strangest of friendships arise in extreme circumstances, and in the ten days it took for Cletus and Maia to walk from Puteoli to Roma, they made a bond that was a surprise to both of them. Cletus had expected Maia to complain her way to the city: can we eat now, can we rest, I'm thirsty...yet she surprised him with her vitality and resolve, and with her cooking skills too, producing a decent meal from whatever he supplied, always without complaint.

Maia had expected Cletus to force himself on her, just like Philo the Greek had at Pompeii. She would have endured it to reach Roma but was relieved when he made no sexual move, even when she had gone to him for warmth on the nights they'd slept in the open. He had pointed out the constellations to her as they lay together, explaining how to find the north star and she had felt both vulnerable beneath the vastness of the sky, and protected in his arms.

They'd followed a path along the coastline, keeping the sea on their left until they reached the Via Appia Antica at Sinuessa. This great, paved highway connected the capital with the port of Brundisium on the eastern coast. Crested in the middle to allow water to run off into the ditches on either side, the road was wide enough to allow two chariots to pass. Retaining walls protected the drainage ditches. It had been easier to find food and lodgings in the caupona along the highway, but Maia had preferred it when Cletus had searched out a comfortable location in the countryside instead of using the inns. When she'd questioned him on safety, he'd answered with a grunt, stating that the cauponae were more likely targets for thieves than a properly searched out camping spot. She'd not once felt unsafe with him.

They fell into a routine of walking mostly in silence, commenting on the birds occasionally, or the vista, and Clete would name some of the flowers if Maia asked. But most of their conversation was beside the camp fire as they ate in the evening.

"There have been women but I've lived the life of a legionary," he replied when she questioned him. She learned he had campaigned in Britannia with the Legio Secunda Augusta, joining them in AD53 following a big recruitment drive to bolster the legion's numbers after a defeat by the Silures tribe. Other than being stationed at Isca Augusta for the final six years of his service, and Glevum before that, Maia was unable to find out more. "If you were there, you know. If you weren't, I can't explain," was all he would say when she asked him about the campaigns. He would tell her about the land, describing it's verdant hills and damp woodlands, explaining how the cold could seep uninvited into your bones with mist hanging in valleys for endless days, to then break into the most glorious of warm sunshine that transformed a dank, fern-lined brook into the most beautiful, lush stream dancing with sparkles of light. "Those days were worth the hundred wet ones."

Maia had initially been reluctant to tell him anything of her life in Pompeii, settling for relating events from when Claudia had taken her home, stressing the kindness she and Dom had shown to her, explaining about the glassware business and how thrilled she had been to have a role in expanding the business.

"I had my own source of income for a short time," she said sadly. "I had such plans, for money gives you status, and money you earn seems to higher that status...in your own mind at least," she laughed ruefully. Cletus had asked of her plans and she had willingly told him about Ebele and Hadassah who had helped her when she was fleeing from the eruption, confirming that she had lived in Pompeii as he had guessed. It was the first time she had mentioned the slave girls to anyone and before long, she had also explained how she felt the gods had saved her, above saving others, so she knew they must have a purpose for her. "I thought that purpose was to buy freedom for Ebele and Hadassah. I was so happy to work hard at the warehouse, to play my part in making Dom's business a success and to share in the spoils. I didn't get far with my savings," she added with a sad snort of laughter.

"Many people survived the eruption," replied Clete. "I doubt the gods gave them all a purpose."

"But I am thrice saved!"

"Thrice saved?" he questioned with a grunt. He saw a lour wrinkle her forehead and it was as if it creased her soul at the same time and the tunnel of trust they had been building became blocked. He understood horrors too great to speak of, he'd seen it in some comrades following battle and had touched the slick hound of black despair himself. He continued to whittle the stick he was working on, deftly using a hunting knife that looked over-sized for the job and had been used earlier to skin the hare they'd dined on, and would be used later to remove the stubble from his chin and the dirt from beneath his fingernails. He didn't mind when Maia changed the subject without answering his question. She would tell him in time if she wanted to, and if they ran out of time, he just would not know.

Cletus may be a man nearing old age, and Maia only a girl on the cusp of womanhood, but they had grown comfortable in each other's company during the trek. Not familiar enough for Maia to talk of how she was exposed by her family though. The shame of it tied her tongue, perhaps it always would. She was also careful not to show her bare feet to him, too aware of how the build-up of rough, hard skin still shouted 'slave', preferring to keep her freedom shoes firmly on.

"I saw Emperor Titus!" Maia's expression changed to a cheeky grin that was met by a jealous grunt from Cletus.

"Those of us employed to keep the Emperor safe were too busy grappling with the low-lifes to see the parade, which, as it happens, was cut short because of the fire in Roma, so you were lucky to see him."

"I don't mean I glimpsed him from the crowds, no...I *spoke* to Emperor Titus!" Clete raised an eyebrow at that. Maia loved the way he did so. "He visited the warehouse, the evening before it burned. A secret visit. We were so happy that night, then by the morning everything was gone."

"Why did the warehouse warrant a visit? And why in secret?"

"Claudia's sister has connections with the Senate and somehow my story reached his ears. He was keen to meet a survivor from Pompeii. It was only secret because of security, I think. He stuttered when he first spoke to me, the Emperor did..." she gave another cheeky grin,"...and I thought I would be the one to swallow my words with nerves."

"So this is why you are travelling to Roma; to rekindle your relationship with the Emperor," he teased. "That is actually a rather cunning plan. A far better idea than abetting that Greek thief, Calix. Perhaps the Flavian dynasty is your destiny, or perhaps you are of Flavian descent. You have the golden hair for it." Even though he was joking, Maia's heart leapt to her throat at his words, her hand going up to her hair in a reflex action. Could it be so? Was that why the word 'Flavian' was next to her slave-name Decima on the Frieze of Rufina? "Hope is the pillar that holds up the world," quoted Clete, as if reading her mind. "The Naval Commander, Pliny spoke those words during an address he gave when I returned from Britannia. A pity the Commander died, he was an interesting man but I've heard his nephew is upholding his family's reputation. Pliny the Younger people are calling him."

"Does his nephew still live in the villa on the Cape of Misenum?"

"He does. Hope is the pillar that holds up the world," he repeated. Maia was indeed heartened, optimistic that if Master Gaius lived, so did Ebele and Hadassah and she may still fulfil her vow. "Keep hoping, Maia."

Chapter Nineteen

They knew they were approaching the city gate by the increasing number of catacombs and cypress trees lining the route. They could clearly see the two cylindrical towers of the Porta Capena rising above the level of the Servian Wall. This must be where Claudia's parents are buried, thought Maia, her heart beating fast. She was growing more nervous the closer they came to the greatest city in the Known World, a storm of emotions resulting in the most demanding of companions...anxiety.

A blustery wind had arrived with the afternoon sun and a scuffle of dust was swirling across their path and Maia felt she could taste the ashes of the burnt city in her throat. It was suggestive of the horror of Pompeii and in a strange way steadied her disquiet by reminding her she was a survivor; thrice saved by the gods. Nevertheless, she moved closer to Clete as they neared the city gate, so close that her shoulder brushed against his arm. A solid frame supporting a lattice.

"Is Roma so large that I'll never find you?" she asked timidly, keeping her eyes looking ahead and not at him.

"Well it's certainly grown since I was here last. It's bursting beyond the wall now." Clete grunted with distaste at the new homes sprawling across the ground to their right. It's like the city is leaking through the cracks in the wall."

"And we will be swallowed up by its size."

"No tears!" he growled, sensing her distress.

"No tears," she promised, flaring her nostrils with pride to keep them at bay. They continued to the gate in silence, with Maia chewing at her lip and wishing she had not been so foolish as to think she was brave enough to find Laurentia's villa alone in a city so big. Her stomach was churning with the worry of it when they reached the gate which seemed so high with its added towers that she felt like an acorn fallen from a giant oak.

"Are you a reservist?" the guard asked Cletus, summing him up by age and appearance.

"Yes, been recalled to help with the crisis."

"Give your name and legion to the clerk," said the guard, waving him through and pointing to a tent to his left. "And your business in the city?" he asked Maia.

"I have family here."

"Address?"

"On the banks of the Tiber near Capitoline Hill."

"That section is out of bounds to anyone but military or hospital volunteers, by order of the Emperor. It's in ashes," he said thoughtlessly.

"Oh!" Maia's hand went to her mouth in despair. She had no other plan and Cletus had disappeared into the tent. For some unfathomable, foolish reason, she had assumed the fire had burned the insulae, the tenement homes of the poor, not the spacious villas of the rich. Burying Pompeii had clearly not appeased the anger Vulcan was displaying towards the indulgence of the opulent.

"The city is still in a state of emergency," continued the guard, his patience beginning to fold with Maia's dalliance. "Only military personnel or volunteers for the asclepion can enter that section," he repeated. "Are you prepared to work in the new hospital in the Temple of Asclepius on the Isola Tiberina? If not, you must proceed to the eastern section. You will be turned away from entering the Capitoline region without the required password."

Maia recalled Claudia telling her how the dry bridge at Puteoli's asclepion was modelled on the bridge at Isola Tiberina. It was a link, albeit a small one, with her beloved, kind Claudia and it was enough to tip her decision.

"Yes...I...yes, I will help at the hospital."

"Register with the clerk in the tent," he said ushering her through the arched gateway, with a noticeable shake of his head as if he thought her crazy to volunteer for such a job. To Maia, it seemed a much better idea than sleeping on the narrow, unsavoury streets of an unfriendly city. She was not afraid of the plague and would at least have shelter and food.

*

After registering with the clerk, Maia left the tent repeating the given password, Canis lupus, over in her head, picturing a grey wolf with its teeth bearing down to eat her in a desperate measure to commit it to memory. Cletus was leaning against the side of a wooden building waiting for her and despite herself, she smiled at the sight of his calm disposition and solid, reassuring presence.

"My plan has changed," she said directly. "I am to report to the asclepion on Isola Tiberina. It's acting as a hospital." Clete raised a questioning eyebrow at that announcement. "It was the best option given my choices," explained Maia. "The Capitoline Hill area is closed by order of the Emperor to all but military personnel. Laurentia's home is most likely burned and..." she gave a small shrug and a sadness puckered her expression, "...well...you know," she tailed off unwilling to voice that Claudia's sister may have burned with it. *Everyone leaves me*, she thought miserably but this was no time to indulge herself in self pity, she must concentrate on getting to the island. "I have been given a password," she added with a positive nod.

"Me too," said Clete. "They've set up a temporary camp in the Circus Maximus for reservists and building specialists. I'm to report to the administration centre there. I'm damned pleased I'm not being housed in the Castra Praetoria with the Praetorian Guard. I'm not sure how temporary this camp will be mind, seems I'll be assisting with the rebuilding work once the burying of the dead is under control. Our Emperor has some grand projects in mind. Pompey's Theatre has burned, and the Temple of Jupiter. I'll be here for the gods know how many full moons. That's assuming I don't succumb to this wretched pestilence," he grunted. "Can't say I care for the smell on the wind."

"The plague starts with a fever. If you get a fever, come to the Isola Tiberina straight away, for you will need the help of Asclepius to recover," Maia said solemnly.

"Are you not afraid of catching the pestilence?" asked Clete, quietly admiring of her resolve and steely determination.

"The plague will not take me, the gods have a purpose for me yet," she said with confidence.

"Death is certain, the day uncertain," he quoted, nodding in response to her reply. The pair stood awkwardly silent for a moment; Maia rubbing her forearm and inspecting a mole near her wrist as if it was the first time she had seen it; Cletus scuffing at the dusty ground with his worn, studded boot. "Come on," he said decisively, "let's get going before we forget our passwords. The end of the journey is just down there for me." He nodded towards the curve of the southern end of the Circus Maximus which could be seen ahead as they left the shade of the Servian Wall. The afternoon shadows were growing longer on the ground, matching those creeping over Maia's heart at their imminent parting. *No tears,* she reminded herself. They walked along unspeaking but it was not the comfortable silence of their earlier trek.

Two legionaries in full military regalia were guarding the entrance to the camp. Maia was drawn by the sight, the sunlight reflecting off armour, shields and the tips of the long pila that were being held upright at an angle that mirrored the other.

Maia and Clete both started speaking at the same time, stopped, started again, then broke off once more. Maia's pulse was racing, sensing an important moment between them as they locked gazes, Maia mesmerised by those eyes she found so disconcertingly difficult to lie to. They seemed to read her heart better than she could. But before the moment could be explored, a heavily accented voice called out breaking the awkward intimacy.

"Cletus Tettidius Castus! By the gods, as I live and breathe, it is you!" A giant of a man, in height and girth, was striding towards them, a smile as wide as the Via Appia Antica amidst his bearded face.

"Well I'll be...Emrick, you old goat." The two men clasped arms, laughing with the joy of a reunited comradeship. "What are you doing here?"

"The same as you no doubt. Here to dig graves for the masses by invitation of the Emperor."

"I thought you would stay in Britannia."

"As much as I love the weather in Isca Augusta..."

"And the women!" interrupted Clete.

"Yes, and the women," conceded Emrick, with a flicker of a frown, "you had spoken so highly of your country that I felt I must see it."

"And what do you think of it?"

"It is too hot, my friend! So hot, it burns its own cities. It is fortuitous that my curiosity has brought me here when you most need my assistance!"

"Not fortuitous to be in Roma during a plague, Emrick, though it is good to see you!"

"It is indeed a double disaster, but I could not ignore the Emperor's request. My comrades need me. I will dig faster and deeper than all of you, you know it to be true."

"Bollocks! Size does not indicate stamina. You'll rush at it like the raging savage you are for half a day, then share the rest of the time between the popinae and the whorehouse. And don't go thinking the popinae are like Britannia's alehouses. They do not serve ale!"

Maia was feeling tiny in the presence of this bear. Tiny and overlooked amidst their banter.

"It is a great fortune to find you outside the camp though," said Emrick, clapping Clete on the shoulder. "If we report together, we should share a barrack." Cletus laughed with his old friend at memories from a previous existence, excluding Maia further.

"I must take leave of you," she said, a spike of resentment giving a boldness to her tone and, with that, she turned and ran as she had down the Via del Vesuvio in Pompeii, her rangy legs once again kicking up dust to a new life ahead.

Cletus, taken by surprise by her sudden bolt, flinched to run after her, but stopped in the presence of his comrade, choosing instead to shout the name of his favourite popina after her.

"Find me in the Carpe Vinum." Maia did not reply, nor check her stride and he didn't know if she had heard. Neither could he see her tears.

Chapter Twenty

By the time Maia reached the northern end of the Circus Maximus, her tears were under control, anger replacing resentment. How dare Clete ignore her like that. She wouldn't go looking for him in the Carpe Vinum...what a ridiculous name for a drinking house!

The sight that met her as she rounded the bend put an abrupt end to thoughts of Clete. Two legionaries, their faces hidden by cloth strips tied across their noses and mouths, were placing an animal hide over a cart piled high with dead bodies. Maia must have been upwind of it for the stench was not noticeable where she was standing.

Beyond the cart was a line of travertine blocks barricading the way to the Capitoline Hill and the sector where Laurentia's villa had stood. Maia could see some blackened remnants of buildings from the fire. Taking a deep breath of courage, she approached the nearest guard.

"I am a hospital volunteer," she said. "How do I get to the Isola Tiberina?"

"What's the password?"

"Canis lupus." Maia was relieved to see a nod of acknowledgement from the legionary who proceeded to give her directions of how to reach the island by skirting the edge of the closed fire-damaged section of the city.

"Straight down to the river, turn right, then keep to the

riverbank until you see the bridge on the river bend" Maia thanked him with a nervous, flat-lipped smile as he let her through the cordon, pointing to guide her towards the river. "Fortuna be with you at the asclepion," he added looking at her with a mixed expression of respect and bewilderment, just as the guard at the city gate had. It did nothing to settle Maia's increasing level of anxiety. Had she been foolish in making this decision? The legionaries seem to think so, yet a timely rumble of hunger from her stomach said otherwise. Food and shelter were awaiting her at the hospital.

The Tiber was an inspiring sight when it came into view, untouched and unaffected by the fire, defiant with its nonchalant watery beauty which was in stark contrast to the charred buildings nearby. The river's surface was as smooth as the glass vials made at Dominico's warehouse, except where the moving barges were creating streamlines. Maia shaded her eyes with her hands and could see the Isola Tiberina upstream looking every bit like the sleek trireme that she'd seen with the navy commander on board leaving Misenum, but without the tiers of extended oars. On approach, she could see the island had recently been clad with large slabs of white travertine sandstone, the same rock that was being used to cordon off the Capitoline Hill, to purposely resemble a ship's prow.

The bridge came into view and it cheered her to see something familiar, a connection to Puteoli, in an otherwise alien city. She conceded the bridge looked better with water flowing beneath it.

Maia was challenged for the password again when she reached the bridge. A flash shot of a leaping wolf reminding her what it was.

"Canis lupus," she said to the guard who looked incredibly similar to the previous legionary, the uniform and training masking individual traits.

"Report to the clerk in the atrium," he said letting her through. Entering the temple was like walking into an oasis of calm, just as it had been in the asclepion in Puteoli. The atrium was decorated with cool marble, flickering lamps lighting the corners and

Maia felt her tension slide away, especially as she looked up at the statue of Asclepius, looming larger than life-size, solid and steadfast in his duty of healing the sick. The clerk registered her with just the merest of perfunctory questions.

"Thank you for coming, Roma needs you," he said solemnly. "We are short of helpers. They..." he broke off realising his words 'they keep dying' was not a good welcome. "I will show you to your pallet in the small ante-chamber. Come." The clerk led Maia to the room, explaining her duties as they went. "Your main job will be to assist with the laundering of linens and tunics. We have set up our own temporary fullonica here as our closest washhouse was lost to the fire. Cleanliness is strict, so there is plenty to wash. You will be released from there in time to help prepare the evening meal in the kitchens. We have a score of volunteers as well as recovering patients to feed. Praying at the statue must also be done. We will assign you a row of pallets to pray for." Maia thought he made it sound so impersonal: a row of pallets. Those pallets contained sick people fighting for life beneath the animal skins, members of a family that would surely be missed in their homes.

"Do I pray at the statue of the healing god in the atrium?" she asked, thinking back to her visits to the asclepion in Puteoli. "And where do I get the charms to touch to his hand? I have no coin to buy them."

"I see you have experience within an asclepion, that is useful. You will not need money. Despite the plague sweeping the whole of the city, it is only the wealthy who are brought here. The poor must fend for themselves. That is the way of it. A charm hangs at the end of each pallet for you to use, already purchased by the family."

There were eight pallets in the ante-chamber and Maia could see that three were vacant, the other five clearly in use, although there was no-one in the room as they entered. A ewer of water and a single dish stood on a low bench at the end of each pallet. Small but pretty arched openings high in the walls gave the room good ventilation as well as allowing natural light to slant in.

"How many sick people are here?" asked Maia.

"More than we have room for! We simply do our best," replied the clerk with a sigh. "I will leave you to wash and change into the clean tunic provided. Return to the atrium when you are ready and I will show you to the kitchens and introduce you to the other volunteers. Oh, I almost forgot; shoes are not to be worn inside the asclepion. Leave them in the wall niche, You won't need them again until you leave the island. We go barefoot to show our dedication to our servitude."

And so it was that Maia was barefoot like a slave once more.

Chapter Twenty-One

Cletus gave the customary legionary salute of a fisted forearm across the chest to the gate guard, after being allowed entry on providing the day's password and directed to register at the Principia. He and Emrick started walking towards the centre of the camp, knowing with confidence where to find the headquarters building as the layout of the temporary camp on the Circus Maximus, despite its elongated shape, was the same as all legionary forts across the lands, allowing any soldier to find his way around with ease. The familiarity was comforting too, giving a feeling of home no matter where you were and the aura was working on Clete.

"Futuo, it feels good to be back inside," he said, raising his arm high to slap the back of his friend's shoulder. Emrick stood a foot taller than Clete. The camp was bustling with veterans recalled to assist with the relief plans of their Emperor. "I wonder who else is here from the Secunda Augusta. A few other than us must have made it to retirement."

"Look front, Brother..." said Emrick.

"...and I have your back," replied Clete, completing their old battle motto. "Futuo, it feels good."

After registering at the Principia, they were sent to the drill hall to collect their gear, complaining at the amount that would be deducted from their first pay packet.

"The price of sandals has gone up since I last bought a pair," grumbled Clete. "They had better be studded with new nails. It's extortion!"

"I just want them to fit," added Emrick. "The leather chaffs when they are too small."

"I doubt there's a hide in the land big enough to wrap around your great platters. How you control feet that size I've no idea. Oh yes, I remember...you don't when you've had too much ale, you great ox!"

"Decent ale is another thing I miss from Britannia!" quipped Emrick, laughing at old memories before becoming serious. "My woman died in childbirth, the pup too." His head hung low as he spoke the painful words. Cletus responded by exhaling a puff of air between his lips before speaking.

"You leaving Britannia makes sense now. I'm sorry for your loss, Comrade." For some reason, this news brought Maia to mind and he found himself recalling the memory of her curling beside him at night during their journey from Puteoli. It was Emrick's turn to slap Cletus on the back, a slap that was more of a swipe that caused him a faltering step forwards.

"Do you have a woman keeping furs warm for you, my friend?" asked Emrick

"Three at the last count," smirked Clete.

"Only three hearts to break? You have slowed down with age! Who was the maiden who ran away at the gate?"

"Not one of the three! A thief, a liar and a puzzlement that one." Emrick raised a questioning eyebrow at the comment but Cletus chose not to explain. "Life is too short for puzzles. Let us concentrate on simpler matters. We'll collect our gear then find food! I could eat a horse."

*

Each man was issued with a bedroll, spade, cooking pot, hand mill, two woollen tunics and a pair of caligae, the heavy-soled military sandal-boots studded with hobnails. As this was not a campaign, battle weaponry, armour and marching gear was not considered necessary. The Praetorian Guards were the only people allowed to carry weapons within the city walls.

Gathering the small pile of clothes and equipment, Cletus and Emrick left the stores to find their assigned barrack in the north west quarter of the camp.

"Shall we climb over the Spina or walk its length?" asked Cletus. The Spina was a brick wall barrier twelve feet wide and four feet high running most of the length of the Circus Maximus. Ideal for the chariots to race round, not so practical in the middle of a camp but with so many extra men to accommodate in the already busy city, the space had to be utilised as best it could. Desperate times call for improvisation. The arena would be returned to the chariot racers when the state of emergency was lifted.

"Let us walk the distance. A tour of the camp is customary is it not."

Nodding at the men they passed, it didn't take them long to reach the base with its rising three columns that marked the end of the Spina.

"Unfortunately, our contubernium is downwind of the latrines," said Clete wrinkling his nose as they reached the tent assigned to them, the seventh in the row of eleven including the bigger tent which was normally occupied by the Centurion. Pulling back an open corner of the animal hide, Cletus ducked inside the tent with Emrick following, grunting with the effort of dipping so low.

"I could do with a larger flap," complained the big Celt.

"If the wind doesn't change direction we'll have to stitch the flap up and dig a tunnel to exit by!" Cletus stood upright, letting his eyes adjust to the darker light inside the tent.

"Hail, welcome," said a man, rising from his bedroll to greet Clete and Emrick with a legionary salute. He gave his full name and legion but Clete and Emrick only remembered Felix of the Legio Septima Gemina from the lengthy introduction.

"Hail Comrade, Cletus Tettidius Castus formerly of Legio Secunda Augusta, as is my friend the big man here, Emrick."

"Are you Briton?" Felix asked Emrick.

"Dobunni tribe by birth, attached to the Legio Secunda Augusta as a local guide. Both have my heart."

"A legend in his own lifetime," said Clete with genuine respect. "And hates the Silures tribe more than you could love a brother!"

"I get confused by all the tribal names of Britannia," admitted Felix with an apologetic shrug. "Spent my time in Hispania until being medically discharged for this." He tapped at his left thigh. "Still capable of digging graves with it though and I re-trained as a mosaic layer so should have skills enough to keep me in work here for a while I hope."

"Who else are we tented with?" asked Clete, nodding towards the four vacant bedrolls that were neatly laid out with folded kit on top. There was room for eight men in a contubernium, so Cletus and Emrick made claim to two of the three remaining spaces.

"All quarrymen from the north west. They're not from the legions but were ordered to come as they have experience of working with marble. Our Emperor obviously has grand designs in mind for the rebuilding of the capital. That suits me fine as grand always includes bigger and fancier mosaics."

Cletus nodded his understanding. "And who have we in the top tent leading us?"

"We'll find out tomorrow. You've made it here just in time for the big camp briefing. We're to muster at the Principia at first light for an address by Emperor Titus." Clete raised his eyebrows in acknowledgement of the direct Imperial leadership.

"It will be interesting to see how they manage a mixture of legionaries and civilian workers," replied Clete. "I'm guessing the majority here have been through basic training at least, but it may come as a sharp kick in the balls to those that haven't, especially if they're unlucky enough to be attached to a group of Praetorian Guards. Can you imagine it, those pigheaded bastards will play with them for sport! I don't see that ending well."

"Then it is a good job I have your back, my friend," said Emrick, rising from rolling out his bedroll. "Thank you for the information Felix, but enough talk as this bear needs food." He patted his stomach. "To the granary with all haste I think. What say you, Cletus?"

"A good idea. Have you got your food rations?" he asked Felix. "Is there plenty?"

"There's enough for everyone. I guess the plague has done the Emperor a favour there."

Cletus grunted at that comment. "For a moment I'd forgotten why we are here. At least the stink from the latrines is disguising the mal-odour of the sickness which has been a constant reminder since reaching the city walls."

Chapter Twenty-Two

By the seventh daybreak, Maia had acquired a routine. Her first task was to collect the discarded sheets and dirty tunics which were left outside the main chamber and take them to the fullonica at the far end of the island. The smell of urine was strong when you first entered the wooden hut but became less noticeable once you had spent some time there. A stack of amphorae stood outside, turfed out quickly when they realised the urgent need for a fullonica instead of an olive oil store.

Marguerita was always there to greet her. A widow of maturing years, whose husband had died in the previous great fire in Roma sixteen years ago. With no income to continue paying the rent of her insulae apartment, she had arrived at the island in desperation and made herself useful by cleaning the asclepion in exchange for somewhere to live. It had been enough to hide away here during her early years of grieving, and, once the grief had passed, easier to stay than to forge a new life away. Thus the years had piled up, turning her hair grey and adding liver spots to a wrinkling skin, regardless of not having lived. The recent fire and plague in the city seemed to bring her a renewed enthusiasm for living, adding a richer purpose to rise each dawn.

"Place the dirty linens straight in the tub please, Maia. I have prepared the solution. We'll be needing more urine for tomorrow."

"I could empty the jars," offered Maia, hopeful of escaping her next duty. "I have the strength for the barrow." The jars were left on the street corners of the neighbourhood for the public to piss in and someone was needed to empty them into large crocks transported on a handbarrow.

"I'll send Julius to fetch the jars. It is a job for a boy with the tabernae seething with legionaries and undesirables!" Maia thought of Clete, half-smiling at the way Marguerita thought all legionaries were unsavoury. "Besides, you tread the linen more thoroughly than Julius. Come on, in you go," Marguerita was waving her arms to encourage Maia into the washing tub.

With a wrinkle of her nose, Maia climbed in to the low, oval shaped tub in to which she had placed some of the dirty linen. The diluted urine solution felt cold between her toes and colder still as it covered her ankles, sending her rigid as she made an open circle with her mouth at the chill of it.

"That's the worst bit," she said to Marguerita. "I'm okay once I'm in." The washing solution came up to her knees and Maia started treading, slowly to begin with, building up a speed and rhythm as she concentrated on turning the linen as she stomped.

"That's a good rhythm that any fuller would be proud of," said Marguerita with admiration. "You've learnt the jump quickly. And thank the gods you have, for there is much to wash. Best not scrimp on the sulphur today when you set the drying, as I've heard a member of the Imperial household has been brought in so we must have the linen as white as possible. We'll have to rub in some cimolian if the fumes from the sulphur doesn't do the job. The poor woman is delirious with fever, I've heard. That's a bad sign. The Palace should have brought her in earlier. It's a bad business this pestilence." Marguerita's mood slumped, her chin dropping with it. "But we must keep with hope and keep our standards high, especially for the Emperor's kin. Make sure she is covered with the best animal skin." Marguerita raised her chin, angling it up with a deft movement of defiance against the sickness, her mood rising up with it. "We must hope Asclepius sees fit to cure her!"

Julius came in and Marguerita turned her attention to organising him to fetch the jars of piss. Maia kept treading, wondering at the age of Julius. He was clearly a few seasons shy of discarding his childhood clothes and the bulla hanging around his neck. Just as well thought Maia, it would be impossible to hold an adult ceremony at the moment with the forum being closed. It seemed a strange thing to discard the bulla as a boy became a man, she mused. If the charm had kept you safe from evil spirits since birth, why not keep wearing it? It was one of life's mysteries that Maia could not unravel.

*

The shadows would shorten and lengthen again before Maia was dismissed from the fullonica. Her next task would be to help in the kitchen preparing food, a job that unsettled her more than any other as it brought memories of the kitchen at Lady Rufina's villa. Memories of being a slave, but she would take a deep breath before entering the room and tell herself this was not forever and nobody knew her past.

It was always a relief to finish the cooking chores, after which she was allowed time to wash and change before collecting the charms from her assigned row of pallets to take to the statue of Asclepius. It was important to present yourself in a tidy state before the great healing god. Once she was cleansed, Maia would take a moment to touch her shoes, the precious freedom shoes put aside in the wall niche. They were a tangible reminder that she was here voluntarily and free to leave if she wished. *I am helping the sick to recover. I am working for Emperor Titus. I am not a slave.* With these words in mind, Maia would go to the main chamber.

Despite the many ill people, the main chamber was a place of calm for Maia. She was not afraid of the sickness as many were, and the room itself was beautiful. The floor was made of marble, which sparkled with its inlaid minerals and was cool and smooth under her feet. A surface that was a pleasure to walk on barefoot. Matching marble columns rose majestically to the high ceiling, solid and reassuring as they stretched upwards, light and air seeming to slide down them from the upper open arches. The whole chamber was at peace with itself.

Making her way quietly along her assigned row so as not to disturb those sleeping, and being careful not to hinder the more senior volunteers attending the sick, Maia unhooked each charm from its pallet. A score in total. There was a lot of fuss being made of a woman in the adjacent row and Maia guessed it was the new patient brought in by the Imperial Palace. Having collected all the charms assigned to her, Maia crept up the aisle that would afford her a view of the lady, curious for a glimpse.

A senior volunteer was tending her by placing wet strips of cloth across her forehead, the skin the same dark colour as Uday's. A woman from the land of lions in the Imperial Palace must surely be a household slave. Despite her dark skin, heat from the fever could still be seen, burning her dry.

"Help me here," said the senior volunteer handing Maia fresh strips of damp cloth. "We cannot leave her and I must visit the latrine. I'll be as quick as I can."

Maia put the charms aside to nurse the patient who was muttering unintelligible words. At Maia's first touch the lady opened her eyes.

"Malita!" she cried with clarity. "My Malita, my heart, how good of you to care." She wrapped a hand around Maia's bony wrist, her grip surprisingly strong for someone so ill. "You will blossom more beautifully than that devious woman and the child will be a girl, so there is nothing to fear." Suddenly, her hand went limp and dropped away, her clarity slipping with it. Maia's hands were trembling as she changed the cloth strips for freshly soaked ones, and droplets of water splashed across the lady's face. There was no reaction and Maia's chest surged with concern as she placed the back of her hand beneath the patient's nostrils to feel for breath, her shoulders sagging with relief as she felt a soft stream of warm air tickling across her knuckles. The senior volunteer returned.

"She is so hot," stated Maia.

"Her fever needs to break in the next few hours or I fear Asclepius will not be able to visit her dreams tonight. And if not tonight, I think he will be too late to save her."

"Who is the lady?"

"She is from the Imperial Palace. Her name is Eshe. That is all I know."

"She called me Malita. She seemed convinced I was she. *My Malita, my heart* she said."

"The ramblings of a fever. Take no heed."

"It was said so earnestly, and with such clarity, not like her other mumblings."

"Take no heed, the woman is very sick."

"May I return to sit with her after I have touched these charms to the hand of the healing god's statue?" The senior volunteer looked up from her nursing to study Maia for a moment, weighing her sincerity.

"It would help me if you could," she responded, seeing what she thought was compassion in Maia's expression. "I am weary beyond belief and feel I could sleep for a Moon."

Maia took her leave, promising to return once all her prayers were completed. The compassion was actually self-interest. Who was Malita? Was she another clue to Maia's bloodline, another suggestion of a Flavian connection, of a high birth? Dare she hope? Eshe had spoken almost prophetically. And who was the devious woman and baby girl the Imperial maid spoke of. Maia would sit with Eshe as long as possible in the hope she would speak clearly again and give Maia some answers to these confusing questions.

Chapter Twenty-Three

The air was warm even at first light as the camp had roused itself for the scheduled briefing the day after Cletus and Emrick had arrived. There was no breeze, as if the dawn was still sleeping despite the pink hues colouring the sky. Cletus and Emrick were mingling with the crowd at the Principia when a bugle pierced the air with its wholesome sound announcing the arrival of the Imperial party. The chatter from the gathered men ceased immediately, replaced by the dawn hush, the silence shouting as loudly as the bugle had, such was the contrast.

"The Emperor!" announced the bugler.

There was a collective shuffle of feet as all the military men in the group stood to attention placing a fisted forearm across their chests as Emperor Titus came to the dais. Those without military training stood straighter, some awkwardly copying the salute, others keeping their arms at their sides, but all were listening intently as the Emperor gave praise for their response to his summons, thanking them for making the journey.

"You have come from across the length and breadth of our land, leaving your homes, your farms, your businesses. Roma thanks you. I thank you. We thank your families for their sacrifice in our great city's time of need." A centurion raised a cheer which was answered by the crowd. Titus waited for the din to subside before giving the grim tally of deaths in the city and updating his audience on the extent of the fire damage, before rousing them into another thunderous cheer by his promises to rebuild the capital. "It will be your work, your efforts, your sweat that rebuilds the heart of our precious Roma!" Soldiers and civilians alike cheered and clapped, Emrick included. The noise was so loud in the still morning it reached Maia on the island, waking her from sleep. The Circus Maximus fell quiet once more as Emperor Titus completed his speech by pointing to the row of Praetorian Guards, pristine in their white togas, standing to the right of the dais. "I have appointed my Praetorians to act as your Centurions in these strange times. You are to return to your barrack row and report immediately to your Centurion's tent to receive your duties. Let us rebuild Roma!" he cried, his right arm raised above his head with his fist clenched. The crowd cheered again but more out of duty this time, their spirits dampened by the news that they were to be commanded by the Praetorian Guards. The Emperor left the dais and the cheers faded into mutterings as the men made their way back to their respective tents.

"*Futuo!* A Praetorian for a Centurion! I'm not liking that," Clete said to Emrick.

"What is so wrong with the Guards?" asked Emrick, the question bringing a grunt of disrespect from Cletus.

"Pigheaded, overpaid peacocks that think they own the city. Bastards, all of them." Clete spat on the dirt to emphasize his dislike. "Have you seen a peacock, Emrick? Noisy, bombastic birds who vaunt their own worth with those feathers that fan open with a hundred eyes upon you."

"Yes, I have seen one. A handsome bird. Once seen, not forgotten. I thought the peacock was revered in your mythology, yet you do not speak highly of it."

"It is the sacred bird of Juno and symbolizes immortality because the ancients believed the flesh did not rot after death. I have seen one rot."

"So you are in discord with your Queen of Gods," Emrick raised an eyebrow in query.

"Only regarding the peacock. I know what I have seen." Emrick nodded in concession to his friend's logic. "Never turn your back on one, for they peck viciously without provocation."

"So we dance to the Praetorians' songs without singing their words."

"Very poetic..."

"We don't have to trust our lives to them, we are not on campaign," reasoned Emrick.

"You'll see...I'll give you a sundial segment before you're restraining that temper of yours. A day, and you'll be puce with rage. A week, and you'll be screaming at that Celtic god of storms you so love to strike them down."

"Taranis the Thunderer!"

"That's the one. You'll be wanting to make a sacrifice of our Praetorian Centurion. Mark my words!"

*

Cletus was right. Their acting centurion had lived up to every aspect of the description he'd given to Emrick, who now referred to the Praetorian as the Peacock, often with a stream of derogatory expletives before and after. By the end of their first back-breaking week of digging graves, the big Celt's temper split. Fortunately, he had held it in check until the two comrades were alone.

Their unit was working a thousand paces outside the city walls preparing mass graves. Funeral pyres were being restricted for fear of further fire in the city. It was an onerous job, made bearable by the comradeship, joshing and joking with banter honed from generations of campaigning, as it was passed from veteran to recruit. It was an army tradition, a right of passage, a survival technique. But the Peacock had been irking both Cletus and Emrick all morning, his pompous attitude as irritating as a persistent fly. Clete had managed to repeatedly swat that fly away, but Emrick seemed to have swallowed the insect and it was crawling around in his guts. A blight he couldn't treat.

He had dug deeper and harder, slicing his shovel into the dry soil and discarding the load to the side, quicker and more feverishly, hoping the sweat running down his back in rivulets beneath the high sun would cleanse him of the anger and bury his temper in the graves they were creating. It didn't. The anger was still within him when they were given orders to go to the city gate to receive the body cart.

Carts were banned by law from the streets of Roma during daylight hours due to the size of the population. There just wasn't room for the number of carts and people to share the same streets at the same time. The body carts were a necessary exception and would trundle around the city collecting the dead and deliver their grim cargo to the grave-digging soldiers twice a day. The driver of the cart would be relieved at the gate and allowed to wash at the pump which the engineers had temporarily provided by tapping into the underground aqueduct.

Emrick threw his shovel aside at the order and began striding with intent in the direction of the city gate, roiling along like a fire billowing with smoke just before it bursts into flames. Mindful of the fines for losing equipment, Clete retrieved the discarded shovel and placed it with his own in the designated storage area, then jogged to catch up with his troubled friend.

"I see why we were not issued with a gladius," hissed Emrick, in control of his ire just enough to keep his words muted whilst still in earshot of his officer. Emrick, still striding ahead, sensed Clete smirk and raised his arm as a warning to him. "Do not say it! Do not gloat! I agree you were right but I cannot stomach you gloating about it. The Peacock is a bastard! An ignorant bastard!" The last word was said with feeling and was followed by a bestial growl which had the effect of dislodging the fly in his guts, allowing his temper to ease, and dissipate with every step they took away from the Peacock. Cletus succeeded in drawing a guffaw from his friend by the time the city gate came in to view.

"I was ready to flatten his head with my shovel, you know?" said Emrick. "It's a bad business when you let a man annoy you that much. I wanted to make pulp of his brains. I was close to breaking."

He shook his head at the memory, perturbed by his own anger now that he was calm again.

"Here," grunted Clete, passing a strip of linen to Emrick, knowing that anything he could add to his friend's confession would be inadequate. Emrick would settle his conscience in his own time. "It will help with the odour of the cart." Emrick raised his eyebrows with appreciative delight at the scent of the linen as both men placed the strips over their nose and mouth, tying them securely behind their heads. "Soaked in lavender oil and allowed to dry in the sun," Cletus explained, his voice muffled by the covering.

"From the serving wench at the Carpe Vinum?" Despite the cloth masking Clete's face, Emrick could see the smile as it creased the corners of his eyes but noted that the sparkle of a sexual conquest was missing from them. He arched his eyebrows at that as Clete grunted an answer. "What was that? You are muffled?" Emrick replied, cupping a hand around his ear to show that he couldn't hear well. "But I would wager a bet that you said 'the wench is pretty but she is not Maia'." The comment brought forth a louder grunt from Clete, the laughter creases disappearing with it. They'd not spoken of Maia since she'd run away at the camp gate and Clete was surprised by the strength of the jolt in his chest at the unexpected mention of her name. He shouldn't have been surprised by the insight from Emrick though.

"You know me better than I know myself!"

"Silence on a subject tells plenty. That, plus your reluctance to drink in any other popina than the Carpe Vinum, despite it being a flea pit, a dust pit, with wine like piss and serving wenches you've not yet humped. That's not like you." The last comment put a grin on Clete's face. "Maia will find you when she is ready. Meanwhile, I would suggest accepting more than just the lavender linens from the serving wench. It might settle your lust and make you more bearable to be with." Emrick clapped his friend on the shoulder to show he was teasing.

Clete let out a soft whistle through his teeth, nodding towards the body cart which had come into view. The height of the pile of corpses beneath the canvas sheet was sobering.

"We'll need a ewer or two of wine tonight," said Clete, enunciating slowly to ensure his words were clear this time.

"A ewer or four! Let us get this job done, Comrade."

"And do not let the Peacock raise your blood again. The last thing we want is extra duties for poor discipline."

Chapter Twenty-Four

Several weeks passed before the pestilence began to release its hold on the city. The number of sick in the asclepion started to fall, the cots clearing more quickly due to a lower daily intake combined with a greater recovery rate compared to the early days of the plague.

Maia was sitting at the foot of the giant statue of Asclepius just gazing up, in awe of his healing power, taking strength from his silent presence. Having touched the large, marble hand so often, she felt an intimacy with the statue, a closeness that allowed her to ask questions without fear of reproach. She was trying to make sense of the number of people Asclepius had not healed. Why let so many perish? Why save one over another? Why allow Eshe from the Imperial Palace to die when Maia had prayed so diligently, so fervently? Was it because her prayers were sent with selfish reasons, for she had wanted to learn more about Malita from Eshe? The questions tumbled over themselves, chafing at her mood until she sighed with frustration at the lack of answers. There was no fathoming it, she would just have to accept that the god who towered above her knew better than she did. Acceptance. It helped, but a husk of annoyance over Eshe stubbornly remained as she returned to the shared sleeping chamber.

Maia was pleased to see the room was empty. With less patients to attend, she had finished her duties earlier than usual and was not needed until the next day. It felt very strange to have time to fill, to even have time to think, but she welcomed the solitude the empty room was offering.

Unpinning her hair, she let it fall loose, noticing it now reached as far as her forming bosom, evident as a small sloping rise beneath her tunic. The flaxen colour, as pale as ripe corn, made her think of Clete and the time he'd joked that she could be related to the Emperor. It seemed an age ago that she'd left him at the Circus Maximus without saying a proper goodbye. Her resentment had softened, confirmed by a rising panic in her chest when she couldn't recall the sound of his voice, his grunt; she missed his grunt of all things.

She closed her eyes and could see his face in the darkness and with the vision came his voice, the timbre, the chuckle, the grunt. It *was* still all with her and a smile of relief simpered on her lips, replaced quickly by a frown. Strange that she felt entirely confident that he was still alive in a city pocked with death. The unbidden thought brought sudden doubt, plunging a spike of fear, like a rush of broiling lava, through her chest to settle uncomfortably in her guts.

Taking a deep breath and admonishing herself for thinking the worst, she concentrated on raking her fingers through her hair, teasing out the tangles until they lost their resistance. The concern for Clete was not so easy to disperse, the tendrils of doubt more stubborn. Perhaps she should look for him at the Carpe Vinum. "Stupid name," she muttered, feeling happier as the idea had fixed as soon as it was presented. She would ask Marguerita for a clean tunic.

*

"You cannot go to the popina alone. I forbid you to go. The streets of the city are not safe for a lone woman of your age at night," lectured Marguerita as she collected and folded the dry laundry in the fullonica. "Here," she said passing a clean tunic to Maia.

"Then come with me as my protector," stated Maia simply.

Marguerita looked up sharply, raising her eyebrows at the suggestion and was surprised to find a flutter of excitement at the offer. The plague had been a reminder of the fragility of life and seeing Maia, a girl on the cusp of blooming into womanhood, Marguerita realised she had let the island steal away her vivacity with its safety. It was time she ventured beyond its walls. To Maia's delight she agreed.

"I have been afraid to live for fear of dying. It is time I changed that. We will put on our shoes and cross the bridge together."

At the mention of shoes, Maia automatically looked at her bare feet with a rush of the slave she had been filling her. It would be wonderful to put her freedom shoes on again. It would help to remind her of the status she had stolen.

"Thank you, Marguerita," she said earnestly. "I must know if Cletus still lives."

*

Cletus and Emrick had noticed the lowering of the dead tally too. The body cart was delivering just once a day at sundown and the strain on the canvas covering was lower too. Despite this, Praetorian Guard Tulio Tiberius Livius had not relaxed his rigorous digging orders and was still raising the blood of the big Celt, and without the noon delivery there had been no break from his relentless pecking.

And so Emrick's temper split.

Clete was returning from the latrine pit when the Peacock displayed its tail. He could not hear what was being said but the language of his body, the sententious swagger and malignant expression of pleasure, were enough to alert Clete to trouble. Knowing Emrick as well as he did from their shared time in the legion where a comrade becomes a second self such is the bond of comradeship, he broke in to an immediate run, grunting, as was his way.

It was this quick reaction that saved Tulio from being struck by the big Celt and saved Emrick from a snake pit of trouble. Cletus came in with a roar, rushing at Emrick from the side, tackling him at hip height as the Celt raised his shovel preparing to swipe at the Peacock's face, his reasoning gone in a veil of wild anger.

Clete attacked with speed and aggression, knowing that was the only way he would be able to wrestle his big friend to the ground. Surprise was on his side as Emrick's focus was on Tulio. The breath was knocked from Cletus as he impacted with his comrade. It felt like he'd run in to the Servian Wall and an agonising pain bolted through his shoulder but the wall gave way as he kept his momentum. For a heartbeat the pair seemed to float and the world was silent before they crashed like grappling Titans to the hard ground.

The shock of the unexpected attack expunged the ire from Emrick, his focus diverting to his immediate predicament. He gave a growl of pain as something solid bruised his ribs and the loose dirt raked his forearm as he landed, grinding grit deep into the skin. Dust billowed and men shouted and before he could make sense of the chaos, he was pinned down. Roaring like an injured bear he struggled to shake the men from his back, but despite his size and strength, they were too many.

"Stay still," hissed a voice he knew in his ear. He couldn't place who the voice belonged to with his face being pressed forcibly to the ground, squashing his left ear and cheek, but it struck a chord as friend not foe which seemed incongruous with events and the tone being used. Through a blurred periphery vision, Emrick could make out other men dragging his attacker to clear ground. The man was not resisting as far as he could tell. "Lucky for you that Cletus is the faster runner," came the same voice.

"Felix, is that you?" growled Emrick, his words disappearing into a distorted mumble into the dusty ground. "Let me up, you dolt!"

"Stay still!" repeated Felix. "Don't make things worse." The tension in the atmosphere was not missed by Emrick now his temper was gone, and there was little else he could do other than comply.

Chapter Twenty-Five

Maia had taken care with her appearance, sweeping her hair into a twisted bundle and securing it with pins revealing an elegant nape. Marguerita had let her choose a tunic from her meagre collection. There had not been a yellow one to match the freedom shoes, so Maia had picked a white one with a teal green, satin edging around the hem, neckline and armholes. The neckline and armholes were cut straight with no gathering at the shoulders. The tunic was a little big on Maia, so the armholes gaped open to her waist so she wore a closer fitting tunic underneath to cover her small breasts. A matching green cord drew the material in at her waist, lifting the stola just enough to keep it from touching the ground.

Marguerita was wearing a similar tunic but with a double band of red braiding at the hem. Maia couldn't see if the neckline and sleeves were decorated as well, as a palla of pale blue wool secured by a fibula brooch made from iron and studded with garnets was around Marguerita's shoulders.

They greeted each other in the atrium with a hug.

"Blossoming to beauty," said the older woman, standing back a little to study Maia. The phrase brought Maia back to the clear words Eshe had spoken before she died. *You will blossom more beautifully than that devious woman and the child will be a girl, so there is nothing to fear.* Maia was no closer to understanding the riddle.

*

In the lowering light of the early evening, Maia and Marguerita stepped on to the bridge that connected Isola Tiberina with the city. The air was still, as if the oncoming darkness was holding its breath until the sun dipped out of sight, hoping not to be noticed before it began its mischief. Bats were swooping on insects still playing on the river. A fausty mixture of smells was clinging to the last of the day's heat.

"We must not forget today's password or we'll not be allowed back in to the Capitoline region," said Marguerita.

"No need to worry about that," laughed Maia. "Honey-cakes! I shan't forget that password, I love honey-cakes." Despite her outward joviality, Maia was nervous. "Are you sure you know the way to the Carpe Vinum?"

"Yes, I know it." Maia had slipped her arm through Marguerita's and the older woman patted the small hand reassuringly. "I used the Carpe Vinum often for our evening meals, before..." she hesitated, frowning at memories that were no longer raw but still painful, unsure how to phrase her loss and settling on, "...before the Great Fire. I always preferred the cooked food from there to that from the thermopoliums. They had a family recipe for their garum and it was the best I have tasted. I am curious to know if the Carpe Vinum is still run by the same people. I doubt it, but I do know the way." Marguerita gave a big smile. "Oh, Maia, something inside me feels alive tonight. I had grown used to the loneliness of my existence, but I am ready for some mischief." Her eyes were twinkling like a faceted, deep blue jewel.

"I hope Cletus is there," said Maia.

They walked alongside the river, retracing the route Maia had used on her first day in Roma, turning left to the Capitoline Hill sector. The travertine blocks were still in place but most of the damaged buildings had been taken down. A lot of clearing work had been going on whilst Maia had been attending the sick.

"Emperor Titus will rebuild the city bigger and better than it was before, just as Emperor Nero did," said Marguerita. "I am sure they will do the same with Pompeii once Roma is done."

"No!" Maia's chest bounced with fear at the sudden thought of it. "They must not, it was too dreadful. Pompeii is buried."

"Surely it can be cleared. Look at how quickly they are rebuilding Roma. Anything is possible."

"No...please do not speak of it, Marguerita. You were not there, you did not see the death-cloud. The mountain exploded with the most fearsome anger of Vulcan. Please do not speak of it. Let Pompeii keep its secrets beneath the ash." The older woman was taken aback by the sudden tirade.

"What strange words to say. Do you have a secret to hide?"

Maia chewed on her lip, upset with her own loose tongue. Marguerita's simple question was a reminder of how careful she must be. It was always when she felt comfortable with someone that her guard would drop. It was dangerous to relax.

"My family are beneath the ashes," she lied, turning eyes as soulful as a young doe's to her friend. "My life is buried there." That, at least, was not a lie.

Marguerita gave a thin smile, patting Maia's hand again. "I am sorry for speaking of Pompeii. We will concentrate on rebuilding your life, just as the soldiers are rebuilding the city. Both will be more beautiful when we are done. You will see."

"I hope so." And she realised how much she wanted Cletus to be a part of that life.

They had reached the Circus Maximus and Marguerita cheekily called out a greeting to the legionaries guarding the gate in an attempt to bring back the mood of their earlier gaiety. She was rewarded with a wink and responded with a flirtatious smile, warming to the fun she could have and bringing forth a wry grin from the guard. Marguerita giggled conspiratorially with Maia and kept up a flow of chatter as they continued to walk alongside the temporary camp. By the time they reached the corner of the Circus Maximus where Emrick had stolen Cletus from Maia, a certain level of the evening's excitement had returned. The concrete arches of the aqueduct commissioned by Nero came into view.

"This part of the aqueduct was one of the improvements Nero made to Roma after the Great Fire. It brings water to The Temple of the Divine Claudius."

"It looks like a border of lace on a grand scale," said Maia as she gazed at the structure of arch upon arch upon arch.

"It does, you are right. No doubt it will serve the Flavian Amphitheatre too. Such a shame the opening has been delayed by these disasters, but perhaps it has fallen well for me, for I would not have been interested in them before meeting you. I feel as if a fog has lifted from me. Truly."

The amphitheatre came into view as they rounded the corner of the tile-topped wall that surrounded the lush gardens of The Temple of the Divine Claudius. The sight of it stopped them in their tracks.

"It's huge," said Maia, her eyebrows rising in wonder.

"And beautiful. So many arches, it is mesmerising." The evening sun was blushing the stone an unusual shade of dusky pink with golden tones.

"I am so sorry that Dom and Claudia did not get to see it," said Maia sadly, suddenly feeling their loss like a quern stone weighing her down.

"Come, it is not far to the Carpe Vinum from here. Cletus will lift your heart."

Chapter Twenty-Six

Emrick's ribs were sore. Clete had a headache.

"Digging again but digging shit," complained Emrick. "You should have let me flatten him. He is scum." Cletus gave a grunt. They both knew the punishment for assaulting a superior would have been much worse than extra latrine duties.

"Be grateful there were witnesses or that bastard Peacock would have lied through his penis to get us charged with more than just an affray. Assault most likely, despite his not having a feather out of place. *Futuo*, I hate the Guards! We were lucky and owe Felix for keeping you out of further trouble whilst I was out cold." Clete had been knocked unconscious when they'd hit the ground. It was his head that had bruised Emrick's ribs as they fell.

"My sense returned when you impaled me with your head. Did you have to rush me so hard you Roman thug?"

"*Brittunculi!*" Clete knew this derogatory name for a Briton would rile the Celt and gave a wry smile as he used it, keeping his head down as he worked so Emrick couldn't see.

"Taranis the Thunderer! Strike all these obnoxious Romans down." There was a silence between the two men as Clete hid his merriment at seeing his comrade trying to control his anger.

"Look front, Brother..." said Clete once he felt Emrick had suffered his teasing long enough.

"...and I have your back," growled Emrick, as he realised

Cletus had been playing his temper. The spoken battle motto was enough to settle the air. "My life is in your debt once more, my friend. I will repay you."

"Never mind that, a jug of the Carpe Vinum's best wine will do it." Cletus spat on the palm of his hand and extended it towards Emrick. The Celt nodded his thanks, spat on his own palm and sealed the deal with a handshake. "A jug for Felix too," added Cletus before releasing the hold.

"Deal! I will settle my debt as soon as we are released from extra duties."

"One day down, six to go. Now let's see if we can work on a strategy that will stop you from losing your temper with the Peacock. I really would like us both to survive this stay in Roma!"

*

The Carpe Vinum was on the corner of a narrow street not far from the statue that had been erected by Nero, of himself, but was now the body of Nero with the head of Apollo, the original head having been knocked off when the Senate made Nero a public enemy, a little before his suicide over a decade ago.

A few people were standing outside the Carpe Vinum enjoying the breeze that was funnelling along the street stirring the hot evening air. One group of three men were laughing at a shared story. Another man, not in uniform but with the deportment of a legionary, was leaning against the wall, an erection evident. No doubt the result of watching his colleague who had his lips closed around the nipple of an amply endowed woman and was working his hand beneath his own tunic. The woman was leaning against the wall looking bored.

"He's not outside," said Maia.

"Then we go inside," replied Marguerita.

With a confidence she thought had gone, Marguerita pushed through the huddle of men who were standing inside. The popina was crowded in the area by the door, but further inside were some empty benches so she led Maia to one of those. Maia's eyes were scanning the faces. She was a rivet of nerves and it felt as if her heart was hammering that rivet into her stomach. Nervous of seeing Clete, yet more nervous still of his not being there.

"I can't see him, Marguerita. I don't think he's in that crowd by the door. His friend, Emrick is definitely not here, he's too big to miss."

"We will wait a while. The serving girl will be sent across to take our order I'm sure."

"Oh, I have no coin. I didn't give it a thought."

"I have," said Marguerita, patting a fold in her stola at the top of her thigh. "I will show you how to stitch a hidden pocket for when you have your own sestertii." Maia already had this skill, just no coins to fill the pocket.

"I should begin looking for some work. I don't think I'll be needed at the asclepion much longer, but how can I earn enough to rent an apartment?"

"Surely you would look to marry? I mean...I know you have no family to arrange a contract, but you can put yourself forwards. Cletus sounds a solid financial opportunity and he will soon be free of his legionary service. Is that not why we are here?" Marguerita frowned in confusion.

Maia, too, was momentarily confused before realising she was thinking like the slave-girl she had been. Decima could not marry a citizen but Maia could. It hadn't crossed her mind as an option, a remnant of her upbringing on Pompeii. How stupid of her! She must act like the free citizen she was claiming to be. Society expected her to marry.

"I have no dowry to offer," Maia replied, escaping further uncomfortable talk on the subject when a group of men entered the room. She studied them keenly before shaking her head at Marguerita as Cletus was not amongst the group. A serving girl came to their table and Marguerita ordered a platter of food with wine for them to share. Maia could only pick at the food such were her nerves. The evening drew on, the level of boisterous noise increasing as the wine took charge. Men came and men went with no sign of

Clete or Emrick. A couple of buxom whores entered, causing a stir as they skilfully displayed their barely covered bosoms in a manner that invited custom.

"Are you sure Cletus said the Carpe Vinum?" asked Marguerita after a while.

"Definitely! It's not a name you forget."

"We'll ask the serving girl if she's seen him when she comes this way again. It's surprising how many customers they get to know."

Unfortunately, Cletus Tettidius Castus did not register with the wench.

"What about Clete?" asked Maia. "He doesn't usually give his full name. Or Emrick? He is so big you couldn't miss him and speaks Latin with an accent." The serving girl declined knowing either of them explaining that she had only started serving the evening shift the previous day.

"Fortuna is against us tonight," said Marguerita.

"Or maybe not," said a man who was sitting at the next bench. He was dressed in the uniform of a Praetorian Guard and formerly introduced himself. "Tulio Tiberius Livius. I overheard your enquiry and know the men you are asking after. They are in my working unit."

"They live, they are well?" Maia's relief was evident in her eager voice and bright eyes.

"Yes, they live."

"Are they coming here tonight?"

"It is unlikely." Tulio's mouth twitched but he kept his amusement at Maia's disappointment from showing. He was thinking several steps ahead. Waving at the serving girl, he ordered more wine. "A ewer of your best posca mixed with brine and three cups." Turning his attention back to Maia and Marguerita he moved across to their bench. "Cletus and Emrick are on duty tonight, but perhaps you will share a drink with me in their absence? I am in the mood to celebrate." He made no mention of their duty being at the latrines but was feeling a twang of arousal at their double misfortune; not only were they digging shit, they were missing this treat too.

"What are we celebrating?" asked Marguerita.

"The survival of friends and the rebuilding of our great city. Two stout and sturdy reasons to raise a cup to our lips I would say." The serving girl returned with their wine, diluted with sea water to cut away the sickly sweetness of the posca. Tulio half-filled each cup and handed them round.

"To Life," said Marguerita.

"To beautiful Roma," said Tulio.

"To both," said Maia, and all three of them drank.

"So...you are friends of my friends," said Tulio.

"I know Cletus; Emrick only by name," replied Maia. "I was hoping he would be here tonight."

"I can pass a message to him for you." Tulio was looking steadily at Maia, who hesitated in replying. She wasn't certain Clete wanted to hear from her. "I see my offer gives you a dilemma," added Tulio, leaning back nonchalantly and raising his left foot so that the side of his boot was resting on his right knee.

"I do not mean to be rude. I just do not know what message to give. To see him would be easier."

"Then I will tell him you will be here the day after tomorrow. Can you make it here for then?" Marguerita gave an imperceptible nod, more a blink of her eyes than a nod, but Maia understood the subtle gesture. With a hopeful look in her eyes, she nervously agreed.

"Thank you, yes, if it's not too much trouble." Tulio's gaze was sure and steady and Maia sensed his desire and looked down to her hands in her lap rather than keep eye contact with him.

"No trouble. Let us raise our cups again to old and new friendships." After taking another draught, he raised his eyebrows in appreciation of the wine. "That's pretty good juice from the vines," he said studying the cup with wonder. Turning his attention back to Maia and Marguerita, "and tonight is a pretty good time for making new friends." Giving his most charming smile he launched in to a series of stories which made Marguerita giggle from the start and finally drew a genuine laugh from Maia.

As the evening grew aged and the night was born, Tulio tapped his gladius which was sheathed and tied to his hip.

"Let me escort you to your residence. The darkness can act as a shield to the lowlifes, but the sword of a Praetorian will deter the scum," he said proudly. They chatted amiably on the walk back through the city, Maia, remembering the password of 'honey-cakes' as they reached the barricaded section, just as she knew she would. The legionary let the three of them through and they walked beside the river in companionable silence. It had turned out to be an evening of merriment, one of those joyful evenings you hadn't expected and didn't want to end.

"Honey-cakes are scrumptious," she announced suddenly, and for no reason at all. They all laughed far too hard at a statement that wasn't funny. That mirth lasted until they reached the bridge across to the asclepion.

"We are here," stated Marguerita. "Thank you, Tulio."

"It has been a pleasure," he replied, tipping his head slightly in acknowledgement of his words. "I will tell Cletus you will be at the Carpe Vinum the day after tomorrow at dusk." The words were said with a smile. The words were a lie, spoken from one liar to another.

Chapter Twenty-Seven

The same faces were in the Carpe Vinum when Maia and Marguerita arrived for their second visit. Except for Tulio, he was nowhere to be seen. The same faces were also absent from the Carpe Vinum. Sitting at the bench they'd occupied before, with a clear view to the door, Maia declined the offer of food. Her stomach was too knotted to invite a meal. Nerves fill an appetite as effectively as any banquet.

They waited with hope.

Just as it had previously, the noise in the popina grew louder as the evening grew older until the voices became a thrum pitted with cheers from a group of legionaries who were gambling over a game of tali. Maia picked incessantly at a hangnail on her thumb. Marguerita, who had begun the evening trying to keep the mood light, gave up when the thrum became too loud for conversation. Twice she had needed to firmly swat away a drunken pass, something she did adeptly, but they were mostly left alone. It was hot.

They waited with fading hope and rising humiliation.

The door to the tavern opened and Maia saw a face she recognised. It was Tulio. He stood aside the door for a moment making it clear he was scanning the room. Shrugging his shoulders he held his arms crooked with palms upwards in a gesture that asked *where is he?* Maia shook her head in response. Tulio beckoned them to him.

"We have an escort home at least," said Marguerita, raising her voice above the din. "Let us go home." They nudged their way to the door which Tulio held open for them. It was no cooler outside. There was no breeze and the torridity was oppressive, giving a thickness to the air that remained heavy with the heat that hadn't faded away with the sun.

"Where is Cletus?" asked Tulio, knowing full well he was still confined to extra latrine duties at the camp. Maia's expression was enough of an answer. "He does not come despite my message to him. I am sorry."

"The fault is his."

"Indeed, yet I regret the anguish his actions have bestowed on you. You deserve better."

"I do," said Maia firmly. "I deserve better!" And she brightened a little, as uttering the statement seemed to make it a more solid proposition. Tulio built on this foundation by once again tapping his gladius and offering to be their escort.

"It is my mission not only to get you home safely, but to restore you both to the fine state of joviality. By Jupiter, by Jove, let our great god of the sky lead us to laughter."

"Yes, let us be jovial as our great god's name intends," agreed Marguerita. Maia nodded and found Tulio's charm did make her smile.

*

Clete was up to his ankles in a slough of mud, urine and excrement and splattering the foul-smelling morass up his bare legs, covering the tattoo of his legion, the Capricornus, the sea-goat on his left calf, as he hefted a spade in to the sticky mess, cussing and grunting with displeasure as he worked at speed to dig an extension to the latrine trench. The Circus Maximus was not suited to having a latrine for this many men. Running water was needed, not just the improvised set up they had here. *Two days to go, five done, two more,* he said to himself, using the words as a working mantra.

Maia...

"Futuo!" he cursed aloud, his black mood made darker by the unexpected thought punching in and disrupting his concentration. He had no need to worry about the girl, and yet he did. She was a liar and a thief and a puzzlement, so why did she matter to him? *"Futuo!"*

Emrick heard the repeated swearing from where he was working and looked across to his colleague. Leaving the water fixing he'd been trying to improve, he picked up his shovel and went to help with the digging. He said nothing, just squelched beside Clete and put his strength in to extending the trench. They worked together in silence until the job was completed, sweat soaking their tunics.

"We stink," grunted Cletus, his demeanour still dark.

"The bathhouse before barracks," replied Emrick.

It was an hour past curfew and the camp was at rest as Clete and Emrick made their way to the makeshift bathhouse. The sleeping camp was an oasis of peace amidst the city that never rested, Roma as busy overnight as it was during the day with the carts delivering supplies, the prostitutes roaming for business and the policing of the Urban Cohorts kept active by the darker professions of the night.

Hearing the snores and muted voices of the men as they passed the tents invoked memories of their time serving in Britannia and Clete's mood became a little lighter, easing him to a more amenable humour...until they saw Tulio walking towards them along the Via Principia.

"The stench just got worse," he growled.

"Still in uniform," noticed Emrick. "Where's he been then and how has he skirted the curfew?"

"Fucking Praetorians are above the rules remember. He'll have been up to no good that's for certain."

"Never turn your back on a peacock." Emrick recalled Clete's earlier words. "The night air is heavy enough for a storm, so I believe we have Taranis the Thunderer nearby should we need to call on his services. Five days done, two to go. The Peacock will not beat us tonight."

Clete was well aware that Emrick was warning him to hold his temper as Tulio approached and the irony of the reversed situation was not wasted on him. When they were within six paces of their officer, Cletus and Emrick stopped, stood to attention and saluted by placing their right forearm across their chests. Tulio acknowledged their salutes with one of his own, then wrinkled his nose and contorted his face.

"*Putere*...you reek!" Then he smirked. "Your evening has clearly not been as agreeable as mine. The sweet smell of honey lingers with me despite your best efforts to smother it. The smell..." he paused for effect, staring directly at Cletus, "...and the taste." With great effort and drawing on his years of military discipline, Clete kept his face expressionless and didn't break his officer's stare. The trick was to look towards the eyes but focus on the nose. Tulio wrinkled his nose again to show his distaste. "Get to the bathhouse," he ordered. "And be thorough!"

Emrick and Cletus held to attention until Tulio had walked six paces away then dropped their salutes and continued on to the bathhouse.

"The Peacock has been displaying its tail. Am I right? Is that what those birds do when they are mating?" asked Emrick.

"Yes but the birds have beauty, that cocksucker has only guile. What woman would go with him?" Then, with the clarity of a mountain stream flowing over pebbles, he knew and his dark mood became blacker...Maia!

Chapter Twenty-Eight

Tulio made use of the next two evenings knowing that Cletus and Emrick were still confined to the camp. He arranged to meet Maia and Marguerita at the bridge to the asclepion whilst there was still daylight and made use of his privileges as a Praetorian Guard to take them on a tour of the damaged part of the city that was being rebuilt.

"Roma is recovering rapidly from the double disasters. Emperor Titus is doing well and the people love him for it. Look how quickly we are raising new structures. With the plague waning we can release more manpower to the rebuilding so our work rate will increase too." Tulio was speaking with passion and choosing his words to impress. "I have some men who specialise in laying mosaics under my command. They are from Segusio in the north west. The province of Alpes Cottiae. Have you heard of it? The finest marble is quarried there." Maia shook her head although the question did not need an answer for Tulio was continuing with his passionate tirade. "They are assigned to repairing Pompey's Theatre. Nay, more than repairing, they are assigned to *improving* the floors of the theatre. Our city will be grander than before the fire when we are done and the chariot racing will return to the Circus Maximus with all trace of our temporary camp there gone. I pledge to take you to those races Ladies, if you will do me the honour of accompanying me."

Maia's arm was tucked into Marguerita's as they walked. Squeezing it gently she gave her friend a warm smile. She was enjoying the tour. There was a lot to be hopeful about. Marguerita smiled back and it pleased Tulio to see the exchange. He enjoyed playing the charmer, laying the bait to draw the women in. He was good at it and had discovered that it suited him better to work for the reward. He felt his groin pulse at the thought of a threesome. Both women could be compliant, he sensed it. But the main driving force to this particular challenge was the knowledge that he was stealing a conquest from Cletus Tettidius Castus. The corner of his mouth twitched with delight at the humiliation it would inflict on a man he hadn't liked from their first meeting.

*

"You like Tulio don't you," Maia said to Marguerita when they were back working in the fullonica the next morning.

"He has shown us kindness these past few days, buying us meals and showing us the regrowth of Roma. Yes, I like him."

"He wants to take us to the Castra Praetoria on the Viminal Hill and show off his military barracks."

"How will he get us in? Women are barred from entering."

"He will find a way, a bribe no doubt. A coin is more effective at opening a locked door than a key."

"You are learning," laughed Marguerita. "Being a Praetorian guard means he will have plenty of coin to cast around. Did you know they receive three times the pay of a regular legionary? A larger discharge bonus too and all for less years of service."

"What is the Speculatores Augusti?"

"A branch of the Guards, the Emperor's personal cavalry bodyguard. Why do you ask?"

"Tulio was saying he wants to wear the boots of the Speculatores Augusti."

"He has ambition then. Not many reach those heights. Do *you* like him?" Marguerita asked, passing a pile of laundered linen to Maia to fold.

"He makes me smile with his wit." It was an evasive reply and Marguerita paused in her work to give Maia a quizzical look.

"Does that mean you like him?"

"He has a joy for life which I like."

"But...?" persisted Marguerita, sensing the reluctance to answer directly. Maia shrugged, turning away to take the folded pile of linen to a bench.

"Do we have enough urine and sulphur for tomorrow's laundry?"

"Now you are changing the subject young lady, but whether you like him or not, we should consider making a marriage proposal. A Praetorian Guard can legally marry, that's another perk they have that a regular legionary does not, so you would not have to wait." This was a reference to Clete without his name being spoken. An acknowledgement that Tulio was a favoured proposition. "And we know it is high patronage only in the Guards so his family must be reputable. How fortuitous your meeting was. You could do much worse than marry a Praetorian Guard. Juno is carrying you at her bosom."

Julius came in with a new pile of dirty linens, fewer than of late, and the talk of marriage, which still made Maia nervous, was halted by the message he gave that Maia was to report to the clerk in the atrium.

"As soon as you can," added Julius. Maia shared a concerned glance with Marguerita. Was this the summons to tell her she was no longer needed at the asclepion?

*

It was. The number of sick in the city was declining daily and Emperor Titus had officially declared the state of emergency as over in Roma. This meant the asclepion would no longer receive funds from the treasury to feed the extra volunteers. Maia would need to leave within the week. She had asked for longer to find new accommodation but the instructions were clear; seven sunrises.

Alone in the small ante-chamber that had served as her

sleeping quarters, Maia was sitting on the end of her pallet with her head in cupped hands and elbows resting on knees, staring at the floor watching the shafts of sunlight dance in patterns where they slanted in through the high, arched openings. Chewing on the inside of her lip, she considered her options. They were limited and Marguerita's words were screaming at her: *you could do much worse than marry a Praetorian Guard. Juno is carrying you at her bosom.*

Was she being saved by the gods again? Had they sent Tulio to keep her from the destitution that was awaiting her beyond the security of Isola Tiberina? She'd looked to Cletus for that safety but it seemed he had abandoned her. It was painful to accept but there was no choice but to play the tali pieces she was given...but she was afraid of marriage, or more precisely, of her past that may be unearthed during the process of marriage. Would questions be asked? They may not, she reasoned. She must not let her guilt cloud her vision. Nor must she act like she had something to hide. *What you do, is who you become. And who you have become, is expected by society to marry.* She must keep faith with that.

"No tears," she whispered to herself. "Cletus doesn't like tears." And with that, her eyes welled up and a tear-drop spilled over. Wiping it away with the back of her wrist, she stood up with a determination to think of anything other than Clete. Seeing her freedom shoes nestling in the wall niche reminded her that she still had an obligation to fulfil. The plague had kept her from this purpose, it was time to renew her attempt to gather enough coin to free Ebele and Hadassah. Marrying into a wealthy family such as Tulio's seemed her best chance of succeeding. The gods were replacing Cletus with Tulio in her life for this reason. It was a clear nudge.

With her thoughts reconciled to her path ahead, Maia went to find Marguerita to discuss a proposal. She had little to offer and everything to gain from the union. Her hopes were balancing on the strength of lies that buried her roots under the ash covering Pompeii.

Chapter Twenty-Nine

As was customary, Maia did not attend the meeting to put the marriage proposal forward, but that was as far as custom went in this time of strange events. It was usual for the fathers to meet at one of the family houses, instead Marguerita would champion Maia's cause and she had chosen to talk directly to Tulio at the basilica. She felt the public building would add formality to the proposition, something that she hoped would make up for the hurry Maia was in.

"Maia is the only member of her family to escape the disaster in Pompeii," she explained. "Her father wore the ring of an equestrian and you would have found his tunic and sandals to be finely stitched. Indeed, you can see this in her own shoes." Marguerita spoke the lies of Maia convincingly for she did not know they were not the truth. "The family's fortune is still at Pompeii and will, I'm sure, be recovered in time. The property may be lost, but the treasures within, the jewellery, gems, coin, all belong to Maia as the sole heir. It was shouted at the forum that the treasures will be reunited with any survivors."

"It has also been shouted that Pompeii will never be recovered," countered Tulio.

"I cannot imagine that will be the case, can you? There are many riches there." Marguerita raised an eyebrow as if to say the temptation is surely too great to be ignored. Tulio's greed thought the same but he remained silent, so Marguerita continued. "Such a devastating event to be involved in and yet it has made Maia both strong of mind and humble. Her work with the sick in Roma has been tireless, proving her ability to keep a house and she is young enough to bear you many children to ensure a male heir."

"You present her case well."

"It is easy to make a gilt purse given gold. Times are so strange that I hope you will forgive my directness to you instead of your father. Maia needs a home quickly." Marguerita kept an unswerving gaze on Tulio as he considered the proposal. Leaning back in the throne-like chair, tapping his thigh with busy fingers and pursing his lips, he took his time, keeping the fact that his father was dead and his family distanced, to himself.

Talk of an heir was appealing. The plague had been a stark reminder of how precarious life was and his joints had been reminding him of his age of late. The lack of a dowry was a problem, but the treasures of Pompeii were a high possibility. Surely they would be retrieved.

"Let me think on it," he said eventually.

"Of course, but I must press you for an answer swiftly due to Maia's situation. Shall we meet here again tomorrow?"

"The day after." Tulio stood up indicating the meeting was over.

"The day after," conceded Marguerita. "You have much to offer each other and I trust you will make the right decision."

*

The Circus Maximus was busy when Tulio returned to the camp and so it must have been fated that the first person he saw as he came through the gate was Cletus, who had just finished his final shift of extra latrine duties. The big Celt was not with him which was unusual. An unexpected opportunity was presenting itself and a glimmer of unkind satisfaction brightened Tulio's expression.

He'd been mulling over Marguerita's proposal as he walked from the basilica to the Circus Maximus, unable to settle on a decision, but on seeing Cletus, he knew that he would marry Maia for it would be the ultimate steal. The greater the hatred, the sweeter the spite.

"Hail hearty to you Comrade," he greeted Cletus with the highest of spirits which was met with a grunt and open suspicion. Ignoring this, he continued with his jollity. "Your duties are finished just in time to help me celebrate. I am to be married."

Maia's name wasn't mentioned but Cletus knew. *Why was the girl intent on choosing such poor male company? And why did it matter to him?* The unanswerable questions bruised his skull. A blood pact with the lowlife Calix had been bad enough, now an engagement to the Peacock! His mood had not recovered from its previous plunge and Tulio's smug expression was pushing it to black depths that smuggle away a man's composure. He'd seen it happen to Emrick but always thought he had more control. He was wrong and Emrick was not there to return the favour of stalling the attack as he swung his shovel at his acting centurion.

Unfortunately for Clete, there were witnesses.

Tulio was quick enough to dodge the strike, stumbling a few paces backwards as he did so, but although the momentum of the missed swing put Cletus off-balance too, his dark rage gave him an unexpected turn of speed. Dropping the shovel and lunging forwards with a bestial roar, he easily grappled Tulio to the dirt ground, billowing dust surrounding them as they landed. Tulio lashed out at Clete's head, managing to grab his left ear but all that did was twist Cletus enabling him to raise his right arm for a punch. Before he could land his fist on his acting centurion's chin, men were pulling him off and as his fury subsided in their strong grip, he sank to a new low at having lost control, silently damning Maia for entering his life.

*

Emrick was allowed to visit Cletus who was being held on charges at the Principia. Two legionaries in full military regalia were guarding his cell, the only stone building in the arena. It may only be a temporary camp at the Circus Maximus but security was taken as seriously as if it was on a frontier.

"What by Mars did the Peacock say to rile you?" asked

Emrick without preamble and in hushed tones. He would not be allowed to stay in the cell long.

"He breathes is all," replied Cletus in a growl.

"Brother, I regret not being with you. Nay, I regret not killing the bastard earlier. He has a way of worming into your blood and before you are aware, his stench has infected you entirely. I know it." The men shared a look of understanding. "Friend, I have bad news..."

"A court martial?" interrupted Cletus.

"I fear nothing as just as that!" Emrick flicked a look towards the closed door, wary of being overheard. Hunching his shoulders as if he could escape inside the cave they made, aggrieved at the news he must give his friend, he continued in a heavily muted voice. "The talk in the barracks is that Emperor Titus is planning lavish celebrations for the opening of the Flavian Amphitheatre. A reward to the people of the city for their hard work."

"I know of this. Has a date been announced?"

"The games are to start on the next full moon."

"Was the moon full two days past?"

"Three."

"So perhaps my trial will be delayed until the games are over."

"Worse...I fear you will not be afforded the decency of a court martial. Rather, you are already condemned to be a part of the mass executions planned to satisfy the blood-baying crowds at the games.

"Men for fodder," muttered Cletus thinking of Calix.

"A lot of men, my friend...the games have been extended, they are to last a hundred days."

Clete stood up and walked the couple of paces to the cell end and slapped his hand against the stone wall in frustration. With his back to Emrick, he leant both palms and his forehead against the wall, silent for a moment as he struggled to compose his thoughts and control the tendril of fear that was spreading through his guts as he began to grasp Emrick's concerns.

"A hundred days?" he said, still looking down the wall towards his feet. "That's an unprecedented amount of fodder."

"Rumours from the barracks are that they have begun filling the empty warehouses in the city with the men who are to be that fodder. I fear they will sweep whoever is unlucky enough to be in cells across the land at this time, despite their crime or innocence, into the warehouses in readiness.

"Wrong place, wrong time," said Cletus gloomily, turning towards Emrick with a grim expression. The Celt nodded his agreement.

"In the darkest hour, when the demons come, you can call on me Brother and we will fight them together." The cell door was suddenly pushed open and the guard inclined his head indicating Emrick's visit was over. There was time only for a legionary forearm clasp and a whispered parting from the Celt. "Keep faith, I will get you out. We know some of these guards."

But Cletus's faith was to be sorely tested as he was taken from the Circus Maximus cell to the warehouses that night, allowing the Celt no time to bribe the guards at the camp, nor time to plan an escape. The condemned were caged and thrown food just like the beasts some of them would fight in the arena. The lucky ones would die quickly.

Chapter Thirty

The new moon brought cooler conditions to the city and, although the temperatures were still high, the contrast led Maia to feel the evening chill as she walked back to the tenement that Tulio was renting for her in the Subura district. The room was pokey with one small window left open to the elements, which at this time of year left it hot and claustrophobic, and she shared it with mice. Mice that sounded as if they were wearing hobnail sandals as they revelled in the roof space in the quiet of the night. It was the worst room she had known but it was better than the streets and for that she was grateful. Tulio was also providing her with enough coin to buy food. It was barely enough, but again she was grateful for it.

It is temporary, she told herself, twisting the newly given ring on her finger, an iron band to signify strength of commitment, and the only tangible sign of Tulio's agreement to their marrying. There had been no engagement party, no meeting of families and no marriage contract had been written. Tulio's sudden, and unexpected, promotion to the Speculatores Augusti had swallowed all plans, at least that was what Maia had told Marguerita, hiding the nagging concern that he was using the promotion as an excuse to delay the wedding. She knew he'd dreamt of wearing the boots of the Emperor's cavalry and when Marguerita pointed out that gaining such a prestigious position at a young age was true indication that Tulio's family was of high standing and in favour, Maia pushed the doubts away and was happy for him.

The lack of tradition was not a bad thing mused Maia, as nothing about her past was traditional! She had his ring, somewhere to sleep and coin so she would not starve. She must resign herself to living with the mice until after the Inaugural Games. There were so many unlucky days in the calender to be avoided too, and she feared the days would be lengthening again before she was wed. A careful study of the calendars posted at the temples would be needed to pick a favourable day for the wedding. She would check when she next passed by.

In the meantime, she would enjoy the spectacle that the Emperor was planning for all the people of Roma. Although large for an amphitheatre, the largest free-standing one to be built she'd heard, it could not seat as many people as the Circus Maximus. The building was more beautiful though and would surely give a more intimate atmosphere. It would be wonderful to see inside.

Ripples of excitement could be felt in the city streets and that was a blessing after the days of the double disasters. There was much to look forward to.

Thinking about the planned games made her think of Calix and she wondered if he would be made to fight in the arena as Cletus had suggested. If he still lived that was. And what of Cletus, where was he? His snub remained painful.

The noise in the Subura district grew in response to the amount of wine that was imbibed in the tabernae below the apartments. There were plenty of seedy drinking bars and fast food outlets in this area that could do with a good scrub in Maia's opinion. Rats scurried freely in the dirty alleyways. One had almost scampered across her foot yesterday and it made her grateful to only have mice in her room.

Maia sighed at hearing a couple in a nearby tenement arguing. There was little privacy with so many apartment buildings crowding together. The strong, fishy aroma of the garum being served with meals was floating on the breeze and she noticed her hunger. She would venture down to the tabernae and see if she could buy a small platter. It was lonely having only mice for company.

*

Maia had lain awake until the early hours, kept from sleeping by the scrabbling rodents and her own disquiet, finally falling asleep, then not waking until the daylight was old. It put her out of sorts and the day ahead was stretching long with no routine. She could not see Tulio until he was released from training and she doubted that would be before the games began. She knew Marguerita would welcome her at the fullonica but a restlessness was unsettling her. She decided to walk it off.

Leaving the Subura district, Maia headed towards the new amphitheatre, shading her eyes with her hand as she stepped out of the shadows of the street in to the sunlit open space where the new building was still being worked on. Tulio had explained it was built on the site of the Golden Palace which was pulled down and the land returned to the people of Roma by Emperor Vespasian after Nero's death. She enjoyed it when he shared his knowledge of the city.

She paused to study the beauty of the amphitheatre. Arch upon arch upon arch. Rising straight from the flat ground rather than being nestled into a hillside.

A small crowd was forming near the end of the Via Sacre, the road that was lined with shops for the rich that led you from the amphitheatre to the Capitoline Hill. Renovation work following the fire would continue for a while yet, but the area was no longer cordoned off. Maia's curiosity led her towards it.

The reason for the gathering numbers became clear when a file of chained men, being harried along by the whips of guards, came into view. The watching crowd began a slow hand-clap as the line of condemned men grew closer. Maia was both fascinated and a-feared by the spectacle with its eerie accompaniment of a slow, flat beat of clapping. Calix could be amongst the chained and if he was, she didn't know if she would feel sympathy for him or spit on him.

As the moving column neared, the crowd neatly parted to create a human avenue and the clapping became louder as the number of onlookers swelled, the beat increasing in tempo too, matching Maia's racing heart. The file of men was long and she scanned the faces of those who were passing. Grubby, rank-smelling men, some with pale skin that didn't look like they had seen sunlight in months, others whose skin was burnt and blistered, then a score with skin as dark as Uday's from the land of lions.

"Are these men all criminals?" she asked the bystander next to her, raising her voice to be heard as jeers and whistles were added to the clapping.

"Criminals or prisoners o' war. Some o' them slaves be from the mines judgin' by their pallor," he shouted back, revealing a mouth of rotten teeth. "They've been bringing 'em in every mornin' for the last two weeks. Holding 'em in the warehouses at the Aventine docks like the cur they are. Must be enough down there to fill a small town already," he said cheerfully. "The Emperor ain't holding back with these games." The man turned his attention back to the line, throwing an over-ripe tomato and cheering as it splattered its pulp across the shoulder of one of the condemned men.

Maia felt a shudder walk her spine. Prisoners of war became slaves and she couldn't help but feel sympathy. Some slaves were being condemned just to make up the numbers for the mass executions it seemed. How precarious life was. And how fortunate she was to have escaped that status. A reminder that she still had a vow to keep. Leaving the crowd with renewed determination not to sit around waiting for Tulio's wealth, she would look for work of her own. The clerks would be shouting in the forum so she went to listen hoping she'd not missed today's recruitment news.

*

The forum was always bustling, but it was a relief to Maia when she found there was room to move around freely this day. She'd not enjoyed the jostling of her previous visit when the whole place had been heaving like eels captured in a basket. There had been nothing silent about the wriggling masses either, with the hum of chatter and laughter from the stallholders, the shouts of the clerks on their platforms, the crying of babies and barking of hounds, grunts from pigs and the clucking and flapping of chickens trying to escape capture. This day was definitely easier.

Thinking how proud Dominico and Claudia would be to see her coping with the city hustle, she went with purpose to the area where the clerks were shouting from their platforms.

"Coin is available from the personal chests of Emperor Titus the Most Generous..." shouted one clerk, his words drawing Maia's interest. "...for those willing to assist with the Inaugural Games at the amphitheatre. Food sellers, drinks sellers, ushers, sweepers, scribes. Multiple positions available. Present yourselves immediately at the water fountain by the main entrance for a chance to be included in the team for the Emperor's most bounteous, most ambitious, most exotic of entertainments." The clerk's voice was high with excitement by the end of his speech and he bent down into a deep bow, making a wide, flourishing sweep of his left arm, that pointed in the direction of the amphitheatre when he stood up straight again.

Sending a prayer of thanks to Venus Pompeiana, who she felt must still be holding her in favour by guiding her to this shouted message, Maia walked back to the site where the Golden Palace had once been. The queue at the water fountain was short and within minutes Maia was giving her name to be added to the wax tablet by the scribe. In return, she was given a small length of yellow ribbon fixed to a pin, with instructions to return an hour after sunrise tomorrow wearing it on her tunic. A coin was placed in her palm.

"An As in advance from the Emperor, Titus the Most Generous," explained the clerk in a tone that indicated he'd explained the gesture many times that morning. Maia was thrilled. It was only a small coin but a welcome gesture of faith and it was with a lighter heart that she made her way back to the Subura district.

And the sun was to shine on her again that day before the dark storm clouds gathered.

Chapter Thirty-One

It was the same peculiar walk. Unmistakably the same gliding gait with the chin tilting upwards to compensate for the forward lean. The same half-twist in the hips. Maia's heart lurched at her throat in a sudden stab of grief. She knew immediately that it was Claudia's sister, Laurentia. Her chest swelled with love.

Without thinking, Maia bounded straight up to the woman she felt she knew despite not having met. A woman she thought of as family, and one she thought had died in the city fire. Laurentia drew back in alarm, her tongue silenced by surprise, as Maia grasped her hands and lowered her forehead to rest on them, dropping to her knees at the same time.

"I am Maia, Claudia's Maia," she said looking up.

"Oh my child, the waif from Pompeii!" replied Laurentia, gathering her wits enough to find her voice but losing it again as quickly with the shock of who was before her.

"I came from Puteoli to find you but your home was gone to ashes. I feared the worst but took heart that you were with my dearest Claudia. She was the kindest, kindest person. She and Dominico gave me the happiest of days." Maia's words were coming in a rush. "And now I find you alive and well. How joyous this day is."

"Come, Child...no, a child no longer as I see you are wearing a ring of a bride to be. Come..." Laurentia drew a hand free and stooped, placing it beneath Maia's elbow thus raising her up, "...I will take you to my new home. We have much to talk about."

*

Laurentia's new home was a spacious domus, not far from the Temple of the Divine Claudius and the aqueduct of stacked arches that brought water to the temple. They entered along a vine covered portico into a cool courtyard. A statue of Juno stood in front of verdant ferns surrounding a small pool with a column fountain at its centre made of the white travertine stone that was so popular in Roma. The stone had been carved with leaping fish, each one spraying fine arcs of water over the foliage making the fronds glisten and drip like the dampest woodland nook.

Following into the house, Maia gave a gasp when she saw a glass vial decorated with an image of Venus.

"Is that from Dominico's warehouse in Puteoli?" she asked with delight, knowing it was by the style.

"It is. Emperor Titus presented me with it after his visit."

"It brings both joy and sadness to my heart to see it. It was a special day to meet the Emperor."

Laurentia gave Maia a long look.

"Recline," she ordered, holding her hand palm up towards the couch in invitation. "Bring us fruit and wine," she said to one slave. "Leave us," she said to another. Maia did as she was told, frowning questioningly at Laurentia, sensing something important. "I received correspondence from Emperor Titus following his visit to Puteoli. Despite the emergencies in the city, such was the impact you made upon him that he made time to write to me asking for my help. Can you believe that? He confided that you look like his sister, so much like her as a teenager before she blossomed to beauty that he could not shake you from his mind." Maia looked up sharply at that phrase, remembering similar words from Eshe in the asclepion before she died. Laurentia had Maia's complete attention. "Do you know of the Emperor's sister?"

"No," replied Maia in a small voice, caught between being nervous and curious.

"She was Flavia Domitilla and died in her early twenties but not before marrying her cousin, Titus Flavius Clemens, cousin also to the Emperor of course. She bore two sons. Her death hit the Emperor hard."

"How long ago was this?"

"Fourteen years, yet you stripped those years, and several more, away when the Emperor set eyes upon you. A remarkable likeness apparently." Laurentia gave Maia another long look before continuing. "So at the request of Emperor Titus, and, I admit, to satisfy my own curiosity too, my sister had given you a home after all, I made enquiries." Another drawn out silence. Maia was struggling to keep her composure, wanting for all the world to run as far from this conversation as possible but rooted by the desire to know what Laurentia had found out. "I have many connections, in Roma, in Puteoli and in Pompeii, yet I found nothing about a Maia who survived the disaster whilst her whole family perished. I would ask questions of you but I know from Claudia that you will not answer them."

"I cannot," stated Maia, shaking a little. Laurentia pursed her lips, holding back a retort as her head-slave brought in the fruit and wine. Dismissing him with a nod, she continued.

"I learned of many sad stories during my enquiries. The gods have shown their displeasure with the capers and the merrymaking of the rich. It is as well that they leave the indiscretions of Pompeii under the ashes, yet some stories refuse to be buried." Maia declined the dates she was offered, in too much turmoil to eat. What had Laurentia unearthed? "Do you know what the term 'exposed' means?"

"N-no," stuttered Maia, shame colouring her cheeks at the sudden mention of her closest secret. For an accomplished liar, she was not coping well with this untruth.

"To be exposed is to be abandoned, legally dead and therefore available to be taken as a slave. I learned of a woman on Pompeii who bolstered her number of household slaves by taking in children who were exposed on the slopes of Vesuvius. Her name was Rufina di Pompeieana."

"Does this lady still live?" Maia's chest was tight with anxiety, her voice like a taut leather string.

"Her entire household perished in the disaster." A stitch of hope for Maia, nay, an entire cloak of stitches, for there was no-one to claim her as a slave.

"I am sorry to hear it. It was terrifying. Please...I cannot bear thinking of it...please..." Maia was on her feet appealing to Laurentia as she would have Claudia, but Laurentia had a less gentle nature and was not to be silenced as easily as her sister.

"Please sit down. Histrionics are unbecoming of a lady." Laurentia waited until Maia was sitting and quiet again. "My enquiries nearly stalled here until I learned, quite by a chance conversation as it happens, of a frieze in Puteoli's basilica; the Frieze of Rufina. A coincidence possibly, but it is wise to be thorough where the Emperor is concerned, so I continued with my enquiries. It was not a coincidence. Rufina di Pompeieana had a turbulent, and rather colourful, few years in her younger days. Pompeii has...had...a way of attracting the ambitious. The allure of Pompeii seduced Rufina as she began seducing the rich, her father disowning her for the sake of his family's reputation. Pompeieana was not her true nomen. A recurring theme from my enquiries it seems." Laurentia paused to give emphasis to the words. "I'll go on...in her youthful bloom, Rufina was reasonably successful in her chosen profession but clients were less interested as she aged. Rescuing exposed children was a way of bolstering her household without parting with any coin, thus she was able to maintain the appearance of success. A clever ruse to look wealthier. Ten souls this woman saved. Remarkable."

"What has this to do with me?" interrupted Maia bravely.

"Plenty," was the sharp retort. "It is time to stop pretending for I have invested much in to my enquiries and the stakes are high. One who aids the Emperor will be well rewarded but we dance a fine line when we choose the politics of high power. Failure is ruin. This is not all about you." Maia was beginning to understand Laurentia's ambition. "Rufina may have been disowned but her paterfamilia was not disconnected. He paid his spies well to keep aware of her affairs and was clearly moved enough to leave instructions for the commission of the Frieze of Rufina on his death. The frieze lists merely the slave names given to these children by Rufina, except for the tenth child whose family name was recorded, for this child was of Flavian blood. Decima..."

You were nameless when I found you. I designated you Decima, my tenth lost soul saved. Lady Rufina's voice rebounded in Maia's head transporting her back to the day she'd escaped Pompeii as a slave-girl. The day she learned she'd been abandoned by her parents. Shame washed over her anew, the colour rising in her face as she absently touched her fingers to where she had been struck on the cheek. There was no visible sign of the wound the ring had made but the scars remained within. Maia felt beaten once more.

"How did the paterfamilia know this child was of Flavian blood?"

"Through the acquaintance of Poppaea Sabina. I will come to that later. My enquiries took me full circle back to the Imperial Palace from where the trail was begun. I spoke to Domitilla's maid, given citizenship as a free woman by Emperor Titus after his sister's death and allowed to reside at the palace as a cherished family member. She has sadly been taken by this dreadful plague, but before she became sick she confirmed a girl was sired by Titus Flavius Clemens during a short dalliance of lust with a woman of scheming ambition. A girl who was to bear a remarkable resemblance to her father's cousin as is often the way in families. The Emperor's cousin was not told; Clemens knew nought of this child. Had the girl who became known as Decima been a boy, I believe there would have been a challenge for the Imperial seat. The mother would have made a claim."

Eshe came to mind again. Was she Domitilla's maid? The question became smothered by Maia's overwhelming desire to know her own parents and learn of why she had been exposed. All she had uncovered herself was matching Laurentia's account.

"Did you learn the mother's name?"

"Not her name," replied Laurentia giving another drawn out stare as if calculating what to reveal. " She was a friend of Poppaea Sabina. Do you know of her?" Maia shook her head. "A hateful woman, devious in nature and ambition. She used her guile to become Empress, first to Otho, then to Nero."

"Oh, the Empress Sabina. I *was* taught of her." Maia recalled Philo the Greek speaking about the wife of Nero. It wasn't a schooling as she was implying, but one of the tales he liked to orate before penetrating her. It used to excite him speaking of the intrigues of the ambitious rich. Or had he known about her parentage? Was that why it excited him? Her flesh crawled with maggots at the thought.

"Poppaea Sabina died before you were born, but this friend, the mother of the girl called Decima, was of a similar nature according to Domitilla's maid, but, of course, she would be biased. And yet...from what I have learned, I agree with her. Devious, ambitious and cruel enough to abandon a child for being a girl." A shaft of pain splintered Maia's heart. This was the truth. This was where her journey had brought her. She was born to an uncaring woman of scheming and a father who knew not of her existence. How could her imperial blood serve her well under these circumstances?

"It is a sad story, " mumbled Maia, chewing at the inside of her lip.

"It is," concurred Laurentia. "A girl of Flavian blood who was exposed and enslaved before she perished in the most terrible of ways with so many in Pompeii and Herculaneum."

"Why are you telling me of this girl...this Decima?" asked Maia trying to hang on to her lie.

"I have spent much time considering my findings and am wondering if the story has not ended as told. Perhaps the girl, Decima, escaped the dreadful eruption. Perhaps the gods sought to protect her. And if she lives and knows her own story...well, a life at the Imperial Palace is awaiting her...if she has guile enough to present herself." Laurentia had turned away from Maia and was silent as she picked up the glass vial from the warehouse of Dominico di Stefano Siciliano Glassware and examined it. "Fortune could await her too," continued Laurentia after a moment. "Emperor Titus the Most Generous would undoubtedly endow much favour upon this girl if she could prove her lineage, and what greater proof is there than the features of a face."

The words of Emperor Titus resounded in the silence: *so much like her as a teenager before she blossomed to beauty.*

Maia's head was reeling as she tried to fathom the whole conversation. Could she trust Laurentia with her deepest secret? Should she confide in her? Cletus had been right when he'd said she had the golden hair of Flavian descent. Her heart jolted at this unexpected thought of Clete. She hated the lies she had told him. Their trek together from Puteoli to Roma had been the happiest of days, but he was gone. Tulio was her life now and it would surely hasten their wedding if she was embraced into the Emperor's family. She would be secure. More than that, she would have influence and enough money to fulfil her mission to make free women of Ebele and Hadassah. Her citizenship would be cemented and her shameful past buried a little deeper.

Yet she remained mute, for Laurentia could not truly know she was Decima unless Maia confirmed it. Once uttered, it could not be undone. No mention had been made of what would happen if she was not believed. Her confession could plummet her back to slavery and there would be no trial for any injustice as a slave is a commodity without rights. Maia needed time to think. As if reading her thoughts, Laurentia took control.

"I will request an appointment with Emperor Titus and tell him of my findings. Think on what I have said and stay with me as my guest until we receive a reply. I would have you give me news of my dear sister before the dreadful warehouse fire. You gave a measure of peace to her before she died, you know, and I thank you for that. Come...I have a letter from her to share with you."

Laurentia had a disarming ability to flip from stern to kind in the time it took to pluck a hair.

Chapter Thirty-Two

The letter moved Maia to tears as Claudia expressed her grief at the loss of Cornelia and how Maia's need for love had given her renewed purpose. Not a day goes by when I don't grieve for my beautiful daughter, she had written. Grief is a pain that cannot be scoured away, nor masked, nor drowned. I have shed enough tears to know. Indeed, I feel guilt if I allow my heart to lift. Maia could never replace Cornelia but, oh my life, the poor waif has taught me such strength.

I understand her loss; the emptiness in her soul, and seeing her resolve to survive, and to grow, has mended something in me. I am able to be a true wife to Dominico once more and we are trying for an heir. It is strange, but I seem content now that I can marry my grief for Cornelia with the unguilty joy of seeing Maia flourish under my care. Sister, do not chastise me for hanging on to my sadness...I must...for it seems disloyal to my beautiful daughter to let it go. But Maia has given me the strength to function beyond these walls of grief.

"Come, the shadows grow long," said Laurentia gently, taking the letter from Maia. "You must stay with me. I will have my maid take you to the guest room." Maia was too wrung with emotions to do anything but follow.

*

Despite the enormity of Laurentia's revelations, or maybe because of them, Maia slept deeply. The night was cooler, the pallet more comfortable than any she had known and the room peaceful without any scrabbling rodents or raucous revelry. When Maia awoke she thought it was raining before realising it was water from the fountain pattering on the ferns in the unfamiliar courtyard that she could hear.

All at once, the events of the previous day folded in with a rush. Had she finally solved the riddle of who she was? The product of a short-lived liaison between Titus Flavius Clemens, the Emperor's cousin, and a companion of Poppaea Sabina whose devious guile was so strong it continued to influence her friends from a grave turned cold by two winters. A part of her could scarce believe she had Flavian blood, yet it fitted with everything she had learned, but could it be confirmed beyond her remarkable likeness to the Emperor's deceased sister?

A thought, which must have stirred in the quietude of sleep and waited patiently for her to wake, jumped forward making Maia sit quickly upright. *Malita*, she whispered. Her thoughts were interrupted by Laurentia's maid entering the room.

"The mistress will be leaving shortly to visit the public baths and requests you join her." The maid stood dutifully just inside the door with her hands clasped in front of her, just as Maia had been taught to stand by Lady Rufina.

"Is there something else?" asked Maia, a little unsure. Her confidence was low and it was affecting her comportment and she found herself wavering between being servile or noble. *What you do is who you become. Do not falter now,* she silently urged herself. It was ironic to think that all the time she had thought she was born a slave she had been able to act as a free citizen. Now that her imperial bloodline was revealed, she was in danger of acting like a slave.

"Mistress Laurentia wishes me to measure you for new clothes. I have a length of cotton tape."

"How kind," said Maia, rising from the cot and gathering resolve to act as she must. "You may braid my hair before you leave too."

*

Laurentia was already in the atrium and greeted Maia warmly.

"The litter is waiting at the front of the domus, come," she led the way outside, pulling her palla up to cover her head, and wrapping the ends of the shawl across her shoulders for warmth. The morning air had an autumnal bite, the first chill of the season always striking colder than it really was. "I have heard the Baths of Agrippa are still only partially open but we will have to make do," she said, once they were in the litter. "The fire damage was extensive and I am told the repairs are delayed for lack of a particular marble which they quarry some distance away. We can bathe but only in the one pool, so the range of water temperatures is not available to us. It is unfortunate, but as I said, we must make do."

They were carried beneath the aqueduct, the drapes of the litter left open for all to see their affluence and Maia caught a glimpse of the amphitheatre at the end of the street.

"Oh!" she exclaimed. "I signed up to help with the preparations for the Emperor's games and was supposed to present myself at the amphitheatre an hour after sunrise today."

"You can attend later," replied Laurentia with a nonchalant wave of her hand.

"I've been given coin in goodwill of my attending," fretted Maia, which drew a sharp look from Laurentia who sniffed disdainfully. The sniff prickled Maia's pride, which in turn, brought some boldness back. "I would like to attend as soon as possible please, for I made an agreement and do not wish to lose the trust of Emperor Titus."

A simper of a smile played at the edges of Laurentia's mouth.

"Dominico said you were spirited. It is good to see a spark of anger, and I agree that keeping the Emperor's trust is wise. What task are you to be doing for the games?"

"I do not know until I arrive."

"I suggest you present yourself as soon as possible then for the sunrise is ageing and the best tasks may already have been taken." Raising her voice to be heard above the noise of the busy street, Laurentia called to the bearers. "Stop when we near the Flavian Amphitheatre." Dropping her voice again for just Maia to hear, "I will continue alone to the Baths of Agrippa, there is much work for me to do at the baths. Only fools believe the city is run at the Senate." The litter stopped for Maia to alight and Laurentia fixed her with a stare that made Maia's heart thump irregularly. By the gods, it was a look to rival that of the monstrous Medusa. Maia feared she would see snakes writhe from Laurentia's hair and wings appear on her shoulders. "A letter will be delivered to the Imperial Palace today. I will expect you at the domus for dinner, no later. I am hoping for a prompt reply from the Emperor. Boy, go with her and guard her life with your own." The slave dipped his head in acknowledgement of the instruction which really meant he must not let Maia out of his sight or his life was forfeit. "The aqueduct is a true feat of engineering but I do miss the view I had of the river," said Laurentia wistfully looking back at the multiple arches, demonstrating one of her mood swings, transitioning from night to day without a dawn and day back to night without a sunset; a sheer heart, either open or closed. "I hope you receive a pleasurable task for these games."

Chapter Thirty-Three

Three people, two older women and a young lad, all from the poorer classes as was evident in their clothing, were waiting at the water fountain by the main entrance to the amphitheatre when Maia arrived. They were all displaying a pin with yellow ribbon attached to their garments. Taking her own pin and ribbon from the hidden pocket in her tunic which always reminded her of Marguerita, she attached it to her own clothing in the same way and joined the queue. I must visit Marguerita as soon as I am able, she thought.

The clerk ticked off the names of the three people before her, asking each in turn if they could scribe. None could, and they were all detailed to join the food and drinks team. Although her own scribing was weak, Maia said yes with confidence when asked in the hope of receiving work more interesting than catering. It was a half-truth at least. She had spoken much bigger lies, and it was pleasing to have the clerk accept her words without a hint of doubt.

"Good, good, that is good, we are short of scribes," he muttered, making a mark in the wax next to her name. "You will be part of the scribing team." She was given a shard of pottery with XXIII scratched on it. "Go to this gate number, turn left and follow the rise to the second level of the amphitheatre. A clerk there will show you what to do. Return to me for payment at the end of the session."

"Thank you," replied Maia, a nervous excitement fluttering her stomach as she walked in the direction indicated by the clerk,

Laurentia's slave always a pace behind like a shadow.

The amphitheatre was beautiful and she marvelled at the vast number of stone arches, noticing the different designs each level displayed. Growing up in Pompeii, she was used to grandeur, but this surpassed anything she had seen before. *Oh Claudia*, she whispered, *you would love it!*

There were eighty entrances to the amphitheatre, all numbered except for the four main gates aligned to the compass points, and Maia walked round until she matched the gate number to the number on her pottery shard. Taking a deep breath to steady her nerves, she showed her ticket to the clerk who waved her and her shadow-slave in. Turning left as instructed, she took the stairs to the second tier of seating.

Despite being the largest amphitheatre ever constructed, it did have the expected intimacy to it, the shouts and chatter of the men working across the arena reaching her clearly. Maia could easily imagine the amphitheatre jostling with people jeering, booing, cheering and deciding the destiny of a beaten gladiator with a show of thumbs. It gave Maia a shiver of anticipation.

The section of seating above her was filled with crates. Four men were working together on the top row binding the crates closed. Two older men, one bald, the other greying, were sitting in the middle of the tier amongst several open crates, hunching over an object held between their knees. Maia stood quietly watching, not wanting to disturb their concentration as they made etchings of letters on the objects, which were the size of citrons but round. She guessed they were made of softwood by the ease of carving. The bald man looked up.

"Hello, I am here to scribe," she said, over-brightly in an attempt to cover her nerves.

"Well, I trust to Jupiter that you are more capable than the others who have been sent to me," he said sharply, then quickly apologising, rising to greet her and distractedly smoothing a hand across his hairless pate. "Sorry, sorry...come, I will show you what needs to be done." He passed her an etching stylus, similar to the tool Calix had used to make his wax designs in the warehouse. "Pick a wooden ball from a crate on that side," he pointed left, "when it has been scribed, place it in this crate here." He tapped the crate next to him, then fixing her with a look that would freeze water, added, "do not put any balls in this crate that have not been completed. I do not want to sort through them all again. There is not time."

"What am I to scribe on the ball?"

"Food," he said curtly, and to her relief handed her one that was already etched, before turning to shout at the men above who had started binding a different section of crates. "Not those, don't take those, I told you not those. Jupiter pity me!" He rushed away to show them their mistake.

"He had hair as thick as mine a Moon prior," said the greying man with a deadpan expression on his face which would be ideal for playing tali. His mirth was showing in his eyes though, which twinkled with fun and Maia relaxed a shade. "I hope he doesn't start pulling my hair out now he has run out of his own. He is stressed by how much there is to do. Here, use this cushion around the ball. Better to slice the cushion than your knee if the etcher slips. They are sharp. I am Ezio."

"Thank you," replied Maia giving her name and settling down on the bench beside him, whilst her bodyguard settled on his haunches nearby. "What are these for?"

"They are gift-giving balls. The Emperor will throw some to the crowd each day and those who catch one can exchange it for whatever is written on it. That's where the Emperor will be sitting," he said, pointing towards the south gate. "Do you see the podium?" Maia nodded. "Make the most of the view from here though, unlike the Circus Maximus, all women, apart from the Vestal Virgins, will be seated in the top tier," he nodded his head towards the highest rows before returning his attention to the scribing. "As well as food, there are balls etched with clothing, slaves, pack animals...that's a tricky one to scribe...horse, cattle, gold or silver vessels...another difficult one to scribe; too many letters to fit on the ball! Emperor Titus is being most generous, a welcome boost for the city, but the preparations are an immense task. Still, we have some ready and they don't all need to be completed for the opening of the games. I am told these celebrations are to continue until Saturnalia, no doubt with some breaks, but still it is a long time. Can you believe it? We'll be wrapped in our warmest clothes by the time they finish." The man shook his head a little, his eyebrows rising in bemusement. "Strange times," he muttered turning his attention back to his work.

The bald man returned having averted the men from sealing up the wrong crates and the three of them worked in silence for a while, concentrating on their tasks. It took Maia some time to complete her first ball and the letters were not as neat as those on the one she was copying. The straight lines were good, but she was finding the circles a challenge.

"It is legible," said the bald man, taking it from her and putting it in the crate beside him. "Start another. You will improve with practise." It was a compliment of sorts but it still caused Maia to frown. Ezio winked at her and smoothed a hand over his hair. The gesture was enough to make her smile and she started work on a new ball, warming to being a part of the scribing team.

*

It was the middle of the afternoon when Maia collected her coin from the clerk at the main entrance. The early morning coolness had been folded over by the daylight hours to give an unexpected, and unwelcome, scorching heat to match the temperatures of midsummer. Cumulonimbus clouds were rising high and the air was close and thick with tiny storm flies which collected on Maia as she walked. She was surprised to see the sun so far past noon. The scribing had absorbed her and stolen away the hours. There was not time to visit Marguerita today. If she was not back at the domus for dinner, she feared Laurentia would turn the whole Urban Cohort out to look for her, and she feared for the life of the slave if that was to happen. It was not worth being late. She would visit Marguerita when she had a day clear of duties.

It began to rain. Warm, fat drops, sparse to begin with,

dotting the dusty paving, a warning of the downpour to come. Maia looked to the moody sky and quickened her pace when she saw the deep pewter hue of the plump clouds threatening to spill their loads. She would shelter at the Carpe Vinum, the slave would have to take shelter where he could in the street. Within seconds of entering the popina, the rain became harder, falling like a veil across the face of a bride.

"Jupiter favours you," said a man sitting at a bench near the door, slurring his words from too much wine. She started, recognising the accented Latin of Emrick. Her eyes quickly searching the room looking for Cletus. "He is not here," said the big Celt. "Jupiter favours you," he repeated. "Just like Juno favours the Peacock!"

"Where is Cletus?" asked Maia, ignoring his rhetoric.

"He is a prisoner."

"A prisoner? Why? Where?"

"The Peacock put him in the cells."

"The Peacock? You're making no sense! Where is he imprisoned?" Maia grabbed Emrick's forearm which seemed to bring him a little closer to sobriety.

"Your Emperor did a sweep of the cells, he is condemned without justice and will die for the city's entertainment."

"Die in the arena?" Maia was horrified. "Where is he imprisoned?" she repeated.

"At the Castra Praetoria. I could have got him out of the cell or the warehouse, but not the Castra Praetoria. It is a fortress." Emrick hung his head, his whole demeanour one of defeat, then suddenly raised his arm and shouted for the serving wench to bring more wine. "Wine is the juice of Hades," he cursed. Maia sat opposite him and frowned at the depth of sadness she could see in his eyes. "Ale is better," he added lamely. "He cares about you, you know." Emrick put the fresh ewer of wine to his lips and downed half its contents before coming up for a breath. "The Peacock put him in the cells. I vow I will kill the Peacock!" Wine was dribbling into his beard and Maia knew she would get little more sense from the Celt until he sobered.

The rain ceased, Jupiter raising the veil of the bride as swiftly as he had covered her face. There was still time to reach the domus for dinner with Laurentia if she hurried.

Chapter Thirty-Four

Maia woke early from a restless sleep full of anxiety, her problems immediately squabbling for attention, making her heart beat irregularly. There had been no reply to Laurentia's request for an appointment with Emperor Titus. Cletus was being held as a prisoner. For what, she had no idea, but there was every possibility he could be put to a public death. Mauled by a bear or gored by a bull, with the cheers of a baying crowd in his ears. It was all too troubling.

Anxiety is a demanding companion and Maia could not sit still. Chewing at the inside of her lip, she realised she was clenching her fists so tightly her fingernails were digging at her palms. She had to take action, she would go to the Carpe Vinum and see if Emrick was still there. He may be able to tell her more if he was sober. Yes, she would do that, the decision to act staying the anxiety to a manageable level.

Leaving a message with Laurentia's maid that she was attending the amphitheatre to scribe, Maia hurried to the popina, picking her way along the uneven paving of the streets, avoiding deposits of debris collected and dumped in the dips by the previous day's storm, some of the more unpleasant deposits already attracting the flies.

Emrick wasn't at the Carpe Vinum and Maia's eyes filled with tears, another symptom of the anxiety that she was trying to contain. Cuffing away a rogue tear-drop that spilled over, she left quickly not wanting to invite curious stares. She couldn't go scribing in this state, she wouldn't be capable of concentrating, so she turned in the opposite direction and found herself walking the streets not knowing where to go or what to do, just as she had in Pompeii the day the peak had exploded.

"Marguerita..." she whispered. She would go to her friend.

*

When Maia entered the asclepion, the building seemed to wrap its arms around her in a warm hug. She needed its calmness this day. Marguerita did the same when Maia entered the fullonica.

"I have missed you," said Marguerita. "Are you well?" she asked, leaning back to look at Maia as she kept her hands on the girl's shoulders, arms outstretched. She was met with a worried gaze.

"I have such problems," replied Maia. "I cannot settle."

"Come, we will talk and I have the perfect job to help ease your troubles." Marguerita pointed at the washing tub. "The fuller's jump is the best cure for a restless body and mind. Come on, in you go. Julius still does not tread the linen as well as you." Marguerita encouraged Maia into the tub with a wave of her arms as she used to and Maia did as she was bidden. Marguerita waited until her rhythm of treading was right before speaking again. "What is grieving you?" she asked.

"Do you remember me telling you of Cletus's friend from Britannia, Emrick?"

"Yes, I remember."

"I met him by chance. In the Carpe Vinum. I sheltered there during the storm yesterday evening." Maia stopped treading the linen and looked at Marguerita with a thin-lipped expression. "He told me that Cletus has been falsely imprisoned and is to be executed in the arena. It is too horrible to think of. I am afraid for him."

"Keep treading," instructed Marguerita and Maia took up the fuller's dance again. Was Emrick sober when he spoke to you?

"No," admitted Maia. "I returned to the popina early this morning, before coming here, in the hope he would still be there but he was gone."

"What is Cletus's crime, I wonder."

"Emrick did not say, just that he is condemned without justice and will die for the city's entertainment." Maia climbed out of the wash tub and Marguerita passed her a linen cloth so she could dry her legs and feet.

"Come, we will set this lot to dry then take a walk along the river and think on your problems again. The river is a comfort and full of answers." They continued working in silence and Maia was relieved to feel calmer by the time the laundry was finished.

*

"I know what I must do," Maia said to Marguerita as they walked beside the river.

"See how the Tiber gives us answers."

"Whether it is truth or lie that Emrick speaks, I must help Cletus. He saved me from making a terrible mistake, a foolish mistake, with..." Maia was absently rubbing the pad of her thumb where she had shared blood with Calix, visible now only as a fine line, "...with..." she was struggling for the right words, "...with a rogue. Yes, a rogue," she said decisively.

"How do you plan to help?"

"I do not know," worried Maia.

"Where is he imprisoned? You haven't said."

"At the Castra Praetoria."

"Really? That is most unusual. You do mean the barracks of the Praetorian Guards?"

"Yes. I think the city is over-run with prisoners so they are using the fort. I'm told the Emperor's games are to last until Saturnalia so a lot of condemned men are needed."

"I wonder if Tulio can find out what Cletus is accused of."

"Tulio is still in training at the Imperial Palace and will not be released until after the games begin. I fear that will be too late."

"Can you not go to him?"

"At the palace, you mean?"

"Yes, make up a reason to speak with him. Request a meeting. An urgent family matter perhaps. You wear his ring after all."

"I...I'm not sure I have the courage to present myself unannounced."

"You won't know unless you try. Nought ventured, nought gained and Cletus is Tulio's comrade, he will surely want to help. The elite cavalry arm hold sway amongst the Praetorians, it's possible he could influence his release."

"Oh...I hadn't thought of that," she gasped, grabbing at her friend's wrist as if she needed a stay to keep her from falling. Maia's mind was racing with this new possibility, and flashing through ideas beyond. She'd not told Marguerita of her hopeful Imperial connections, too afraid they would reveal her shameful past. If Emperor Titus recognised her as kin, she would have influence of her own, despite being a woman. Power and influence; traits that were far removed from anything she had ever been and frightening in their unfamiliarity. From slave-girl to one with Imperial patronage, it made her head spin but she must hold herself together, for herself, for Cletus, for Ebele and Hadassah. The enormity of the responsibility for their lives brought the anxiety back with a sudden gush, rushing through her like the rainwater from the storm had slushed along the street gulleys. "I must go and pray at the statue of Juno," she said, full of urgency. "Forgive me, Marguerita, but I must take leave of you. I will be broken if Cletus is put to a brutal death. I must go," she implored.

"Hearts can make fools of us," replied Marguerita sharply, regretting her rebuke when she saw the fragility of Maia. "Go...let Juno guide you, but do not forget you are to be wed to Tulio. That is where your prosperity lies."

Chapter Thirty-Five

The early afternoon sky had steel grey streaks of cloud sweeping across the azure blue driven by a brisk breeze from the east. It was warm in the sun and cool when the clouds took charge. The sunlight broke free to shine on Laurentia's domus as Maia reached the entrance, and she took that as a good omen. There was a statue of Juno in the courtyard but Maia wanted to find Laurentia first in the hope that Emperor Titus had replied with an invitation. Maia had formed the semblance of a plan after leaving Marguerita. If an audience with the Emperor went favourably, it would negate the need to involve Tulio. Reach to the top first. She would risk her freedom to have Cletus saved from death.

"Where is the mistress?" she asked the slave-boy who was on his hands and knees scrubbing the flagstones in the courtyard.

"In the tablinum," he replied, looking up briefly from his work, but quickly averting his eyes as he had been taught to do. Eyes that intrigued Maia, almond in shape and as dark as the mineral jet. "Her mood is bad," he added, foolishly risking a lashing for speaking ill of his mistress. Perhaps he sensed Maia would not punish him.

Maia nodded and went directly to the study. Laurentia received her immediately, the room reminding her of Dominico's study in Puteoli with its crates of papyrus rolls neatly filling the shelving that lined the walls. Laurentia was sitting at a desk with a wax tablet and stylus before her and greeted Maia without a smile.

"There is no word from the Palace," she said without preamble. Maia thought it best to remain silent. Laurentia shared more than just a walking style with her sister, and Maia recognised the signs of worry by the tilted angle of her chin. "I have been considering the implications. I am surprised there has been no swift reply bearing in mind the content. It is possible I have angered the Emperor, but I cannot think how and conclude that perhaps that is my insecurities thinking the worst. The stakes are high after all. I am therefore left with the concern that my letter has not reached the Emperor as it should. I will write again and deliver it to the Palace myself so I may see whose hands receive it. You will accompany me. Please be ready in the atrium in one segment of the sundial. I have ordered the litter."

"I will be ready. May I have permission to pray at the statue of Juno before we leave?" asked Maia politely. "The auspices have shown me a peacock and I wish to understand why." Maia was thinking of the conversation with Emrick. "That is the sacred bird of Juno is it not? The bird with a hundred eyes in its tail."

"It is, and you would be wise to pray for guidance. I cannot stress enough the precarious path we are dancing. Do you know how the bird got those eyes in its feathers?" Laurentia asked, her mood suddenly softening. Maia shook her head. "They were once the eyes of Argus, Juno's watchman. The Queen of Gods left him to guard her shiny, white cow but he fell asleep and the cow was lost. Juno was so cross that Argus couldn't keep even one of his many eyes open that she gave them all to her peacock, saying the bird was wiser than the watchman, for the bird always knows when anyone is looking at him. If you have been shown a peacock, then you are wise to pray to Juno."

*

Laurentia remained thoughtful after Maia left the room, her elbows on the desk and hands steepled beneath her chin, staring at the door which had just closed. When Maia had so unexpectedly found her amongst all the people in the city, it had seemed like a roll of three sixes in a game of twelve. A top score that could not be beaten. But had her judgement been ill? Had she overestimated Emperor Titus's interest in Maia? The lack of an appointment was indeed troubling. Perhaps time had changed the Emperor's memory of meeting Maia, or perhaps his focus was taken with the forthcoming games. Frowning, she gently shook her head, she had been so sure her letter would be well-received, so sure. It was galling how quickly fortunes could slide.

No refusal had been received, she countered, and if Maia had been shown a peacock, that could be interpreted as a sign from the gods that her letter had not been seen by Titus. Sending her own swift prayer to Juno that this was the answer, inhaling deeply, Laurentia picked up the stylus. Her path was trodden, she would ask again for an appointment and ensure the delivery of this letter.

*

It didn't take long to reach the Imperial Palace and Laurentia showed her ring, entrusted to her by a friend from the Senate, to a guard who waved the litter through the gate of the outer wall. Two storeys of magnificent, white columns greeted them, standing like giant sentries towering up to a high roof of tiles the colour of dancing flames.

Turning away from the main palace entrance, they continued towards the western side of the building, passing the elegantly curved crescent of columns and continuing around the corner, where the wonderful aroma of baking bread was filling the air. More towering, white columns lined the western side of the Palace, with two sentries guarding the entrance halfway along, their red capes and military regalia standing out like rose hips against snow.

The sound of men training on horses was drifting on the wind from behind the columns and Maia pictured Tulio astride a horse practising the skills of the Speculatores Augusti and it brought reality to what he did, what his promotion meant, and a flush of pride that she would be a part of this world when they married. It also brought acknowledgement of the suspicion that he was deliberately delaying the wedding preparations. Their union was far from cemented. The patronage of Emperor Titus would undoubtedly improve her status. How fortunes can change on a door-swing.

The source of the aroma was a bakehouse. A small, but equally decorative building, displaying scenes of chariot racing on its gables. It was sensibly sited outside the main complex to reduce the chance of fire destroying the Palace. A preventative measure copied from the military forts where the bakehouses were kept away from the barracks.

For the second time that day, Maia was reminded of Dominico and the glass warehouse in Puteoli, this time by the heat inside the bakehouse. It had the same intensity, expunging the breath from your lungs until you adjusted to the rise in temperature. That was the only similarity though. The bakehouse was much smaller, smelled wonderful and was stacked with breads of different shapes and sizes, some topped with seeds, others with olives.

Ignoring the slaves working at the ovens, Laurentia led Maia to the far end of the room where a woman was riddling seeds at a bench, sorting and sifting as she did so, tossing the unwanted blackened seeds into a trug beside her.

The slave-woman looked up as they approached and the blood drained from Maia's cheeks. A beautiful face was made ugly by the branded F on her forehead, marking the woman as a recaptured runaway slave. A face with almond shaped eyes the colour of the mineral jet. Intriguing eyes, that should have averted their gaze but instead bore through to Maia's soul.

Maia could not take her gaze from the unsightly branding. The blood that had drained from her, returned with a gush screaming her own slave-name: *Decima, Decima, Decima*...she was a runaway too! She watched as Laurentia passed a papyrus scroll, sealed with a drop of wax, imprinted with an insignia, to the runaway. She saw the minutiae with clarity, as if time had slowed, but could hear nothing other than her slave-name reverberating in her head. Maia's legs became unsteady and she stumbled against a bench, the knock breaking her trance, the noises of the bakehouse returning.

"The heat is distressing," mumbled Maia by way of an explanation.

"My business here is done," replied Laurentia, supporting Maia's arm as she escorted her out. "Take us to the public baths," she instructed the slaves before settling in to the litter and addressing Maia."Are you recovered from the heat of the bakehouse?" The long, hard stare that accompanied the question told Maia it was a rhetorical question that needed no reply. Laurentia knew it was the branding that had upset her and Maia realised this was why she had been brought here. Her reaction confirming Laurentia's suspicion that she was Decima, the tenth lost soul saved. Maia looked down at her shoes, still a comfort to her when her freedom was shaky. "I am frustrated that I did not think to present my first letter by this route," continued Laurentia with a little thump of her fist to her thigh, making no mention of the confirmation. There was no need. She had shown her upper hand. "You are wondering how I can be so certain of this letter being delivered to the Emperor aren't you? Did you not notice a resemblance to another you have seen?" Laurentia raised her eyebrows questioningly. Maia kept her eyes looking downwards. "A word to the wise: success is in the detail. If you are to flourish within the Palace, you will need to be observant." Another pause. "I have her son within my household, a gift from Emperor Vespasian," explained Laurentia. Of course, thought Maia. Those eyes, she *had* seen the same; on the boy scrubbing the courtyard flagstones. "She will not cross me."

Chapter Thirty-Six

Talk at the public baths was all about the games, especially of the big fight between Priscus and Verus, two highly popular and experienced gladiators, that was scheduled to go ahead. It had been shouted in the forum that they were to fight on the opening day, and despite tickets being given freely by the Emperor, there were reports of large bags of coin swapping hands as some were selling the prized tickets to those fans who'd missed out in the lottery and were rich enough to buy them.

The city was abuzz with the preparations and rumours rebounded on what other spectacles were being organised. Some would prove to be correct, others wildly wrong. Laurentia passed a coin to the eunuch employed by the state to work at the public baths.

"How are the repairs coming along?" she asked.

"We are hopeful of a delivery of marble in the next few days, Mistress" replied the eunuch.

"It will be good to have the full range of pools open again, I do miss the temperature range. Please keep a sharp eye on my jewellery," she said passing across a necklace and matching bracelet, especially chosen to wear to the Palace and both more valuable than her usual choice of gemstones for a visit to the baths. "A larger coin is available for you when I safely collect them." The eunuch tilted his head in a respectful nod. "What news have you heard?"

"All the talk is about the upcoming games, Mistress."

"Anything noteworthy, other than this tedious fight between

Priscus and Verus?"

"There is talk of the Shirt of Medea in the arena, Mistress."

"Really? I thought that cruelty had stopped with Emperor Nero's death."

"I only know there is much chatter about it, Mistress," said the eunuch averting his eyes to show deference. His role was to give information, not offer an opinion.

Maia glanced towards a girl, similar in age to herself, who was standing behind waiting to hand her own valuables to the eunuch and Maia's heart lurched in her chest, for the girl was clutching a choker inset with golden-brown topaz in the same pattern as the one she had been given by Philo the Greek. The same choker that Lady Rufina had wrongly accused her of stealing. She had thought it unusual in style but perhaps there were many of the same design, she reasoned. Nevertheless, it was a shock to see it.

How full of anxiety this day was.

"You look as if you've seen the shade of an enemy," said Laurentia astutely, leading Maia through to the pool.

"I was thinking about the words of the eunuch," lied Maia. "Is the Shirt of Medea where the condemned men are made to wear a flaming shirt?"

"Yes, but I cannot think that Emperor Titus would resurrect such a practice so associated with Nero. Many whispers of the lower classes are exaggerated. Let us see if we can learn anything that may be of use to us."

*

The visit to the baths did not produce any gossip of interest, much to Laurentia's frustration.

"It is all talk of the games," she complained as they returned to the domus. "Nothing useful at all. I shall be glad to get these festivities started and finished so we can return to sensible talk of political use. What do I care which gladiator wins. I prefer the chariot racing."

Maia was only half listening, preoccupied with her own

concerns: Cletus, the Shirt of Medea, the patronage of Emperor Titus, her shaky wedding plans, that choker...she kept seeing a vision of the choker. Then a peacock jumped in to her fractious thoughts, the iridescent blue and green colours and it's eyes in the tail feathers staring at her so vividly, shouting...but what were they shouting? It was all so confusing. When would the gods relent? As soon as the question formed, she knew the answer...when she fulfilled her vow. Thus it was a great relief to be greeted at the domus by Laurentia's head-slave with an invitation to the Palace.

"Thank the gods," breathed Laurentia as she finished reading the invitation. "My perseverance has been rewarded. We are to be presented to Emperor Titus this very evening. His tone is not as favourable as I had hoped but you have an audience with him and he will soften on seeing you. I know it. Oh, Claudia, my dearest, dearest sister..." Laurentia closed her eyes and covered her heart with both hands, "...you found the greatest prize from Pompeii." When she opened her eyes, they were shining with greedy excitement. "Titus the Most Generous will favour me for bringing his own dead sister's face back to life."

Maia felt suddenly uncomfortable.

*

Two guards in full military regalia escorted Laurentia and Maia through a high-ceilinged room, decorated predominantly in white with sections of orange, gold and green separated by latticework windows that allowed the sunlight to shaft through creating wonderful patterns as it danced on the polished marble floor. It was as beautiful and magnificent as was expected of an Imperial Palace of the greatest city in the Known World.

They passed between two rising columns, also of marble but in a contrasting rich brown, and shimmering with golden flecks and continued along an avenue of white statues, each one mounted on a plinth sited two paces apart. At the end of the avenue was a series of verdant hedging screens, clipped into precise squares and growing in ceramic pots so they could be positioned wherever privacy was required.

Behind the screens was a large rectangular pool with a grand, central fountain sending water cascading down an intricate design of waterfalls. The guards were standing to attention either side of a trellis covered in vines that acted like curtains around an area of seating that was draped in purple silk cloth, indicating that Laurentia and Maia should enter. It was an unexpectedly private nook in the palace gardens and Laurentia felt a thrill of delight at the intimacy of the meeting place chosen by Titus.

She was not to enjoy the surroundings for long however, as Emperor Titus dismissed her from the meeting, not unkindly, but swiftly after formerly greeting them both. Maia was more nervous than she had been in Puteoli. Back then, she had only one agenda which was to keep her past a secret. This time, she was seeking the truth of her past and with much to ask of the Emperor.

"I am sorry to hear of the fire at the glass warehouse," began Titus. "My condolences, you have suffered much loss."

"Thank you Imperator."

There was no stuttering from Titus this time, and he sat quietly and calmly just looking at Maia, his expression kind and thoughtful. It was difficult for Maia to hold his steady gaze and she found herself flicking her eyes down, then looking back up beneath her brow, then looking away again, and finally raising her chin to meet his gaze fully once more.

"Fourteen years is a long time. "Fourteen years, yet when I lay eyes on you, every one of those years, and more, dissolve." He shook his head in wonder. "The likeness to my sister is remarkable. I was taken by surprise when we met at the glass warehouse, but have since had time to reflect, especially upon the detail given to me by Laurentia. This girl, Decima, has quite an incredible story, if Laurentia's conclusion is to be believed, the gods must favour her." He shook his head again as if he was unable to quite believe the story. "I will be direct, you present me with a problem, Maia Secunda. As you requested an appointment, I assume you are claiming this story as yours and wish to be enveloped into the

Flavian dynasty?" Maia opened her mouth to answer but Titus raised his hand to silence her. "Do not speak until I have finished for an admission cannot be unsaid. It is a serious matter to escape slavery, the property should be returned, but to whom? I understand the whole household perished in this unprecedented disaster at Pompeii. The status of slave I therefore have the power to lift." Maia dared to start believing, only to have her hopes knocked back. "To be exposed at birth is not so easy to erase. Your family disowned you." Shame coloured her cheeks anew. Emperor Titus clasped his hands resting them on his belly, and lightly tapped his thumbs together as he contemplated the problem. "If it is true that my cousin sired you unknown, then the decision to expose you was not his." Another lifeline for Maia. "Yet your mother made no claim to Titus Flavius Clemens which suggests your bloodline is not of this family." A crushing knock back. "You look so like Flavia Domitilla, so very like her, but it is not enough to confirm it."

"Eshe thought I was Malita." The words came rushing out. It was the only six she could throw.

Shock registered on Titus's face.

"Eshe rests in Elysium. How can you know that pet name? It has not been used beyond the Palace and not since Domitilla's death have I heard it spoken."

"My Malita, my heart, how good of you to care," quoted Maia, remembering how clear those words had been amidst Eshe's feverish ramblings. "I nursed the maid from your household on Isola Tiberina. I was with her as she died of the sickness. She had a fever, Imperator, but spoke those words with such clarity. She...Eshe...also saw what you see."

"I made a free woman of Eshe on Malita's death. Eshe was a woman of great compassion. A wise woman, a seer of her lands. You were with her at the end, you say?"

"Yes, Imperator."

"A Warrior of Asclepius...as courageous as any soldier." Titus was nodding gently with respect. "I prefer to fight an enemy that can be seen and pray the plague will not return. The people of this great city have suffered enough. Thank you for your service Maia Secunda," he said sincerely. "Did Eshe say anything more to you?"

"She spoke another sentence clearly, Imperator, but I did not understand the meaning of it until Laurentia explained her findings to me."

"Can you recall the words?"

"You will blossom more beautifully than that devious woman and the child will be a girl, so there is nothing to fear."

Titus rubbed at his chin with index finger and thumb, thinking, and Maia watched with hope that her mention of Malita and Eshe was enough to bring a shift in the Emperor's stance. It was.

"You will have my patronage. I cannot publicly accept you to the family, you cannot use the Flavian name, but you will have my patronage."

Maia choked back tears of relief.

"I have been seeking the truth of who I am, Imperator and believe, finally, my journey has ended. You honour me with your patronage and I am grateful, but more importantly, I have your personal belief in the true blood of my father. I can claim the name of Maia Secunda with a clear conscience of knowing I am rightfully a free citizen. I was wronged by my mother who so cruelly exposed me. I will not seek her nomen. I am happy to be Maia Secunda."

"I notice you will change your name again soon," interrupted Titus pointing at her engagement ring.

"Yes, Imperator. I am to be married to a member of your Speculatores Augusti, Tulio Tiberius Livius although I fear he is stalling on our wedding plans," said Maia, her tongue untied now her nerves were settled. "I think a favourable date will soon be found once he hears of your patronage," she smiled, forgetting that pride comes before a fall.

"Deceit is a bad footing on which to begin a marriage." Maia's smile fell away as she tried to pre-empt the direction the conversation was taking. "A slave cannot marry, so you cannot have been honest with him. How much of your past does he know?"

"He knows nought of my life on Pompeii, Imperator. I speak

of it to no-one, it is too traumatic." Emperor Titus nodded his understanding for he had seen much of the aftermath of the disaster and it had affected him too. "The gods sent the ash to bury my slavery, for what purpose I didn't know, but I was thrice saved and for that I felt a duty to survive. Lies have been necessary." It was the most honest she had been since the peak exploded above her.

"Desperate times invoke desperate measures. Am I right in thinking myself and Laurentia alone hold the truth?"

"I have told no other."

"Then the matter is closed for Laurentia will do my bidding and you will become Maia Tiberius with my blessing. Tulio Tiberius Livius has a rising career ahead of him. I will add to your dowry."

"It is as the people say, you are most generous, Imperator. Yet..." Maia chewed on her lip, choosing her next words with care. It was possible they would anger her new patron but her heart was full with the need to speak. "Yet, I have a more pressing use for your patronage than increasing my dowry. I spoke of being thrice saved."

"Go on," instructed Titus when Maia hesitated. Her line was cast.

"I vowed to fulfil whatever purpose the gods wanted of me in return. It was not immediately clear but they showed me in time that I must buy the freedom of two slave-girls that use the names Ebele and Hadassah, who I believe survived the Pompeii death-cloud with their master. I was to work for Dominico and intended to amass my own coin pile but the fire burned that hope. I came to Roma looking for work all those weeks ago with nothing and still have just this coin." Maia showed the As she had tucked in her secret pocket. "Tulio has given me money for food but this is the only coin I can call my own. It is from you," she added brightly. "I signed up to assist with the preparations of your Inaugural Games. I have been scribing the gift-giving balls, it is such fun, but I fear I am failing in my purpose. Your patronage could free Ebele and Hadassah."

"I wonder if the gods have a greater purpose than that for you." Maia frowned at his reply, nervous of disagreeing with the Emperor. Titus threw his head back and gave a hearty laugh. "I recognise that look of disagreement for I have seen it before on my dearest Malita. You are a joy for my heart. I will grant your wish. Who do these slave-girls belong to?"

"The villa is on the Cape at Misenum.

"The nephew of Gaius Plinius Secundas?" asked Titus in surprise.

"Yes, and his mother, Lady Marcella. I was with them on the road as we fled the Cape when the death-cloud fell." Maia dropped her gaze, conscious that although she wasn't speaking a lie, she was withholding some truth. "The Naval Commander was so brave to take his fleet towards the exploding peak," she added hoping to deflect the conversation. It worked.

"He is greatly missed." Titus had become sober again. "I will make free women of those you seek to help. It will be done," he said decisively, rising to his feet. "My guards will escort you to Laurentia who is waiting in the Palace." He shook his head again, looking at her with a smile. "A remarkable likeness."

Maia blushed, partly from the intense scrutiny, partly from the panic that was rising for she was afraid of angering the Emperor with a second request.

"There is a man..." she blurted without further thought, for time was pressing, "...a friend, being held captive at the Castra Praetoria who is wrongly accused. I would plead for his release as I understand the plight of being wronged. His name is Cletus Tettidius Castus."

A peacock, one of four that roamed the Palace gardens, strutted into Titus's view, its tail low and sweeping behind it. The bird squawked its tuneless greeting.

"Juno sends her sacred bird to decide this captive's fate," answered Titus, watching the bird keenly. "If the peacock raises its tail, the man you speak of will be released."

And so it was that one peacock had sent Cletus to his death and another rescued him for the bird at the entrance of the nook fanned its tail feathers in a majestic display.

How remarkable this day was.

Chapter Thirty-Seven

Training of the Speculatores Augusti was always exacting. The regiment prided itself on being elite cavalry soldiers, an honour which required skilful swordsmanship and horsemanship, both of which required constant practise. Joining the unit just before the opening of a major venue had been extremely challenging with intense parade drills. Tulio had thrived during the training sessions, his accomplishments gaining a personal note of achievement from the Praetorian Prefect. He could not have hoped for a better start to his promotion. Confidence was dripping from him as he returned to the Castra Praetoria with his new unit to collect their parade kit for the games. The next two days would be taken up with polishing armour, weapons, boots and horse tackle, including the extra ceremonial items.

Their stay at the camp was short, but he'd gathered his gear quickly to ensure he had time to visit the cells before returning to the Palace. The holding cells at the Castra were by far less appealing places to be incarcerated in than the makeshift cells at the warehouses, and a cruel, smug smile spread across his face as he crossed the parade ground towards them, just as it had when he'd heard along the vine of chatter who was being held there: Cletus Tettidius Castus.

Tulio was feeling kissed by the laurel wreath and all his good fortune was fuelling his arrogance. He could not let the chance pass by, possibly the last he would get, to humiliate the man he had grown to hate. Thinking of Cletus brought Maia to mind and a vision of her naked, bending at the hip presenting her young buttocks to him with her legs enticingly apart made him grow hard with lust. There had not been time to visit the whorehouse during training, nor would there be until the games were well under way. He would reproduce the image later and stroke himself for sexual release. His cruel grin grew larger as his imagination expanded the vision to include Maia standing astride Cletus who was chained by arms and legs, unable to touch the female flesh and forced to watch as Tulio entered Maia, victorious in penetration.

His passion deflated as he neared the foul-smelling cells, for the stench was ripe.

*

The demons had found Cletus. He'd kept positive when he'd been at the warehouse, keeping faith that Emrick would get him out. Then they transferred him to the newly constructed pits at the Castra Praetoria and his resolve had dropped. He tried to raise his spirits by shuffling through memories of his time in Britannia, the campaigns, the women, the drunken fights, the drunken laughter, his comrades and their practical jokes, the endless marches in lashing rain which worked through to soak skin. Strange that he could no longer recall those days of glorious warm sunshine that he'd told Maia were worth a hundred of the wet days. The mind plays tricks when the demons enter. The Castra was more like a fortress than a camp, it's high masonry walls of concrete and red brick facing were solid and imposing. There would be no rescue from Emrick now.

He was being held in one of four subterranean pits, similar in design to the Tullianum dungeon on the Capitoline Hill, and although hastily constructed to cater for the increased number of condemned men that had been brought to the city, the chambers were well clad with blocks of travertine stone held firmly together with cement made from volcanic ash and lime. There were no cracks to pick at and crumble away.

At least the solid, iron door led to a passage that sloped up to the surface in these pits, rather than opening straight to the sewer system as at the Tullianum, mused Cletus. He knew of the story of the famous prisoner, Simon Bar Jioras, who was defeated at Jerusalem by Titus a decade ago. Jioras had been executed then left to rot in the Tullianum before being disposed of in the sewers. Other prisoners had simply been left to starve, perishing in the dark, airless dungeon then shovelled through the iron door to join the city's excrement.

Cletus knew he and his fellow inmates, twelve other condemned souls who he no longer had the confidence or desire to speak to, another symptom of the demons, would not starve, for a man must be alive for a public execution; dragging a corpse to the arena made no spectacle! Cletus heard the metal grid covering the circular hole in the ceiling being lifted and waited for the scraps of food to be thrown in. The hole was the only source of ventilation and light in the cell and also their serving hatch, the iron door having remained firmly closed since they'd been brought in.

Sitting with his back to the wall, hugging his bent knees with his forehead against them, he remained looking down, wondering how long it would take for him to waste away if he refused to eat, knowing it was a futile venture as the guards would force feed him. But instead of the sound of food falling to the ground and hungry men scrabbling for it, he heard his name shouted down in a voice he recognised immediately. He still didn't look up but was suddenly alert and ready to fight for his life which a moment ago he'd been contemplating ending. Hatred can be motivating.

"Castus, you smell as bad as our last encounter," mocked the voice, its timbre confident, smug and cheery. "I have good news." Tulio was laying on his stomach and forearms with his fingers curled over the circle's edge, peering through the hole. Cletus raised his head slowly to see a silhouette of Tulio's head and shoulders, the facial features unclear but the sneer obvious in his tone. "A date is set for my wedding, the first day of Ludi Romani, and with the Emperor's blessing no less. She has his patronage, have you heard? Ha, no, of course you haven't. Isn't it marvellous? I thought you would like the chance to congratulate me before you...how can I put it...entertain us in the arena." Tulio laughed at his own words. Cletus stayed mute, silence his only weapon, but his guts were churning at the news. "We would have had you on our wedding guest list if things were different. It is a shame. I should like to have displayed her as mine before you." *A true bastard peacock,* thought Clete. *Favoured by Juno.* "When I heard of your death sentence, I admit the desire to marry waned," he paused, flashing his most charming smile, "because you would not be around to suffer the humiliation. You prisoners held here at the Castra are scheduled for execution first. Did they tell you that? Ha, no, of course not. But then I realised you will have no funeral, no-one to pay the ferryman, so your shade will not cross the River Styx for judgement. Your spirit will be left wandering amongst us and that brought my appetite for marriage back. Maia is high-born; Maia is mine and you will wander in perpetual distress at seeing us couple together. Sweet Juno, it heats my desire to speak it! Do you recall those extra latrine duties I put you on? Maia was waiting for you at the Carpe Vinum. She asked me to tell you. Ha, there seemed little point as you were otherwise detained. I, of course, did not enlighten her of your foul-smelling duties. Damned decent of me to keep that from her I thought...such a degrading task. I'll admit she was distressed by your snub, but I helped her merriment return."

His laughter echoed round the chamber long after the iron grid was hefted across with a clank to secure the hole. Feeling wretched and ignoring his cell mates, Cletus replaced his head on his knees and allowed the darkness to swallow him. Tulio had meant to crush him, yet the visit had stirred fire into his stomach, and fire is energy. *Look front brother, for I have your back.* He would fight the demons for Maia was worth fighting for. He must find a way to save her from this intended marriage.

Chapter Thirty-Eight

"Will you scribe a letter for me please, Laurentia?" Maia was overjoyed, relieved and excited. Laurentia was feeling much the same way. The meeting with Titus could not have gone better. "I wish to tell Tulio of my patronage from the Emperor. I am hopeful it will speed our marriage."

"As sure as a frog croaks, it will do that," laughed Laurentia. "Your dowry is now a high prize." Laurentia was not aware of the deal Maia had struck with Titus. The act of freeing Ebele and Hadassah was between them and the gods and not to be discussed. Titus had insisted there be silence about the matter, also making Maia swear silence of her suspected parentage. It suited them both. "We will deliver this letter to the Palace bakehouse as before. Have you a day in mind? We must look for a new moon in the calendar."

"I will wait to see what Tulio says. I do not want to tempt fate or something will surely go wrong."

"Wedding ceremonies don't plan themselves you know," answered Laurentia sharply, with one of her sudden mood shifts. "There is much to think of: the guest list, the venue, the procession. I assume Tulio will provide an auspex? And we must order a pig for the sacrifice. Where is his family home? You will need the consent of his father."

"His father is dead, Laurentia, and the gods have buried mine, so we only need our own consent. There will be no contract and few guests. I have only you and Marguerita to invite. I'm not sure who Tulio will bring, but his family moved north on the death of his father."

"That sounds as dour as an unloved eunuch's funeral," tutted Laurentia. "There are customs we must uphold."

"I'm afraid this wedding will be anything but traditional. I don't even have any childhood toys to offer to the household gods."

"Well...we will have a procession at least, I will make sure of it. The wedding party may be a small affair in numbers but we can still make a lot of noise for you. I will supply the boys to play the flutes and we will have torch-bearers to light the way. Bridesmaids too, for someone must carry the distaff and spindle. Your marriage *will* be grandly announced." Maia smiled at Laurentia's enthusiasm.

"A procession would be lovely. Will it be in the evening light?"

"Of course, I have bronze holders for the torches that will catch the light of the dancing flames and they will look so much better in the twilight. And we must have a hemless tunic made for you. New shoes, new palla and a headdress of flowers."

"Oh!" Maia put her hand to her hair. "Can I wear a tiara of tiny flowers like the goddess whose nomen is my own?" She was remembering the beauty of the wax sketch that Calix had deliberately smudged.

"Let us get this letter delivered. We have much to do for I think your betrothed will be eager to set an early date for the wedding when he reads of your Imperial patronage."

*

Laurentia was correct. A reply from Tulio was received that same day telling Maia that the first day of Ludi Romani was lucky in the calendar and urging her to go ahead with preparations for the wedding. He would bring a comrade from the Speculatores Augusti to act as Auspex as his family would not be able to reach the city in time.

"You see, he is keen now," said Laurentia. "So keen he will not wait for his family to attend! Perhaps it is best to get on with it in these strange times," reasoned Laurentia. "I am pleased for you

Maia. It is a good match and will cement your citizenship and that of your future children, as well as ensure your unspeakable past remains buried at Pompeii." Maia knew that to be the truth.

"I wish Claudia and Dominico were here to share the day."

"Indeed...but we cannot waste energy on reflection, we have much to do in a short period. We will create a day that Claudia would be proud of. Now, where will we hold this ceremony? I fear there will be scarce chance of securing a slot at Jupiter's Temple what with the festival and the games going on. There will be so much feasting, we will all end up the shape of large-bottomed amphorae! Where is the apartment Tulio has taken tenancy of?" Laurentia looked at the letter again which gave an address in the city north of the forum.

"Would it be possible to do the sacrifice at your statue of Juno? I should like to honour the Queen of Gods." Maia was thinking of the peacock that had sealed the release of Cletus. She had buried the ruby brooch, the one she had picked up at the naval commander's villa on the Cape, at the shrine in the garden of the domus as an offering of thanks. The gods had been guiding her the day she had planned, but failed, to reach the shrine of Venus Pompeiana in Puteoli. There had been a more important cause for the brooch. Cletus.

Laurentia was looking thoughtful.

"As we are breaking with tradition, I see no reason not to hold the ceremony here at the domus. There is room enough for the few of us attending and your new home is not too far away for the procession."

"Oh, yes please, I would love that!"

"Good, that is settled at least. Now, we must think of your veil." The planning was interrupted by a second delivery which came wrapped in linen marked with the crest of the Palace.

"It will be tickets for the Inaugural Games," said Maia with delight. "Emperor Titus promised he would send some and he is true to his words."

"We'll not be going," said Laurentia sharply. "Did you think we would be?"

"I had hoped to be there for the opening. Dom and Claudia had so wished it."

"I will not be seen seated in the top tier with the dregs of society and neither will you! Such a thing does not apply at the Circus Maximus and neither should it at the amphitheatre. It is extremely galling. I am not rubbing shoulders with the plebs and neither are you young lady. It is not seemly for women of our position."

"Is it not rude to reject the Emperor's gift?"

"We'll not be going," repeated Laurentia firmly. "The tickets will be given to my household slaves." Laurentia scowled at Maia's disappointment. "Pulling a face like that will not make me change my mind. We will share in the atmosphere of the day. My household will need help finding the gate on the tickets and whilst they are inside, we will explore the stalls on Nero's old lake. There is no humiliation in that.

"Nero's old lake?" queried Maia.

"I forget you are not from the city. The ground they have built the amphitheatre on was once a lake in Nero's Golden Palace. Let's hope they have drained it as well as they boast!"

Chapter Thirty-Nine

On the opening day of the Inaugural Games, more people than usual were filling the streets before the carts had left the city. There was much still to prepare and the cockerels seemed to be crowing louder than usual as if they sensed the excitement of this special day.

Maia had chosen her outfit with care and a maid was brushing her hair, taking longer than usual to add an extra shine to the golden locks. Maia was sorry not to be sharing the day with Tulio, and a little envious that he would be at the arena when she would not. He was on duty and would have a fine view of proceedings. Still, there would be time to share stories when they married in four sunrises. *Four sunrises*, she mused. It was no time at all and yet seemed an age. She was planning to go to as many scribing sessions as she could, not only would they help to distract her nerves, but they were a way of thanking her patron. She would ask after Ezio at the old lake and find out where he was working now that the amphitheatre was in use.

As the maid started braiding her hair, she thought of Cletus. His incarceration would be over by now as Emperor Titus had promised it would be so. That should have made her happy, but a sadness came over her instead. Where was he and why had he chosen to abandon their friendship? Thinking of Clete made her think of Calix. That was a friendship she didn't regret losing, but the unpleasant memories lowered her mood further. Irked with herself for allowing her thoughts to tarnish the start of what was going to be a spectacular day, she made a conscious effort to think of the present. The maid was taking great care with the braids.

"Are you trying a new style today?" asked Maia.

"Yes, Mistress, 'tis an important day. You may get a glimpse of Priscus. Some are saying he will parade in the city as well as in the arena. Must have you looking your best before Priscus."

"Before Priscus?" queried Maia. "What about before the Emperor?"

"Oh, Mistress, I would rather be noticed by the gladiator," replied the maid boldly without a flicker of embarrassment. "He's a murmillo, my favourite."

"Is that the gladiator that carries the small shield and curved sword?"

"No, Mistress, that's a thracian. Verus is the thracian, he's from the Balkans. Priscus will be armed with a bigger shield and a short sword, like the armour of a legionary. It's kind of Roma versus Thrace in this combat."

"Is it a murmillo that wears the big helmet with a fish motif?"

"Yes, Mistress, some people call them a fishman."

"I thought that was a retiarius gladiator, the one that uses the weighted net?"

"A retiarius does use a net, Mistress, and a trident, but it's a fishermen he depicts, whereas a murmillo is sometimes called a fish-man." The maid separated the words for clarity, emphasising the difference.

"I do get confused with it all," admitted Maia with a small laugh.

"I will be cheering as loudly as I can for Priscus. They both have many wins to their names, I like them both, but I do favour Priscus...I think. Yes...Priscus to win, and anyhow, he is a murmillo. I cannot thank Lady Laurentia enough for giving me a ticket. This is the best day of my life." Maia did not miss the irony of the situation: as a female slave she could have attended the games, as a privileged woman of Roma she could not. The maid finished the new hairstyle by twisting the braids and pinning them in place.

"You look beautiful, Mistress."

"I will take your word for it as dearest Claudia always told me that too much time in front of a mirror is a weakness."

"Just a quick peep won't hurt," said the maid passing a hand-mirror to Maia who desperately wanted to look. Peering into the polished oval of metal that was set in a wooden surround, she smiled, liking the new hairstyle.

"I'm going to have a tiara of flowers on my wedding day," she said, her mood brightening again.

*

The young slave-boy with the dark, almond-shaped eyes was walking in front of Laurentia and Maia, carrying a basket of citrons that Laurentia would offer to the poor. They had decided not to order a litter today, preferring to surround themselves with their entire household of slaves, all dressed identically to show whose house they belonged to. The crowds were thick on the streets for this first day of festivities and it was a prime day for displaying your wealth. It would be a profitable day for the thieves too, so a high number of slaves would also help with security.

The noise and bustle was increasing as they neared the amphitheatre. Stallholders were selling food, drinks and all manner of trinkets marking the occasion. Jugglers and acrobats were all working their skills vying for attention and coin. Hawkers were mingling through the crowds carrying cheap charms and favours made of ribbon, some orange, some blue, so you could show whether you were cheering for Priscus or Verus in the big fight. Laurentia bought three of each.

"Our household will support whoever is winning," she said, winking at Maia and chuckling as she glided over the cobbles in her distinctive walk, pressing a coin into the hand of a beggar with a stump for a foot. The party made their way towards the giant porticoes of the North Gate, guided by the gilded horse-drawn chariots atop each glinting in the morning sunlight. Reaching Gate

XXXVIII, Laurentia checked the letters matched those on the tickets. "Yes, this is the entrance." It was plain in comparison to the highly decorated North Gate whose paintings and stuccoes doubtless depicted a story but Maia didn't know it. Laurentia called the three household slaves chosen to attend the games to her, giving them the pottery shards and the lengths of orange and blue ribbons. "Remember whose household you represent," she lectured. "You are expected back at the domus before dusk." The amphitheatre was filling up quickly, the many entrances making easy work of the crowds. "This arena is tiny compared to the Circus Maximus," said Laurentia looking up at the arches as she and Maia moved away from the gate. "You'll not catch me in there unless they change the seating structure. I know you can end up sitting next to the most annoying people at the chariot racing too, but at least it is possible to pay for one of the shaded seats to ensure a higher class of neighbour. They clearly don't want women of the upper class to attend the ludi. Perhaps the Senators fear losing their wives to the gladiators!" Maia, in contrast, was in awe of the amphitheatre and desperately disappointed not to be inside. "Come, let us walk round the building and see who is about," said Laurentia seeing Maia's disappointment.

The slave-boy was still carrying the basket of citrons and Laurentia instructed him to hand them out to the poor as they and their entourage made their way towards the other end of the amphitheatre. The basket was soon emptied and Laurentia gave the boy a coin and sent him on another errand to buy drinks from a nearby stall. He returned with two cups of watered wine with added honey and Laurentia suggested they find somewhere to sit near the South Gate to drink them. A trumpet sounded from inside the arena.

"Look, the Vestal Virgins are arriving," said Maia, pointing excitedly towards the group of priestesses being escorted through the crowd of onlookers, her excitement turning suddenly to anxiety as an unexpected remnant of Decima took over, for she knew the Vestal priestesses had the power to arrest the flight of a runaway slave by uttering a prayer. The utterance could rivet the runaway to the spot, providing they'd not gone beyond the precincts of the city. Maia calmed herself by rationalising her anxiety: *the gods have buried your slavery.*

The Vestal Virgins disappeared through the gateway to a roar of cheers from inside the arena. Somewhere from the heights of the western side of the arena came a steady hand clap and a chant of 'Ti-tus, Aug-us-tus, Ti-tus, Aug-us-tus'. The clap and chant was gradually mimicked by other segments until the whole amphitheatre was taking part and calling for the appearance of their Emperor. Even from outside the arena Maia could feel the excited anticipation of the Emperor's arrival.

The crowd inside began to stamp its feet adding another layer of sound, increasing both the tempo and the volume of the chant, the excitement of which transferred to those people mingling outside. Maia began clapping her hands in time with the crowd, and with a small nod of her head, Laurentia allowed her slaves to join in too, although she remained demure. Maia joined in with the stamping and just as the crescendo reached its peak, when Maia thought the arches of the arena would collapse with the noise, when she herself could not maintain the level of energy a beat longer, a bugle bellowed and the crowd took a collective gasp of air before erupting in a wild cheer as Emperor Titus walked on to the podium with his entourage. Maia's eyes and cheeks were bright with the thrill of it all and she longed to be inside the amphitheatre.

"Come, we should make our way round to the Wast Gate with haste for that is where the gladiators and beasts will be brought in," said Laurentia. "The parades will start as soon as the Emperor declares the games open."

"Oh, I really want to see the gladiators," said Maia with excitement.

"We'll try but it may depend on the crowds. I'll not stomach being jostled by a mob for too long, especially as the day rises in heat."

The throng was indeed growing and Laurentia had her strongest slaves forge the way. There were enough in her household to form a protective circle around her and Maia, but it was becoming increasingly more difficult for the slaves to create space for their mistress to walk unimpeded as they approached the West Gate.

"The crowd is shifting back towards us, Mistress" warned one of the slaves at the front. "It is the Speculatores Augusti, they are pushing through on their horses."

"How distressing," complained Laurentia as she was squeezed into a huddle between her staff. "Keep them back," she snapped, but the surge of the parting crowd was strong and Laurentia's household found themselves unable to move forwards, nor backwards, as the people behind continued to press on, unaware of the horsemen ahead. "We shall be crushed! Stop this, stop this!" The situation eased once the Speculatores Augusti reached through to the gate and stopped displacing the crowd. It was made even better by the arrival of foot legionaries, dressed in their ceremonial togas, who cleared the masses from behind as they marched through to join the horsemen, but Laurentia's angry mood was not so quick to disperse. "I am going home! No gladiator is worth this nonsense. You will come with me, Maia."

Oh, Laurentia, please may I stay. Tulio may be nearby. It would be wonderful to see him on duty. There will not be such a spectacle again."

"Thank Jupiter there will not! You will come with me."

Maia's heart fell to her feet with disappointment but she knew it was not wise to disobey Laurentia's ire. She was spiteful in anger. The slaves recreated their protective circle giving the ladies space to walk once more as they drew away from the busiest area. Maia was too short to see past the household huddle, so despite the Speculatores Augusti being on horses, did not see Tulio mounted in the line proudly wearing the special boots of the Emperor's cavalry bodyguard. She did, however, hear a voice she recognized calling above the hubbub. It was Ezio. Maia didn't hesitate for it must surely be a sign from the gods that they wanted her to remain at the amphitheatre this day.

"Laurentia, I have a care to scribe more of the gift-giving balls for the games. I can hear Ezio nearby. He is one of the organisers of the scribing team." Laurentia, still narked by the crowds, scowled at the request but Maia pressed on. "It will give favour to my patron."

"Then I can hardly refuse," stated Laurentia crossly, knowing she could not object to this reasoning. "Boy, accompany Mistress Maia as necessary," she instructed a slave. Maia dipped her head to Laurentia, partly in respectful thanks, but also to hide the excited delight that would only irk Claudia's sister further.

Chapter Forty

Ezio greeted Maia warmly.

"It is good to see you still have a full head of hair," joked Maia.

"There is much scribing still to be done, so I may yet lose it all before these games are over! I was hoping to see the gladiators arrive but these crowds are like a strong river current and I seem to be wading against it. I suggest we go with the flow instead and take safety in the scribing tent which is closer to the East Gate." As Ezio led them away from the crowd, a huge cheer went up and women could be heard screaming the name of Priscus. "Sounds like our murmillo has arrived. I always favour a thracian, as does Emperor Titus I believe. He'll be happy to argue their merits with the crowd no doubt."

"Laurentia has instructed her household to cheer for whomever is winning. They have both orange and blue ribbons to raise as necessary."

"Do I detect a touch of disappointment in your tone?"

"A little," answered Maia.

"I'd wager it is more than a little by that flat response."

"The amphitheatre is such a special place," enthused Maia. "I had hoped to be inside but Laurentia will not allow it."

"Well..." Ezio made a point of looking left then right, "...I don't see her and I have access to a seat inside." Maia looked questioningly at Ezio's smiling face. "It is not the most glamorous seat in the building, neither can you view the action on the arena floor from it, but it will give us access." Maia's expression grew more confused. "As head of the scribing team, I am allowed entry to use the public latrines. With a little guile we can position ourselves at the top of the stairs. The view may be restricted but you will experience the atmosphere at least." In perfect response, a deep, joyous cheer erupted from the amphitheatre, matching Maia's soaring excitement. "And so the games begin. Follow me."

Maia dismissed Laurentia's slave, pressing a coin into his hands. The slave did not hesitate in seizing this unexpected opportunity and Maia smiled as she saw him pull a freedom cap from beneath his tunic as he rejoined the mingling crowd. Many slaves used such tricks in the city to deflect unwanted attention if they were sent on a solitary errand.

Maia went with Ezio, matching his increasing pace as the crowd became thinner as they neared the East Gate. The clerk at the gate knew Ezio and within minutes Maia was inside the arena following Ezio along the outside circular corridor.

The air itself was thrumming with excitement, the stone corridor channelling the applause with the noise bouncing off the walls and echoing the cries from within. The tiny hairs on Maia's nape prickled and she felt the thrill of the event surge heat across her neck and behind her breast.

"The latrines are along this outer corridor, but if we divert to the inside corridor, the stairs will take us to a viewing position. You must keep in the shadows though Maia or we will be ousted by security for breaching the seating rules." explained Ezio.

And so it was that Maia got to watch, albeit with a restricted view, the gladiators, wearing their ceremonial finery, parade the arena in chariots. Sunlight was glinting not only from polished arm and leg guards, but also from naked, muscled torsos and thighs, all glistening with oil, as well as the different shields and weaponry on display. But it was the feathers adorning the helmet of Priscus, the murmillo, that caught Maia's attention. Peacock tail feathers, four of them, fixed atop the wide-brimmed helmet, standing tall and proud with the large eyes of each seeming to stare accusingly at Maia stealing her breath and causing her guts to loop over in fear as she felt the whispers of fate creeping across her back. *Cletus!* Peacocks always led her to Cletus.

The din in the amphitheatre continued but Maia's world fell silent. In her imagination she saw one of the colourful feathers fall away from the helmet and float to the sandy ground. She saw herself running in slow motion across the arena, desperate to retrieve the feather to keep it from harm, reaching it only to have the thunderous wheels of the chariot carrying Verus snatch it from her tenuous grasp. Maia watched with horror as the wheel mangled the beautiful feather. *Was this a warning from the gods? Had the Emperor not made good on his promise to release Cletus?*

The vision faded and Maia looked towards the Emperor's podium but could not see Titus from her restricted view. As if from afar, she could hear the audience chanting the murmillo's name, along with the name of the thracian in reply. "Pris-cus, Ver-us, Pris-cus, Ve-rus..." Ezio joined in, shouting in support of the thracian and hearing his voice brought a reality back to Maia and she refocussed on what was happening in the arena, noticing that all four peacock feathers were safely attached to Priscus's helmet. Mendacius must be sitting beside me, she decided, shaking her head. This was not a day to spoil by allowing the god of trickery to fool her.

"Judging by the number of incense vats around the arena, we're certainly in for a lot of bloodsport today," said Ezio, raising his voice above the din. "I'm not sure which smells worse to be honest, blood or the incense," he laughed. "They have plenty of dark sand down too. That will help disguise the amount of blood. We are definitely in for a treat."

"When will the fights begin?" asked Maia.

"Not until this afternoon. There will be a hunt after the gladiators' parade. After that they'll perform a mime of some description, followed by a mass execution of prisoners. Titus will most probably leave the arena to dine at that point. He won't want to risk a drop in popularity like Claudius did by staying. The big gladiator fight will begin when the Emperor returns, although I have heard rumour of a staged naval battle too. I can't see how that will work on dry land, perhaps they plan to have lightweight craft that can be lifted in to position."

"Perhaps bottomless boats that men will lift to their waists and we'll see their legs as they walk them around the arena. If they wear boots the colour of the ocean, no-one will notice a thing," suggested Maia, her concern for Clete lingering but lessening.

"Who knows," said Ezio, chuckling at her idea. "The soldiers will need to pull the sail across soon. The heat is rising early today."

"When will the gift-giving balls be thrown?"

"At the end of the day, for sure. An enticement to ensure the plebs don't leave early. Empty seats would not be agreeable to the Emperor." The cheers for Priscus and Verus subsided as they left the arena, to be replaced by a collective gasp of delight as two female gladiators, mounted on horses galloped in. "Gladiatrix, you don't often see them. And dwarves to follow too! It is as we thought, Emperor Titus is casting his highest tali pieces at these games. He wants the public to worship him. It's working well so far, listen to their cries of adoration."

Hearing the cheers for the Emperor, her patron, her true kin, steadied her anxiety for Clete further. Titus was loved by the people and a man to be trusted. She put the vision of the peacock feather aside.

"Can we stay to watch the hunt?" asked Maia.

"We'll stay for the hunt but must get back to scribing before the sun is at its highest. There is much to be done."

Chapter Forty-One

As soon as the parade was finished, a legion of men busied themselves in transforming the arena to resemble an exotic jungle of trees and shrubs. The audience was entertained by jugglers with flaming torches and naked tumblers wearing headdresses resembling lions, wolves and bears, making the display a strange, mythical spectacle of cavorting human-beasts. Some of the bigger trees were lowered on hoists which was entertainment in itself, although the greatest applause came when an unfortunate tumbler misjudged his line and collided with the scenery that was being moved across the floor.

With the scenery in place, a dozen men, the hunters, clad in just loin cloths, carrying spears or bows and arrows but no shields, ran into the arena through the West Gate, darting and dodging between the shrubbery until they were dispersed across the floor and hiding in the undergrowth. Then came the beasts they would hunt. Driven by trained animal handlers from cages hidden in the tunnel beneath the Emperor's podium, the big cats loped into the jungle setting, their strength evident, their menace obvious, their hunger expected.

"Now the blood will spill," said Ezio rubbing his hands together with delight. "Let the slaughter begin."

"I have heard of a lion, which is the lion?" asked Maia, thinking of Uday's story from when he lived in Africa.

"The lion has the mane, the leopard his spots, the tiger is

stripy, the panther is not. That's the best way to remember which big cat is which. I can see a lion and a leopard out there. And look, a hippopotamus too. What a size!"

Maia was captivated by the prowling lion, its shaggy bronze-tinted mane that grew darker in colour where it covered the powerful neck and shoulders, swinging from side to side as it moved. The slow motion focus came over her again and she saw the lion in silent isolation. It's intense gaze seeming to lock with her own and she marvelled in the beast's magnificence

An arrow pierced the lion's hide and Maia saw pain in its eyes, pain that quickly changed to anger. The hunter hit its target again and the beast's roar broke through Maia's isolation and she gasped at the thrill of the atmosphere inside the stadium. Hunters were running between the shrubbery intent on gaining a quick kill, pressing home their advantage of surprise, the beasts still bewildered by the unfamiliar surroundings; the scent of man, the noise of man. The crowd wanted the animal's slaughter, but empathy for the majestic creature filled Maia and she willed it to live. And just as the life-blood had risen in Maia when she'd realised the head-slave's intention of cutting her throat in Pompeii, so the life-blood rose in the injured lion. With arrows and spears protruding, the beast launched itself towards a hunter. Maia's heartbeat lost all rhythm as ice scorched her veins, so cold it burned. The hunter was Calix.

After being arrested by Cletus in Puteoli, Calix had been brought to Roma in the round-up of prisoners across the land, and picked out to attend the Morning Camp to be trained as a hunter specifically for the games. The majority of hunters died in the arena, lucky if unconsciousness came early as the beasts tore at their flesh, but a hunter, at least, had a slim chance of survival, whereas a prisoner put forward for execution had none. A hunter could also savour the brief adulation of the crowd, the cheers drowning their own screams in death.

Touching the pad of her thumb where she and Calix had made their blood oath, Maia watched as Calix was mauled, mutilated and mangled, his final moments prolonged as the animal handlers provoked the hippopotamus in to a charge to disrupt the massacre. It was chaos but the charge only delayed the end for Calix who bled out on the arena floor, the dark sand betraying the lush foliage in the jungle amphitheatre, just as Calix had betrayed Maia's trust in Puteoli. It was fitting that he met a grizzly, bloodied, public death. Dead men could not talk. Calix could betray her no further and her own blood pounded through her heart with the thrill of being alive.

"We must take our leave," said Ezio, guiding her with a hand against her bony shoulder. Neither spoke again until they reached the scribing tent, the calmness of which could not have been more contrasting to the atmosphere inside the amphitheatre. Muffled cheers, cries and the general melee of the hunt could still be heard but the aura in the tent was soothing. Ezio and Maia settled down to etch the gift-giving balls. Conversation was minimal as they worked and with the fading buzz of being at the hunt, Maia was able to process all that she had seen that morning.

She couldn't shake off the vision of the damaged feather and fretted over what it could mean. She was convinced the gods were telling her something about Cletus, but what? Had he been freed or had the Emperor been humouring her with that promise? Was Cletus going to meet a similar death to Calix in the arena? If she went to Emperor Titus, her doubt of his word would surely seal her own crucifixion, the same crucifixion that Lady Rufina had condemned her to. Were the gods testing her faith of Titus, the man who sat closely beside them, was that the reason for the vision?

By the time the gladiators re-entered the arena, to the loudest cheer of the day, Maia had tied her thoughts in knots and was tired of churning them over without finding a conclusion. She would let the gods guide her once more. If Priscus won the fight she would know that Cletus was safe, for it was Priscus who had displayed the peacock feathers in their full beauty. Should Verus win the fight, it would be confirmation that Cletus needed her help, for it had been Verus's chariot that had broken the peacock feather.

There, it was decided and before she could tangle her mind again, she sent the decision to Juno, for the peacock was the Queen of Gods sacred bird. She felt immediately better for clearing her mind of an impossible decision.

"Ezio, can we sneak back in to the amphitheatre to watch the big fight?"

"Did you think I would miss it?" he laughed, winking at her. "We will surely need to use the latrines again." Feeling at ease with Ezio, Maia told him about her planned wedding day.

"We have picked a lucky day, the first day of Ludi Romani, which is why we will hold the ceremony at the domus as all the temples are already being used for the other celebrations. I'm rather pleased to be having the ceremony at the house. My husband to be is a member of the Speculatores Augusti so I will be well provided for." Ezio raised his eyebrows in acknowledgement of the prestigious rank, but did not miss the shadow which crossed her expression.

"Is your heart with a different man?"

"There is someone I care for but he does not feel the same. We travelled from Puteoli to Roma together but he has since shown me he does not care. I am engaged to a good man with high prospects."

"It is a fine match, you will be well provided for. Marriages of convenience are often the best you know. The one you are marrying, what is his name?"

"Tulio Tiberius Livius, do you know him?"

Ezio did not reply for a moment. And Maia thought she saw a flicker of recognition at the name and a momentary stiffness to Ezio's posture.

"You will be well provided for," he repeated, and regaining his gentle composure, suggested it was time they visited the latrines.

Chapter Forty-Two

"That was unprecedented," said Ezio, stunned by the outcome of the fight. "A joint victory, palms to them both. What a fight! Both men were on their knees with exhaustion but each time they stood and would not cower. Remarkable spirit, remarkable." Maia could not make sense of the message Juno was giving with this outcome. There was always a winner and loser in combat, never a draw. She was feeling robbed of an answer to her indecision. What should she do now? "We must leave again, Maia. I wish to ensure the correct gift-giving balls are delivered to the podium. There is too much incompetence to entrust another with such a task. Just imagine the embarrassment to the Imperial Palace if blank balls were offered in to the crowd. The crows would be pecking at my eyes tomorrow if that happened. With responsibility comes fear," explained Ezio thinking Maia would be reluctant to leave the games. He was wrong, Maia followed him willingly, needing a chance to think on her predicament.

"I should return to the domus whilst the streets are less busy and daylight remains," she said.

"That is a sensible idea. Keep alert for thieves just the same."

"It is not far. I will be safe." Taking her leave of Ezio, she retrieved her manners enough to call back a thank you but her mind was filling with the problem of Cletus and anxiety soon had her chewing at her lip and nervous of every shadow.

Following the curve of the amphitheatre towards the South

Gate, she could see the Speculatores Augusti on their horses, presumably waiting to control the crowds when the Emperor left the games. Although a lot of their work was clandestine in nature and undertaken in plain clothes, today they were wearing the ceremonial uniform, pompous in its flamboyance and designed to be visible. If she could find Tulio, perhaps he would help. Of course he would help, it was an obvious and simple solution and finding him became her focus.

Where there was a spectacle in Roma, there was always a gathering of people to push through and she wished Laurentia's slave was still with her as she made her way towards the throng that she would need to get through to reach the line of horsemen that fanned out across part of the old lake. A one-armed beggar pulled at her clothes and she brushed his hand away roughly. The beggar was not easily put off and grabbed her tunic again, more firmly this time.

"Please leave me," she snapped. The man bared a mouth of rotting teeth in a mean smile, causing Maia to gag on his rank-smelling breath. "I have nothing to give you." She saw him look to her bosom in lust, the man's sneer becoming a leer. With speed, his hand moved to cup a breast. Just as quickly, Maia stabbed her fingers to his eyes. Her aim was a little awry but the unexpected attack caused the beggar to move his hand to his face and Maia wasted no time in escaping, for once pleased to have a crowd to move in to. Weaving between people with increased urgency, constantly glancing back to check if the beggar was pursuing her, she reached the line of horsemen. Feeling safer with the guards nearby, she turned her attention to searching for Tulio.

Dressed as they were in their ceremonial uniforms, it was difficult to tell one Speculatores Augusti member from another without a careful study of their faces, thus Maia missed the reappearance of the beggar whose lust had only been heightened by her rebuff. Even lacking an arm he was far stronger than Maia, and it was easy to pin her to him by clamping his arm around her chest from behind. She could feel his engorged penis hard against the small of her back as he pressed against her. Too afraid to cry out, repulsed by the stench that came from his breath blowing so close to her ear and sickened by his unwelcome touch, her body betrayed her, fear mimicking sexuality by hardening her nipples and bolting heat to her groin.

"You have plenty I want," whispered the beggar, keeping a tight hold on Maia and discretely moving his hips to rub his erection against her, making clear his intentions, his pleasure all the greater for the secrecy of the act amidst the public, those around them more interested in the guards than the beggar. All except one person. Just as he had appeared in the covered walkway at Puteoli to save her from the knife of Calix, so Cletus appeared in Roma to rescue her from the beggar.

With the element of surprise, Clete easily overcame the beggar, twisting his arm behind his back and freeing Maia in a heartbeat. But in compensation for a missing limb, the beggar had learned to writhe like a pit of restless serpents, and, despite Cletus's strength would have wriggled free if Emrick had not leant a hand. The big Celt took charge, the ruckus causing Maia to stumble forwards and the crowd to move outwards, upsetting a horse which skittered out of line. One event led to another and before Maia had a chance to react to the grunt she knew was Clete's, the upset horse bolted and Tulio arrived to fill the gap in the line of the Speculatores Augusti. Without hesitation, Tulio kicked out at Clete, using the height of his horse as an advantage.

Maia watched in horror as Tulio skilfully manoeuvred his horse to a position where he could lash out again.

"Tulio, no! It is Cletus, your comrade!"

"I know who it is," he snarled, kicking out again. The cocksucker should be baited to the bears." Cletus was ready for Tulio's second attack and, grabbing at the boots that were so distinctive, tried to pull Tulio from his horse. It was madness to attack one of the Emperor's personal bodyguards, even in self-defence. There would be no leniency if he was arrested again. Emrick, acting quickly and decisively, released the beggar so he could pull Cletus away.

"We leave," he said tersely. "We will have our revenge another day as we planned."

There was only time to share a glance with Maia, a glance that explained nothing, as they shoved through the crowd and disappeared from view; Cletus filled with frustration; Maia filled with confusion; Tulio filled with anger. At least she knew Cletus was alive and free. Emperor Titus had kept his word. With her emotions unravelling, she turned to admonish Tulio, uncaring of those around her.

"Why did you kick him? What did you mean he should be baited to the bears? He was helping me."

"He should rot! How did he escape the arena?" Maia took an involuntary step backwards at seeing the hatred in Tulio's eyes. Leaning down his horse's flank, he grabbed her arm. "Did you have something to do with his escape?" he asked menacingly. Maia was saved from answering by a bugler playing a series of two-tone notes that split the air. It was a signal to the Speculatores Augusti to close formation and come to attention. Tulio was forced to release his grip on Maia and focus on his duties. "Go straight to the domus," he hissed. "And don't be foolish enough to return to these crowds without at least one slave to protect you."

Maia backed away, rubbing her upper arm which was red with the imprints of Tulio's fingers, stunned by his vicious reaction. Embarrassed to look at the people surrounding her, she mumbled courtesies as she withdrew, keeping her eyes looking down to the ground, but constantly flicking her gaze up quickly, warily looking for the one-armed beggar and hoping to see Cletus or Emrick.

How emotional this day was, swinging from high to low so many times.

*

Still shaken by the series of events as she walked along the less congested streets, her thoughts were full of the drama as she tried to make sense of it all. Cletus was alive and well and had saved her from the beggar's unwanted attention. It had been such a shock to see him, a welcome one, yet he had disappeared as quickly as he appeared. Did he care after all or was he just doing his civil duty in helping her? Why had Tulio been so angry? There seemed to be hatred between Tulio and Cletus. Why? Or had she misheard Tulio's words? She shook her head at her own wishful thinking. Tulio's actions told her she had heard him correctly and being an accomplished liar herself, she was alert to deception. There was something involving Clete and Tulio that wasn't right.

Reaching the junction where she should turn left for the domus, she hesitated. The Carpe Vinum was a short distance to the right. Would Cletus be in there? She considered going to see, but quickly dismissed the idea as foolhardy. As Tulio had crossly pointed out, she had no slave to protect her and after such a public fracas, Clete would not take the risk of drinking in a popina, especially an establishment frequented by the guards. She snorted softly at herself for even considering a look. "He didn't come to the Carpe Vinum when you asked him to," she quietly reminded herself, "so why would he be there waiting for you now?"

As she turned left to return to the domus, Venus was surely mocking her as Cletus was in the Carpe Vinum, hoping she would come looking for him.

*

"That didn't go to plan," growled Cletus. "Bloody beggar, bloody Peacock!"

"And being here is not a good idea. If you are re-arrested there will be no reprieve issued by the Emperor this time? It will be death in the arena. Is she worth that risk?" asked Emrick.

"Was your woman in Britannia worth risking your life for?" responded Cletus. The Celt pursing his lips, nodded gently and conceded the point by ordering a pitcher of watered wine.

"The brain cannot fathom the heart. Your goddess, Venus, makes fools of all men. Let us hope that Fortuna favours us at least. We need her luck to keep those meddlesome Speculatores Augusti lads busy and away from here. It is a poor place to hide."

"Sometimes it is better to hide in plain sight. Do the unexpected."

"Tulio is no fool."

"We will see. They will arrest you too..."

"I'm staying," interrupted Emrick firmly, cutting off any further talk on the matter." Without knowing it, they were sitting at the same bench that Maia and Marguerita had occupied the night they waited for Clete who knew nought of their invitation thanks to Tulio's deceit. The goddess of love was indeed mocking them.

The two comrades kept a quiet vigil for more than two hours. Customers came and went but no Praetorian Guards nor any from the Emperor's elite cavalry came in. No Tulio. No Maia. A serving wench put a spill to the lamps inside the popina as the daylight slumped away.

"She isn't coming is she?" said Cletus. "*Futuo!* I should have followed her."

"It was impossible to follow her."

"What can we do now?"

"We will keep vigil at the scribing tent. The slow grinding of your Roman administration system will, without doubt, mean there is still much work to do there. She will come and we will choose our moment better this time." Clete grunted in response to that barb.

"If that bastard Peacock had been anywhere else in the horse line..."

"She was looking for him, so it is not that surprising..." interrupted Emrick, who in turn was interrupted by Cletus.

"I cannot let her marry that bastard Tulio. The thought alone curdles my guts."

"We found her once, we will find her again," replied Emrick making placating gestures with open hands, "but Brother, we must avoid putting our heads above the parapet unless there is no other choice," urged Emrick.

Chapter Forty-Three

Maia would have preferred to go straight to the solitude of her room at the domus, but Laurentia was sitting in the shady courtyard garden making it impossible to sneak in.

"No slave with you?" she asked raising a questioning eyebrow.

"He accompanied me to the scribing tent, but it seemed futile for him to stand there all day. I was working and safe with Ezio, so I dismissed him." Maia wasn't sure how much of her day she wanted to share with Laurentia who would be furious that she had been in the amphitheatre watching the hunt and gladiator fight. Feeling shaken and fragile with all that had happened, she wasn't ready for a fight with Laurentia. Neither was she able to cope with Laurentia's sudden mood tacks which were disarmingly effective as an interrogation strategy. One minute kind, then throwing in a cruel jibe, followed by a direct question on a different topic entirely. As soon as the wedding plans were mentioned, Maia's eyes filled with tears that she tried, but failed, to stem.

"My dear, whatever is the matter?" Laurentia jumped up from her seat, full of concern, and taking Maia in her arms, comforted the tearful girl. With a clever mixture of concern and guile, practised and honed in the political arena that masqueraded as the public baths, she cunningly manipulated Maia in to telling much more than she had intended. "Let me see if I have this right. A beggar attacks you, the friend you came to Roma with suddenly reappears to save you from the beggar, and Tulio kicks out at the friend?"

"That's sort of it."

"That's either it or it is not," stated Laurentia with less compassion than earlier. "So which part is upsetting you?"

"Tulio is upsetting me."

"Why?"

"He was so angry, so harsh, I am frightened to marry him."

"Ah...there it is...a young bride's wedding nerves. It is natural. This friend, Cletus did you say?" Maia nodded, wiping her face with the linen Laurentia provided now that her tears had ceased. "He did not see you safely home?" Maia shook her head, frowning. "Not much of a friend is he? Are you sure it is Tulio's anger that is upsetting you or the fact that this Cletus does not meet the standards you demand of a man?" Put to her like that, it seemed the solution to Maia's tears.

"You are wiser than I," said Maia managing a wan smile.

"I am, so listen when I tell you that this marriage to Tulio is a good thing for you. Provision is the wisest bond. Come, we will dine and talk of the wedding arrangements we still need to sort. I have much for you to do over the next four days. I will send for Marguerita at first light tomorrow to help us. It will be good to have her company until you wed. I will ask her to stay." They heard the service door of the domus open and the excited chatter of the returning household slaves. "At last! I may not have wanted to sit with the plebs in the amphitheatre, but that does not mean I am disinterested in the games. Let us hear the gossip. It is important to keep abreast of any event that is organised by the Emperor."

Maia was feeling wrung out but her emotions had steadied a little following Laurentia's counsel. Cletus would not have liked her tears, she mused. Thinking of him brought forth the strange vision of the damaged peacock feather, its meaning still troubling her.

"I heard the big fight was a draw, Laurentia."

"No...really? That must have been some fight. It is just as well I bought both ribbon colours," she laughed.

"I am exhausted. May I be excused to my room for I do not think I can stay awake to hear all the news."

"Tut!" Laurentia was not impressed but could see Maia was tired. "I cannot spare a maid to undress you at this time."

"I can see to myself."

"Then go. I will fill you in on events from the arena tomorrow."

Maia was relieved not to have to sit through the re-telling of the hunt and hear the great gossip of the fight. It would only serve to scramble her thoughts again, and being so tired she was worried she would let a comment slip that would reveal she'd been in the arena. She retired gratefully to the comfort of her cot, but spent a troubled sleep dreaming of a mangled peacock feather.

*

In the days leading up to the wedding, Laurentia and Marguerita kept Maia busy at the domus preparing for the wedding.

For each of those days, Cletus and Emrick kept vigil at the scribing tent, keeping to the shaded areas, initially hopeful that Maia would turn up, but each day became longer as Cletus became more despondent.

The first day of Ludi Romani dawned with an unexpected downpour of rain, soaking Cletus and Emrick who were in position to watch for Maia before it was properly light. Their mood was dour before the soaking which lowered it further and they both felt the chill of the air which dropped in temperature after the rain.

"If she doesn't show by the time the sun is at its highest, I'll be speaking to that tall guy in the tent we saw her go to the amphitheatre with," said Cletus to Emrick in a belligerent tone.

"We've been over this idea before. It's a bad one. He's employed at the basilica, if Tulio has put out a description of us for arrest, he'll know about it."

"What other choice do we have? We cannot wait here indefinitely!" Clete grunted with frustration. "I am tempted to crash that scribing tent at first light."

"We wait," growled Emrick, his thick Celtic accent adding menace to the statement.

"Only until the shadows are at their shortest or the rain falls again. Whichever comes the sooner. I'll not take another soaking." Clete spat on his palm, and nodded when Emrick accepted the agreement with a spit of his own and a shake of hands.

*

It wasn't often Cletus prayed for rain, but he did that morning for he was restless for action, only to be denied his wish. The early morning downpour was replaced by a clear dawn sky of pink hues sliding quickly to soft blue, the tint deepening as the sun rose higher. Cletus and Emrick shivered as the temperature dropped further as it often does with the increasing daylight until the warmth of the sun took over. They watched as the carts finished making their night-time deliveries, leaving the streets free for the day-time citizens of Roma to carry on with their daily routines. The temporary stalls on the old lake were taking on a more permanent look as the hawkers were settling in to a routine with the games. The amphitheatre filled for another day of entertainment. Maia did not come to the scribing tent.

"Mars have pity," whispered Emrick as a particularly loud cheer was raised inside the amphitheatre. "Poor bastards. I am learning your Roman ways; the louder the cheer, the more perverted and gruesome the act. And you call my race barbaric!"

"It is the way of it," grunted Clete non-committally. "The shadows are short, it is time to raise our heads as you put it. I can be still no longer. You ready to move your tallowy arse?"

"Ready," echoed Emrick. "In truth, I was praying for rain too," he chuckled, slapping his friend on the shoulder. "My guts were churning with the wait. Let us see if this scribe knows anything. Remember, if we have to run, we split up. Get out of the city as fast as you can. I will see you at the Port of Ostia as arranged."

*

Ezio had been worrying over Maia since their conversation about her wedding. He had become quite fond of her in a paternal way, but she was not his responsibility and it was not his place to advise her. Yet he worried over whether he should speak of what he knew. As it transpired, the gods had made the decision for him as Maia had not returned to the tent since the opening day of the games...but that changed with the arrival of Cletus.

Cletus had a presence about him that filled whatever room, tent or cell he was in. Ezio turned to look at the ex-legionary as he entered the scribing tent, and putting the wooden ball he was working on aside, greeted him with a touch of suspicion. Ezio's colleague, the bald-headed clerk, was with him in the tent this day, along with two other scribes, so as soon as Cletus mentioned Maia's name, Ezio held his hand out towards the flap indicating they talk outside.

"Why are you looking for Maia?" asked Ezio, eyeing the big Celt who was waiting outside with even greater suspicion.

"We travelled from Puteoli to Roma together. I am leaving the city tomorrow and wanted to say goodbye."

"She is to be married this day." Ezio had none of his usual tolerance for dalliance, the words spilling as if he knew the importance of this moment.

"No! *Futuo!* She must not." Cletus raked his fingers through his hair in despair, cursing the air blue as only a soldier can. Ezio's eyes narrowed, not with disgust at the language, but in measurement of Clete's reaction which had reflected his own, yet the emotion was tenfold.

"She thinks you don't care, yet I see that you do."

"She makes a habit of poorly choosing her men. The one she is marrying has deceived us both."

"Tulio Tiberius Livius." Ezio spoke the name ponderously, rubbing his finger along his bottom lip as he came to a decision. "I knew his father. I liked his father, respected him, but the son has none of his father's morals. He is slippery of character and when his father died, instead of taking on the responsibilities of a patriarch, he disinherited his mother and sisters. A bad business, so it does not surprise me to hear he is deceiving the pair of you. I wish I had spoken up when Maia told me his name, but I did not feel it was my place to give her counsel."

"Never mind the regrets," said Emrick. "Do you know where and when the ceremony is taking place?" Shrugging his shoulders and shaking his head, Ezio looked wretched with himself.

"Maia told me they are marrying at the domus but I do not know the precise location, only that it is near Nero's Aqueduct."

"We may be too late," said Emrick, voicing Clete's fears.

"No, there will be a procession to the marital home at dusk. There is still time to intercept them."

"How does that help if they've already spoken vows before your gods?" asked Emrick, not knowing the Roman customs.

"The union is not complete until the groom carries the bride across the threshold of their intended home," explained Cletus, hope creeping in to his voice. "Do you know where the marital home is?" he asked Ezio. "We need to find the route of the procession."

"I do not."

"Futuo!"

And so it was that Cletus and Emrick found themselves lurking in the shadows of Nero's Aqueduct, with Ezio for company, waiting, an interminably long time it seemed, for the sky to display its red sunset glory, so they may listen for the sounds of a wedding procession.

Chapter Forty-Four

It was not until the shadow of the sundial was long that Tulio and his comrade, Marcellus Petronius Rufus, were greeted at the domus by Laurentia and Marguerita. Both men were dressed in white tunics tied with plaited silk sashes that matched the shade of green found in lush olive groves. Each had a cloak of the same colour draping across his shoulders and a gladius hanging at his left hip, for a Praetorian Guard will bear a weapon even on his wedding day.

Laurentia led them through to the garden where Maia was waiting beside the statue of Juno. She was yet to reach her full womanly blossom, still hanging on to a willowy teenage frame, but looked every bit the Roman bride. A tiara of yellow and white tiny-petalled flowers mixed with marjoram adorned her braided hair holding her flame-coloured veil in place. A rope of entwined ribbons matching the colours of the flowers was looped around her narrow waist securing a white, hemless tunic made from the finest cotton. Maia was dressed as well as any high class citizen yet it was the shoes that made her stand tall. The finely stitched shoes of a bride, a free citizen of Roma, made from leather and died with red saffron to match her veil.

Laurentia clapped her hands to gain the attention of the small group.

"It is with great pleasure, and pride, that I announce that the pig for the Auspex to sacrifice has kindly been donated by the

Caesar, Emperor Titus Flavius Vespasianus as a show of his blessing for this marriage between Tulio Tiberius Livius and Maia Secunda." On cue, a tethered pig was brought to the statue, grunting happily in its innocence of what was to follow. The slave tied it to a peg. Tulio beamed his most charming smile at Maia, showing his delight at the blessing. "I call upon the Auspex to check the gods approve of this union and that this chosen day is favourable."

Marcellus stepped forward, his green cloak replaced by a leather apron, burnished but blood-stained from previous butchering. The pig began to squeal in protest as the slave shortened its tether and deftly tied its head securely above a large, ceramic dish, then added straps to its hind legs and tied them to two more pegs. The squealing from the pig got louder as its protest turned to fear. Marcellus picked up the large ceremonial knife, that was presented to him on a decoratively stitched red velvet cushion with golden silk tassels hanging from each corner. The red velvet serving to highlight the beauty of the polished steel blade that swirled with snake patterns, complimenting the delicately carved asp on the knife's bone handle.

"Juno, Queen of Gods, we ask if this day is lucky," said Marcellus as he silenced the pig by a quick but deep slash to its throat, then immediately slit open the pig's belly letting the entrails spill onto the flagstone whilst the lifeblood was still flowing into the ceramic dish. On his knees, he spent a silent minute examining the gory mess before declaring the auspices to be favourable. "The gods approve the marriage," he declared.

Tulio waited for Marcellus to wash the blood from his hands and arms using the prepared lavender water which Marguerita poured from a ewer, giving him time to remove the bloodied apron and put his cloak back on. When all was ready, Tulio offered his hand to Maia who placed hers upon his and together they moved to stand before the statue of Juno, careful to avoid the sacrificial mess.

"Before Juno, Queen of Gods, Goddess of Marriage, whose many strengths include loyalty as a wife, I declare I am past the age of puberty and that I am a free citizen of Roma," said Tulio using the formal words. He dipped his head in respect to the statue. It was Maia's turn to speak, her moment's hesitation prompting a squeeze of her fingers from Tulio. He thought her shy before the formalities, when in reality, Maia was struggling to break the shackles of her slavery. She thought she had danced free but a solemn declaration at the shrine was not easy.

"I declare I am past the age of puberty," she began, but the next sentence stuck on her tongue and she was grateful for the veil covering her blushing face. "And that I am a free citizen of Roma," she finished, her heart missing a beat, but Juno showed no wrath, gave no sign of the vow not being true and Maia's shaking legs kept her upright. She had danced free and her chest surged with relief.

"I declare our intent and consent to be husband and wife," said Tulio

"I declare our marriage complete upon being carried across the threshold of our intended home," replied Maia.

The solemnity of the ceremony was broken by a cheer from the guests.

"Let the procession commence at dusk," shouted Marcellus, his duty as Auspex now over.

But the Auspex had been mistaken when he declared the day lucky for the bride and groom.

*

Laurentia provided a lavish spread of rich foods and fine wine for the wedding party to dine on as they waited for the sun to sleep. As the sky darkened and the birds went to roost, a taper was put to the torches and the wedding procession left the domus. Tulio and Maia led the way through the streets with three young boys playing sweet music on their flutes as they danced along behind the bride and groom.

Two young bridesmaids, one carrying a distaff, the other a spindle, tools to signify Maia's new role as a wife, followed the flute players, with Laurentia, Marguerita and Marcellus at the rear. Six torch-bearers, more young boys employed for the job, whooped along with the music as they danced and skipped around the procession, creating as much noise and shimmering light as they could. Laurentia had promised them a bonus coin if they made this the loudest procession of Roma. It was a wonderful spectacle and the magic of it helped Maia put aside her apprehension of what was to come, as she smiled and waved at the unknown well-wishers who stopped to clap and cheer the couple on their way to their new life together.

But the couple didn't make it across the threshold for Laurentia's promise of a bonus coin ensured the procession was heard by many, including Clete's group waiting beneath the arches of the aqueduct.

*

Like the Sirens, the half-bird and half-woman creatures from the ancient lore, that lured sailors to destruction with the sweetness of their songs, so the flute-playing and celebratory singing was drawing Cletus, Emrick and Ezio to the wedding party. Being older and less fit than the two ex-warriors, and more cautious of where he was putting his feet, Ezio was falling behind as they ran through the dirty, cobbled streets, which were unusually clear of people, thanks to the feasting of Ludi Romani.

"This way," grunted Cletus, darting down an alley not wide enough to walk a horse along. Emrick followed without question, cursing in his native tongue as he skidded in some unpleasant mess, managing to keep his footing as he bounced off the walls. The narrow alley was amplifying their ragged breathing and echoing the sound of their footfall as well as distorting the singing and music of the procession, so that when they rejoined the wider street, busier than the previous thoroughfare, they needed to pause to determine its direction. "This way," grunted Cletus again, heading to his right.

"Ezio is not with us."

"Futuo!" During the afternoon's wait underneath Nero's Aqueduct, there had been much discussion between the three of them as to what they would do when they succeeded in intercepting

the procession. Cletus was hoping Maia would listen to Ezio's levelled reason. His presence would be key in adding weight to their objections to the marriage. Their plan was weak at best, without Ezio it was hardly a plan at all. "*Futuo, futuo! We can't wait!* We must intercept them and hope that Ezio can find his own way. Listen, we're closer! " The music, singing and clapping was indeed louder. "Next block," Cletus called over his shoulder, weaving his way through the people to the next narrow alley where he was able to pick up the running pace again.

*

Cletus and Emrick burst out of the second narrow passageway just in front of the wedding procession, their sudden appearance causing cries of alarm. Tulio and Marcellus reflexly drawing their swords in response to the unexpected danger, although their reactions were not as sharp as usual due to the strong wine which Laurentia had provided at the celebrations. Emrick, however was fired up by the chase and wasted no time in grabbing a large amphora standing empty outside the shop on the alley corner, and, adding a roar to match his bear-like appearance, ran straight at Marcellus, smashing the earthenware jar over his head, knocking him unconscious with the power of the delivery.

The surprise attack and exploding pottery shards scattered the procession amidst screams and confusion. The musicians ceased playing, the torch-bearers stopped dancing and the well-wishers backed away leaving a scene worthy of a frieze. Maia was standing between Tulio and Cletus, all three of them stunned motionless. Emrick's unexpected frenzy was not yet finished. With another massive roar, and with Marcellus's sword now in his giant hand, he launched himself towards Tulio, and within seconds, Tulio was bleeding out on the cobblestones from a fatal wound. It was as quick as that.

"What have you done?" whispered Maia, still too stunned to move, her breaths shallow and ragged with shock.

"Call the guards," screamed Laurentia. "Call the guards, call the guards!"

"What have you done?" repeated Maia as she stared at Tulio's lifeless form.

"The Peacock got what he deserved," replied Emrick, breathing heavily from his burst of wildness but his voice and eyes displayed no remorse. "I told you I would kill the Peacock."

"The Peacock?" Maia was remembering the conversation she'd had with Emrick when he was drunk. "Tulio was the Peacock that put Cletus in prison?"

Emrick nodded. "I have fulfilled my vow."

"I knew nought of that vow," said Cletus, recovering from the shock of what his comrade had done. "Another plan that didn't go as expected. We need to leave Roma, and quickly or you will be arrested for murder. Come with us Maia."

"What? I cannot. I have the patronage of the Emperor. I cannot leave Roma." Maia's mind was a jumble of everything that had happened since reaching the city. The vision of the broken peacock feather now making sense. It was foretelling Tulio's death not Clete's. Looking up at Cletus her world became silent, everyone and everything ceasing to be important as she locked gazes with those caring eyes she so loved, the eyes she found so very difficult to lie to. "You didn't come to the Carpe Vinum when I sent for you. I thought you didn't care."

"Tulio did not give me the message. He knew we were on latrine duty for seven days."

Was it as simple as that, thought Maia. Those eyes said it was. Laurentia, having recovered her composure from the unexpected disruption, disagreed.

"Detain these men until the guards arrive," she called to rally the bystanders. No-one moved. The Praetorian Guards were notoriously disliked in the city. That, and the sight and size of Emrick wielding a gladius kept the onlookers still. "There will be a reward," she added crossly but it was not enough to prompt any action.

"Come with us Maia," urged Cletus.

"But the peacock is Juno's sacred bird," worried Maia. "Juno will be against us for this killing. There will be no happiness."

"He will rot. If there was time you would see that he is not sacred. He will rot. We must go!" Cletus saw a ripple in the crowd as someone was pushing their way through. "We must go! There will be no second reprieve from your patron if we are arrested."

"I saw Calix die in the arena. Put to the wild animals, just as you predicted."

"And you wish that death on me?"

"No! But..."

"Then come!"

"It is Ezio," said Emrick with relief.

Ezio burst through the crowd, frowning as he saw the dead groom, blood soaking his white tunic.

"That wasn't as we planned," he said, taking Maia in his arms, something Cletus had wanted to do but was afraid to for fear of Maia's rejection." Maia, I am so sorry for your spoiled wedding day, but trust me when I say Tulio Tiberius Livius was not good enough for you. I knew his family. You deserve better, you deserve happiness. Forgive me for not speaking of what I knew when you told me his name. There was no time."

Maia was still undecided. It was too much to comprehend. She had found her blood kin, her true family, here in Roma and had been so close to ensuring citizenship for herself and future children. Cletus had stolen that from her. In truth it was Emrick but she was blaming Cletus. Yet, she was remembering the joy of Clete's company on their journey from Puteoli, his quiet, protective strength. But Juno would surely not allow them happiness after this.

Maia was wrong. Juno still favoured her.

She saw the choker first, the topaz gemstones catching the light of the torch flames and glinting with hues of golden-brown beauty. It was around the neck of a young girl who was watching the drama with innocent curiosity. Then Maia was looking directly into the eyes of Philo the Greek. Maia's heart missed a beat as she saw his cruel smile. The life she had tried so desperately to escape from was revealed by Philo in four short words.

"A slave cannot marry," he called out loudly, stepping forwards to be seen. A hush descended. "A slave cannot marry," he repeated in to the silence. "I know this bride to be a slave from Pompeii." The whisper of Decima was chiming loudly again. Her buried life was unearthed.

*

Ezio's arms dropped away in surprise. Marguerita fainted. Laurentia melted in to the crowd to publicly disassociate herself from what she already knew but had gambled on hiding. She would need to work quickly to disassociate herself from this scandal if she wanted to keep her current high status. Marcellus began to stir from his unconscious state. Cletus took charge of the situation by grabbing Maia's hand and leading her quickly through the spectators in the direction of the docks.

"We are going to Britannia," he said gruffly. "I am done with the hypocrisy of Roma. The Dobunni tribe are missing their man," he said nodding over his shoulder at Emrick who was right behind them. They will welcome us without the questions.

"Wait, Cletus, wait..." He stopped running to look at her. "I am not Maia Secunda."

"You are Maia to me."

"I am not a Roman citizen. I am a slave...worse...a runaway slave."

"I know...I don't care."

"What? How did you find out? When?"

"You would never take your shoes off to sleep. That was the first clue. You were far too capable at cooking. That was another clue. There were no tears and you didn't complain during the hard walking and rough sleeping, not once... and I can tell when you're lying."

"You never said anything."

"Neither did you. Now can we get going before the guards catch us?" Maia felt her heart swell as she lost herself in his gaze. She'd forgotten how much she liked those eyes, honest, caring, demanding. Her own welled up. "No tears," he grunted.

"No tears," she promised, cuffing them away.

"We must make haste out of this damned city. There will be little rest tonight. It's a long walk to the Port of Ostia."

"It is not far compared to Puteoli," she smiled.

Thus she ran with Cletus, her rangy legs throwing up puffs of dirt just as they had when she'd run to the port in Pompeii, but this time she was not alone and her feet were not bare, she was wearing the saffron-red shoes of a bride. A new life was waiting across the water. Her new home would be Britannia and she would cross that threshold with Cletus and Emrick.

The End

Author Notes

As with any historical novel, Juno's Peacock is a blend of fact and fiction. I have made every effort to be accurate with the facts but errors and omissions will have occurred. These are entirely my own fault and I trust they do not detract from your enjoyment of the story. My main aim was to produce an entertaining tale that immerses you in the world of ancient Rome. I hope I achieved that aim.

People have asked me where I get my ideas from for my Roman novels...they come from research, lots of research. Once I have a framework of facts, I create some characters and place them in the situations thrown up by the research. Then off we stride together with the characters leading me in their willful ways.

I'd like to take this opportunity to thank the following people (in no particular order as I know how competitive you all are!):
My cousin Terrie Sidnell for the amphora weapon suggestion – inspired.
My cousin and beta reader Mary O'Connell for her useful feedback which helped me to polish and improve this story.
My friend from school, and for life, Wendy Clemens for proofreading the manuscript.
My immediate family for putting up with my exasperation during the formatting process – I enjoy the challenge really.
I love and appreciate you all.
My readers too – what a great source of support and motivation you are. Thank you.

Reviews...yes please, they're welcome on Amazon, Goodreads, Facebook, anywhere. If your critique is favourable I will write another book. I have a whim to link Juno's Peacock with Wall of Stone. Wouldn't that tie things up neatly. It's not a promise as my characters may disagree and lead me elsewhere. We'll see...

Printed in Great Britain
by Amazon